D0394864

# THE OUTPOST

*Recent Titles by Gerald Hammond from Severn House*

# THE OUTPOST

## Gerald Hammond

SANTA CLARA CITY LIBRARY
DISCARD
2635 Homestead Road
Santa Clara, CA 95051

This first world edition published in Great Britain 2004 by
SEVERN HOUSE PUBLISHERS LTD of
9–15 High Street, Sutton, Surrey SM1 1DF.
This first world edition published in the USA 2004 by
SEVERN HOUSE PUBLISHERS INC of
595 Madison Avenue, New York, N.Y. 10022.

Copyright © 2004 by Gerald Hammond.

All rights reserved.
The moral right of the author has been asserted.

British Library Cataloguing in Publication Data

Hammond,  Gerald,  1926-
    The outpost
    1.    Great Britain - Armed forces - Women - Fiction
    2.    Women,  Black - Great Britain - Fiction
    3.    Africa - Fiction
    4.    War stories
    I.    Title
    823.9'14 [F]

    ISBN 0-7278-6121-2

Except where actual historical events and characters are being
described for the storyline of this novel, all situations in this
publication are fictitious and any resemblance to living persons
is purely coincidental.

Typeset by Palimpsest Book Production Ltd.,
Polmont, Stirlingshire, Scotland.
Printed and bound in Great Britain by
MPG Books Ltd., Bodmin, Cornwall.

All the characters in this book are intended to be absolutely and totally fictitious.

This book is a work of fiction, almost of fantasy. I have played fast and loose with geography and politics. The British Army, however, is an incontrovertible fact and I am deeply grateful to Major Graham Linney for helping me to update and correct my recollections of the army as seen from a lowly level during World War Two.

# One

'For Christ's sake,' said the Prime Minister, the Right Honourable Geoffrey York. 'How did you ever come to let this happen?'

His Minister of Defence, Charles Hopkirk, bridled. 'With respect, Prime Minister, may I remind you that it was your suggestion—'

'Never mind that,' the Prime Minister said quickly. Really, Charles would have to go, and soon. 'Somebody should have had more sense.'

'Perhaps,' said the Defence Minister. 'But in all the confusion . . .'

'Well,' said the Prime Minister, 'I suppose it could have been worse. We were lucky to come out of such a major crisis without losing more face than we did. And in the one little war that was all our own, we seem to have covered ourselves with glory. That would be all well and good, except that the media are making this woman into some sort of cross between Joan of Arc and Helen of Troy.'

'You couldn't have a cross between Joan of Arc and Helen of Troy,' the Defence Minister said. 'They were both women,' he explained, in case the PM had missed the point. 'Although in this day and age . . .'

At the next reshuffle, the PM decided, Charles was going to find himself at the Ministry of Pettifogging and Nit-picking, or the nearest equivalent that he could find or create. 'How is the army taking it?' he asked.

'Divided. The Old Guard is horrified, doesn't know what the country's coming to. The younger and more radical element think it's wonderful PR. Even my clerical assistant

1

said that it was the best thing since . . .' He paused, thought and substituted, 'sliced bread.' The young lady had actually said 'flavoured condoms', but there were certain things about which the PM was inclined to be puritanical. 'Anyway,' he resumed, 'there are no particular heads to roll and it would be a major vote-loser to roll them anyway. The whole thing seems to have been fated. In fact, there was an awful inevitability about it from the beginning, like one of those Greek plays. She seems always to have been in the right place at the right time . . .'

# Two

Corporal Angus Brown of the North Wessex Regiment was always as neat and shining as a well laid dinner table. That remained so even when he was drunk. It has to be admitted that, in his earlier years, he enjoyed a drink. Not that there is anything wrong with enjoying it. If drink is taken, it should be enjoyed. It is the taking of drink to excess which is to be deplored, and Corporal Brown fell into the way of it from time to time along with his friend Abe Bathurst.

Once or twice a month, in celebration of nothing in particular, the two would tour the pubs of the small garrison town and blow off steam. At the end of the evening, when the last landlord had firmly closed his doors against them, Corporal Brown, still neat and apparently in control of himself, would guide or support his friend homeward before returning to his own quarters in the barracks.

Corporal Brown was unmarried – he was too silent a man to be tolerated by most women outside the bedchamber – but it was through him that Abe Bathurst met and married the NAAFI manageress, a black but not unlovely lady, tall and lean, with a jolly sense of fun and a blinding smile. Angus Brown acted as his friend's best man. The wedding went with the organized precision of a guard-change and the best man's speech was compressed into less than forty words.

Corporal Brown was a favourite with the ladies. Even in his cups, he was a handsome devil, tall and straight with the craggy features of a cowboy film star embellished by a generous but very neat moustache. His silent nature made him appear a good listener, an attractive characteristic to any compulsive talker. On those social occasions he was rarely inclined to take no for an answer. And so it fell to him to impregnate Mrs Bathurst one Saturday night, something that her husband had never managed to do. They had tenderly tucked the comatose Mr Bathurst in his bed and were about to take one last cup of tea in the kitchen above his shop when Corporal Brown decided in his fuddled, but still disciplined mind that the time had come. Always a man of few words, he gently but firmly manoeuvred the lady across the corner of the kitchen table and had his way with her. She made little protest, possibly because her husband had proved such a disappointment in that activity.

When Mrs Bathurst later announced that she was pregnant, her husband was delighted. Any one of the trio having a suspicion that the baby might not be his had more sense than to voice it.

After the customary delay, the lady went into labour and with little difficulty was delivered of a baby girl. The infant was, if anything, even blacker than her mother, but Abe was enchanted by her and was quick to draw attention to many points of resemblance which he detected between the baby's features and his own. In this, he was eagerly supported by his wife and friend. It says a great deal for the trust between the two friends that they quite accepted the apparent suspension of Mendel's laws of inheritance and never took a second glance at a handsome corporal of Nubian extraction in D Company.

On one subject, the proud mother was adamant. She herself had the first name Hallelujah, a name that had been borne by her mother and her Jamaican grandmother before her, and she was determined that her daughter should continue in the family tradition. Abe, a lapsed Jew, was at first reluctant to see his daughter saddled with a name he considered to be obviously Catholic in origin, but when the regimental chaplain pointed out that the word stemmed from the Hebrew, he seized on the excuse to humour the wife he both loved and, very slightly, feared. As Hallelujah Bathurst she was registered, but when that name was found to be rather a mouthful, as well as a source of barely concealed amusement to their friends, she was invariably known as Hal.

\* \* \*

4

When Hal was a plain little toddler of little more than a year old, Corporal Brown left to do a two-year tour of duty in Northern Ireland. By the time he returned, there had been changes. He was now Sergeant Brown, decorated with a new ribbon on his chest and burn scars on his hands from a petrol bomb. Abe Bathurst was not there to welcome him. Without his friend to see him safely home, Abe had attempted one more pub crawl on his own and had been found in the morning in a snowdrift, dead of hypothermia.

Abe's widow, genuinely sorry without being wholly devastated by grief, had sold his business and, although Abe – who had had a talent for dealing in antique jewellery – had left her tolerably provided for, she continued in her post with the NAAFI and had returned to her old quarters within the barracks, co-incidentally only a few yards from the sergeant's billet. This juxtaposition permitted a more leisurely and less anxious resumption of their affair and brought the sergeant and his daughter into regular contact. Two years later, he married her mother and any question about their relationship became academic.

Young Hal became a favourite with NCOs and men alike. Eventually, she was to grow tall and slim like her parents and, like her mother, she was beautiful in the way that some African women are beautiful, with fine-boned features and grace of movement. Her black hair was straight and shining, and she was bright and gifted with laughter.

Her relationship with her real father was at first rather hesitant and stilted. The circumscribed patterns of military life form a screen behind which a shy personality may shelter, and Sergeant Brown hid a reserved and introverted character behind the facade of a rigid and perfectionist conformity to army discipline. He could be eloquent in teaching his men the elements of drill or in dressing down an offender, but in informal society he found himself tongue-tied. His friendship with the late Abe Bathurst had been founded in part on their shared enjoyment of an occasional drinking bout, but even more on the fact that Abe was garrulous by nature and thereby saved his friend from the trouble of choosing more than a few occasional words of conversation.

Whether the young Hal instinctively divined the relationship between them or was merely drawn to him by his very silence, she soon took to following the ramrod figure about the barracks. Sergeant Brown – Company Sergeant-Major Brown as he was soon to become – at first pretended to be unaware of his shadow except when it was necessary to escort her off the parade ground, to the great amusement of the troops, but her mother could sense that nothing would be allowed to touch her daughter so long as she was within his sight.

Angus Brown had sometimes thought that he might have enjoyed having a son, but in time Hal became as good as a son to him. She might chat or fall silent, but she made no demands on him for speech and his few utterances were accepted gratefully and as gospel. As time passed, he was surprised to find that she had brought a new dimension into his life, transporting him, if not to the seventh heaven, at least to the fifth or sixth.

Away from his military duties, she was his constant companion. They fished together and, although his catch of brown trout from the nearby river was usually larger than hers, he taught her to place a dry fly on the water with an accuracy and gentleness almost equalling his own. On the small-bore rifle range she soon became his equal and, as she grew in speed and strength, she became able, on occasions, to beat him at tennis or squash. At snooker, he remained the usual victor by a small margin. In his rare bursts of loquacity, he boasted of her progress to his fellow warrant officers and tried not to let anyone see that his nose was occasionally put out of joint. When, off duty, he sat with some of his cronies on the bench overlooking the square or on the terrace behind the warrant officers' mess, Hal was often in attendance, unnoticed or accepted, listening wide-eyed as they raked over old actions and argued as to whether old So-and-so should have asked for air cover and wondered how Harry's platoon had come to get themselves enfiladed and pinned down. They were outwardly respectful of their officers but Hal, as she grew older and more perceptive, began to detect an underlying attitude of amused tolerance, as of a mother to a favourite child.

At school, Hal was treated at first as a strange, alien being. There were several Asian pupils at the school, children of local shopkeepers and businessmen, but they kept to themselves. Hal found herself isolated. In part, this was the fault of the teachers. Hal's reaction to the first occasion on which a contemporary addressed her as Nignog was so explosive that staff had to separate the combatants. When the cause of the dispute was explained, the staff were horrified to discover the taint of racial discrimination in their midst. Hal's part in starting the fisticuffs was forgotten in favour of shocked recriminations and lengthy lectures about racial tolerance. The unintended result was that, whether from resentment or trepidation, children tended to steer clear of Hal who, living the life of a partial outcast, went through several phases of being a holy terror.

During her first year at school, however, Hal made a particular friend. Among the children of the regiment she was a familiar face, although most of those who attended the local school followed the line of the others and left her to herself. At the regimental children's Christmas party, the same reserve was noticeable. When the party games broke off for refreshments, Hal nibbled a couple of sandwiches and then helped herself to a plate of jelly and ice cream. Chairs being in short supply, she sat down on the floor behind the nearest table with her back against the wall and assumed the air of one who is above such frivolities.

A newcomer, a stocky boy with sandy hair and a snub nose, soon dumped himself down beside her. 'I'm Tony Laverick,' he said. 'Who are you?'

Hal introduced herself and they shook hands solemnly.

'My dad's the adjutant,' Tony said.

'I have a stepdad. He's a sergeant-major.'

There was a moment of respectful silence. Obviously a sergeant-major outranked a mere adjutant.

'When I'm old enough,' Tony said, 'I'm going to be a soldier like my dad. What are you going to be?'

Hal warmed to him. He was accepting her for herself. She was still of an age to accept childhood as a lifetime occupation and she had never considered the question of a career. She gave it some rapid thought and decided against being an astronaut. There was only one other job towards which she had an inclination. 'I'm going to be a soldier too,' she said.

Tony shook his sandy curls. 'Silly! Girls can't be proper soldiers. They can't join the infantry or the artillery.'

'Then I'll be something else.'

'My big brother says that the women soldiers are just officers' groundsheets.'

Hal had no idea what he meant. Neither of them understood the magnitude of the insult. She let the slur go by. 'I'd like a chocolate biscuit,' she said.

Tony's mother had evidently read him a lecture about being a Proper Little Gentleman, because he got up. While he was at the table, two of the other girls whispered to him. Looking puzzled, he fetched her a chocolate biscuit in his rather grubby fingers and sat down again. He seemed to find her black skin a matter for curiosity. He licked his finger and ran it down her arm. 'It doesn't come off,' he said indignantly. 'They told me it would.'

The two girls were giggling.

Hal remembered that when she had first become sensitive about her colour, her mother had played a little joke on her with cold cream. The folding table now looming above her had been borrowed from the armourers' workshop and, in military fashion, the hinges had been treated with black grease. She collected a smear on a surreptitious finger. 'Yours is what comes off,' she said. 'We're all the same underneath.' She pretended to lick her finger and then wiped the grease on to his forearm.

Tony looked at the black smear and his eyes grew wide. He jumped up, gazed around for his mother and trotted away.

Hal looked at the two girls. 'Not officer material,' she said loftily. It was a favourite expression of her father's.

Tony's mother made a fuss. Tony's father had a word with the sergeant-major and the sergeant-major had several words with Hal's mother. 'Bloody officers,' he said. 'I've shat 'em.' Hal was not supposed to overhear the casual remark, but she filed it away in her mind. Tony's father told him not to be so gullible in future.

Despite that episode, Tony sought Hal's company. She continued to pull his leg and, smiling his cheerful grin, he continued to fall for every leg-pull. On one occasion when they were feeding the elderly horse that the colonel rode on formal occasions, the supply of carrots ran out and Hal persuaded Tony to offer his thumb between two fingers as a substitute. Tony's thumb was bitten and Hal received one of her very few spankings. She was told to stay away from officers' children. The children of other ranks, she concluded, were fair game. She ignored the injunction anyway.

Hal's few friends were nearly all boys. Girls treated her as an alien, whereas boys accepted her as somebody who would join or even lead them in mischief or, later, could bowl tirelessly and play a fierce game of tennis. When Tony's father was posted abroad, taking his family with him, Hal was sorry to see him go. She had other friends but she would never, she thought, have another one so delightfully credulous.

When Hal was entering her last year at school, Angus Brown – now Regimental Sergeant-Major Brown – sat down with her in the small sitting room of their married quarters. He was grizzled now; he seemed to have shrunk progressively as she grew, and he played squash or tennis less often although his voice could still stop a company in its tracks at a quarter of a mile. But he was speaking softly that evening. It was an effort to speak at all.

'The colonel had a word with me today,' he said. 'About you.'

'Me?' Hal said. She thought back. Had she been seen eating crisps on the barrack square? Necking with the quartermaster's son? Putting out her tongue at the regimental goat? She had committed all those sins and more, but not usually until after dark.

Her father nodded seriously. 'He's nobody's fool. He keeps

his ear to the ground. And he's been hearing about you.'

Hal's mouth went dry. 'What's he been hearing?' She nearly went on to say that it was all lies.

'He was hearing how well you were doing at school. Didn't leave many prizes for the others, did you? He made me show him your school reports. He says that if you can get a university place, the army has a fund for helping out with fees and things. Of course it would be better, easier on the funds, if you got a bursary.'

Some saliva returned to Hal's mouth. When she had thought at all about the future it had been in terms of looking for a job in competition with all the other school-leavers. But learning came easily to her and she even found studying enjoyable. 'What do you and Mum think?'

The RSM hesitated. He was treading on dangerous ground but it had to be said some time and she was a big girl now. 'Your mother would have liked you to marry the right sort of boy, settle down and have a family.'

'You mean the white sort of boy?'

'Well, yes. But—'

'But I'm black.'

'I had noticed,' the RSM said with wry humour. 'That's hardly your fault. You didn't choose your genes any more than we chose our ancestors. But it may make it very difficult for you to come to the right decisions. Think of it as a challenge – I've noticed that people who make a success of their lives have usually started from a handicap. Whatever you decide will be both right and wrong. If you ask for advice, you'll get it, but we won't interfere or criticize. Do what you think is best for you and we'll support you all the way. But that's another matter.

'As far as I'm concerned, yes, I'd like to see you go to university. I've been hoping for that. I wasn't sure that we could manage it, financially; they've cut away down on grants, but what the CO said makes it possible. It means that you could have a career, or at least you could have a better selection of boys to make your choice from.'

'I expect,' Hal said slowly, 'that there's somebody

somewhere with my name on him. When he comes along he can be pink or green, for all I'll care. Until then . . . yes, I think I'd like to go to university.' She smiled, a sudden flash of white teeth. 'I'll see what I can do to oblige you. And the colonel, if he really gives a damn.'

'There's just one thing,' the sergeant-major said. 'To be eligible for a bursary, you'd have to commit yourself to an army career. Taking a commission. Becoming an officer.' He smiled lopsidedly. 'Then I'd have to salute you. My own . . . stepdaughter.'

'Would you mind?'

'I'd be proud.'

Hal thought deeply. The concept of herself as an officer was a new one. She had necessarily encountered many officers and, to a small girl peering from between the ranks of the non-commissioned, they had seemed a lordly group, looking down their noses at a little coloured girl. There had been some cutting remarks, though not as many as Hal heard in her imagination, and she knew that some of the children of the regiment had been dissuaded from playing with her, as though her colour might be catching.

'I don't think I'd like that,' she said at last.

'Why ever not?' It was beyond his comprehension that anyone might not want to be commissioned.

Hal remained silent. She had a feeling that any explanation including the expression 'toffee-nosed' might be misunderstood. Her father tried not to look disappointed. 'Never mind,' he said. 'Your . . . your dad left your mum well provided for and she wants the best for you. We can still manage.'

'You're sure?'

'Just about sure. Of course, we could manage a lot easier if you get a scholarship.'

Hal worked hard that year. The thinness of her social life made studying easier than it might have been, and her intelligence had been recognized by a headmistress with a good degree and a talent for teaching. When the exam results were at last disclosed, Hal found she had obtained a good scholarship to Oxford.

She could have joined some of her contemporaries in one last school-organized trip abroad, but she was, as ever, uncertain whether she would be permitted to mingle on equal terms. She decided to remain at home. RSM Brown was arriving at retirement age. For some years he had been organizing his finances and now he was preparing in earnest. Occasionally, when time allowed, the couple journeyed to inspect possible retirement cottages in suitable countryside, near to some acceptable trout fishing but not too far from shops and surgeries. Hal went along with them and became a valued observer of papered-over cracks and the smell of dry rot.

On other free days, the RSM and Hal went fishing.

They were sitting at ease beside a reservoir, finishing the remains of a picnic lunch and enjoying mild sunshine, when the RSM brushed away an intrusive damselfly and said, 'You'll be going away soon.'

'But I'll be coming home,' Hal said comfortingly. 'Maybe not to the barracks, but I'm sure I can trust you to write and tell me where to come.'

Her father was not really listening. 'I expect so,' he said. At times he was becoming almost garrulous. Speaking to Hal had become easier with time. 'You'll find it very different, living away from home. We won't be there to . . . to see you through. We've tried, without being heavy-handed, to guide you in the right direction, but . . .'

'But you can't tell a stepdaughter to move to the right in columns of threes?'

He produced one of his very rare grins. 'Not with any hope of being obeyed. And now you'll have to make the bigger decisions for yourself. You can do that?'

'I think so. Dad, is this about sex?'

The RSM turned faintly pink and looked ten years younger. Hal had never been able to understand how it happened that all the men, including the younger officers, were terrified of him. 'Partly. I left it to your mother to explain the . . . the nuts and bolts of it.'

'She didn't say anything about nuts and bolts,' Hal said. 'I think she told me everything else.' She glanced round to make

sure that they were not being overheard. There were some
secrets that she still wished to keep in the family. 'Would it
help if I assured you that I'm still a virgin?'

Her father's weather-beaten face turned from pink to a dusky
red but he bore up bravely. He had given many a fatherly talk
to young soldiers but talking to this outwardly self-assured
young woman was somehow quite different. 'I was sure of
it,' he said huskily. 'Well, fairly sure. You never seem to
know with young girls these days. The point is, do you know
enough to stay that way?'

Hal wanted to ask whether they were talking contraception
or unarmed combat but decided that the RSM was already
making heavy enough weather of it. 'I can say "No!" in eight
languages now,' she said. 'Did I tell you that I started learning
Swahili last term?'

'No, you didn't. I'd have thought that you'd want to separate yourself from that side of your genes.'

'I'm not going to put rings round my neck or a bone through
my nose, but I'd like to visit Africa some day and see where
a minority of my ancestors came from, and I'd look pretty
stupid as a black tourist in Africa, not knowing at least one
of the languages. So I must keep it up. The next time that the
thirty-fourth son of some tribal chief tries to patronize me,
I'll be able to give him a proper telling off.'

'Just see that you do. It's all very well saying no, but you've
got to keep on saying it. Young men of student age only have
one thing on their minds and you're carrying it around with
you. They can be very persuasive.' The RSM was remem-
bering his own youth. God forbid, he thought, that she should
ever meet up with a version of his younger self. She wouldn't
stand a chance.

'If I keep on saying no indefinitely, I'll never hitch up with
the man of my dreams and yours,' Hal pointed out. Not for
the first time, she seemed to latch on to his thoughts. 'You
were a young man once. Inside yourself, there's probably a
twenty-year-old screaming to get out. Yes?'

'Perhaps,' he said. This was a quirk that the RSM had often
recognized in himself but he had a feeling that admitting it

13

might somehow alter the father-daughter rapport which, despite the unacknowledged nature of the relationship, was developing. But he was too proud to deny the accusation outright.

'Well then. You're in a position to advise me. When a young man tells me all the right things and does all the right things, how do I know whether he's serious or if he's just saying and doing them in the hope of getting me into bed?'

'Nobody said it was easy,' the RSM pointed out. 'That's why so many girls get in the family way and ruin their lives, because when the right man does come along he may not want to take on somebody else's sprog. And then their mothers come running to me, as if I should know which of the men was the culprit.'

'You usually find out, though.'

'How would you know that?'

'I hear a lot of things.'

'You hear too damn much. I can only say to follow your instinct but be sure that the heat of the moment isn't influencing your decision. And, if he's sincere, he won't mind waiting.'

'Until we're married? I'm not sure that any young man is as sincere as all that nowadays,' Hal said. She looked at her father out of the corner of her eye. 'If he's prepared to wait a week or two . . .'

The RSM jumped to his feet. 'The fish are rising again,' he said.

'No they aren't.'

'Well, they will in a minute.'

# Three

Just off Whitehall, in a comfortable annexe to the Foreign Office, the Junior Minister was receiving the Maverian Ambassador. Maveria was hardly a dot on the East African map – usually described as being about the size of Wales, he corrected himself, which would have been large enough among the British Isles but was almost lost in the vastness of Africa. And anyway, even that small area was only partially habitable. The total population, he recalled, was about that of Gloucester. At one time a British colony, Maveria had achieved independence during the Fifties, to the great relief of both parties. A brief flirtation with democracy had ended in a military take-over, but by then responsibility had been abnegated. Coffee, he had decided, would suffice.

With civil service efficiency, the coffee dead-heated with the arrival of the Ambassador, escorted by the Permanent Secretary. While the Minister's PA poured, the weather was discussed and dismissed. The PA made her escape.

Courtesies observed, the Junior Minister looked down his long nose at the Ambassador. They had known and disliked each other at Cambridge and by unhappy chance they were both wearing the Tie. 'Now, old man,' he said. He called almost everybody 'old man'. It saved him from having to remember their names, especially those damned difficult foreign names that sounded as though the utterer was having an epileptic fit. 'What can we do for you?'

The Ambassador sighed. This was going to be hard slogging, but he was under orders. 'No doubt you are aware, Minister, that we have disposed of the military dictatorship and reintroduced democracy.'

15

'*Disposed of*' was good, the Junior Minister thought. The last few days of the outgoing government had been discussed in shocked tones in the corridors of power, the underlying thought being *There but for the grace of God* . . . 'I meant to send a telegram of congratulations,' he said vaguely.

'You did send a telegram of congratulations,' said the Permanent Secretary.

'That's all right then. Tell me, how did you manage it?' Military dictatorships, once established, tended to be self-perpetuating and therefore permanent.

'Without great difficulty,' said the Ambassador, smiling at the memory. 'It was only necessary to convince His Nibs that the people loved him, which he was predisposed to believe, and that holding free elections with outside observers in attendance would establish him in the eyes of the world and open the door to economic aid. His opponents had the voters primed and waiting and we had control of the radio station. We announced the election result as soon as it was known – or rather, before it was known, to be honest – and His Nibs was on the first boat out, without more than a smidgen of the fortune that he had been salting away. Some of his supporters managed to follow him, but by no means all. They had not gone out of their way to seek popularity, you understand.'

The PS suppressed a small shiver. 'We believe,' he said, 'that His Nibs is now squatting in Liboon, next door, trying to organize a triumphant return.'

The Ambassador nodded sombrely. An armed return, it went without saying. Very few of the original supporters had survived, but those had been in the military. It had been necessary almost to disband the army. 'That is the problem. Liboon always considered Maveria to be part of it – as, indeed, it has been several times in its history, despite ethnic differences, a language barrier and a formidable geographic boundary. The Liboonese are governed by a military dictatorship very similar to the one which we recently disposed of. They need little encouragement to put their own puppet back in charge. For one thing alone, Maveria has a good harbour; Liboon only has cliffs. The situation is unstable, to say the least.'

'I don't quite understand what you want us to do about it,' said the Junior Minister. Mentally, the PS added it to the long list of things that the Minister did not understand.

'We want to become a colony again,' said the Ambassador simply. There! It was out. He waited for the storm to break.

It seemed that there was not going to be a storm. 'You what?' said the Junior Minister mildly. He nearly said, 'But we've only just got rid of you.'

'Want to become a colony again,' said the Ambassador slowly and distinctly. The proposal was not causing the fluster which he had expected. 'Those, it now appears, were the good old days. Stable government, justice and sound management. All right, so a few pockets were lined. Well, why not? The means were legal. There was ten times the pocket-lining under His Nibs, and by methods that didn't even pretend to be legal. Graffiti is now appearing. The most popular slogan, after KEEP MAVERIA MAVERIAN, is BRITISH COME BACK.'

The Junior Minister was aware of an internal swelling of pride. It was nice to be appreciated. For a former colony to ask, actually ask, to return to the fold was unprecedented. He might yet go down in history as the man who laid the foundations for the second British Empire. But no. 'It's impossible,' he said.

'Why?'

'The cost alone . . .'

'Some cost may have fallen on the British taxpayer last time around,' said the Ambassador modestly. 'But since then, minerals have been found.'

'Oil?' asked the Junior Minister hopefully.

'Well, no. Not oil,' the Ambassador admitted. 'Not yet. But valuable metals. Copper and cobalt in particular. A small Australian company is already at work in the foothills but there is ample scope for more development. We need not be a burden to you.'

The Junior Minister looked at the Permanent Secretary. The PS shook his head. 'Quite impossible,' he said.

'But why?' the other two demanded in unison.

'It would be politically unacceptable. "Colony" has become

a dirty word. Even the Russians are coming to accept that the days of empire are over.'

'You owe us that much,' said the Ambassador, tongue in cheek. 'You have armed Liboon.'

'We can't accept that, Ambassador,' the PS said indignantly. 'The Liboonese have been buying American M-Sixteen rifles.'

'Through Britain.'

'Through a British arms dealer.'

'But you issued a trading licence. Also, there was some British artillery involved. That, I suggest, is the same thing.'

'It's not at all the same thing. It's just business. We sell arms to anybody unless we see good reason not to. If we didn't, the French would.'

'And you didn't see reason not to sell arms to a country that is poised to invade a neighbour?'

'At the time of the arms deal, they weren't poised to do anything of the sort,' the PS protested. 'And anyway, what we sold to them had been in service since Aden and the American rifles were ex-Vietnam.'

'They were clapped out,' the Junior Minister said more bluntly.

The Ambassador hid a smile. It was time to assume his fall-back position, which was what he had intended all along. 'Then may I suggest that we become a British protectorate? A British garrison would send a clear signal that an armed invasion would not be tolerated. If you were to help us to develop a larger market for our mineral resources, we could pay our way.' He sat back, satisfied.

'I think,' the PS said slowly, 'that we could introduce you to a man who might help you. It would cost you a substantial consultancy fee, but he could put you in touch with the right people and help to ward off any awkward questions in Parliament.'

The Junior Minister was nodding happily. It was an opportunity to put Stan Motherwell MP under an obligation to him.

# Four

University life was a revelation to Hal. From a garrison town so dominated by the barracks that the tail might very well have been said to wag the dog, she was pitchforked into a cosmopolitan society where academic or sporting accomplishment transcended colour. All nationalities were represented but there was little tendency to clannishness; she was accepted, by all but a small cross-section who considered themselves to be the 'in' crowd, as a fellow student and that was that. She was now expected to study without being spoonfed, but as a habitual reader this came easily to her, while her upbringing had so steeped her in the army mind and manners that the study of military history was little more than an extension of what she already knew.

She devoted the slack in her academic time to languages. She had intended to abandon her brief acquaintance with Swahili in favour of a language more likely to be of use to her, probably Spanish, but the presence in college of a Swahili-literate white girl born in East Africa, and a North African girl fluent in Arabic offered the chance of regular practice, so she persevered, adding Arabic to her repertoire.

Events continued to steer her towards her destiny.

One non-academic subject was added to her studies during her first year. Despite the generally relaxed attitude within the university to matters of race and colour, there had been some cases of racial abuse and several late-night attacks on coloured students, some of them women. In one instance, the classics student had managed to slip out of the attacker's grasp and had proved to be the faster sprinter. In another, sexual molestation, the nurse had known an unpleasant method of robbing her attacker of his motivation for several weeks, if not permanently. Later attacks had been more serious and more successful. One male Nigerian student was hospitalized and an Indian lecturer was permanently scarred. The police were issuing warnings that the attacks would certainly continue and would probably escalate in violence.

In keeping with police advice, Hal made a point of being accompanied whenever she was abroad after dark, but one winter's evening she was among the last to leave the Bodleian Library. Nobody seemed to be going in her direction and she had perforce to walk back to Somerville alone. Before she was aware of another presence she was suddenly grabbed and jerked towards the shadows beside Keble. There was a hand over her mouth. A rasping voice in her ear assured her that she was a black bitch and had it coming to her.

Hal fought down panic. A black girl in a white man's world, she had known that some day this could happen. In the privacy of her own mind, she had decided that her life was worth more than her virginity and that she would submit without a struggle. But in the event, she found that her values had reversed. She had no intention of letting her virginity go easily to a rapist. She drove a back-elbow into her assailant's stomach. The grip was released and she screamed. Heart pounding, Hal span round, determined to get one good look at her assailant before taking to her heels. Instead of one or more white youths, she found a fellow female student, winded but still managing to grin, crouched at her feet. The girl was a notorious practical joker who had made herself detested by regularly going beyond the bounds of the acceptable. She had made Hal a frequent target.

'You've laddered my tights,' she said plaintively.

'Try anything like that again,' Hal said grimly, 'and I'll ladder your spine. That wasn't funny.' She stalked off, leaving the other to pick herself up. Nobody seemed to be hurrying to answer her scream.

A trio of engineering apprentices were caught in the act of molesting a Jamaican medical student a few days later. They were brought into court, unmarked but shamed, and the attacks stopped, but Hal had learned a lesson. She had already suffered from the attentions of several over-physical suitors. She enlisted in a course of self-defence, progressing from the defensive aikido to the aggressive art of tae kwon do.

The university was riddled with clubs and societies, so that almost any activity could be indulged. Hal did a parachute jump for charity and a bungee jump from a high crane for the hell of it. She continued to play squash for exercise. In her final year, she obtained her blue for target-shooting. During her vacations she stayed with her parents, latterly near a major still-water fishery, in the cottage which the ex-RSM had bought and where he was supplementing his pension as a fishing instructor with a steadily growing reputation. During long vacations, they fished; in winter she became adept at stalking rabbits with her father's Anschutz small-bore rifle.

It was in what time was left for a social life that Hal noticed the greatest change. Any pressure that she might have imagined to foregather with girls of similar colour soon faded. Only on very rare occasions did she experience a racial snub.

One such occasion occurred during her second year when a party had been due to attend a May Ball. One of the girls caught the prevalent flu and dropped out. Rather than waste an expensive ticket and unbalance the party, one of the other female students asked Hal to step into the breach.

Despite a mistrust of blind dates, Hal allowed herself to be persuaded. She had been living a studious and frugal life and was due for a little relaxation. Between her scholarship, her grant and an allowance from her parents, she was no shorter of funds than the average student and she had determined that her clothes would not let her down. Other coloured female students, she had noticed, tended to dress in sombre colours, often black, perhaps with some idea of leaving behind their colourful origins and emulating their white peers; but Hal, aware that strong colours suited her, had chosen carefully and invested in a plum-red velvet evening dress. With her hair dressed high on her head and no jewellery, Hal's appearance caused a momentary stumble in the general conversation as the party entered.

When she met her partner for the evening, she was glad to know that she was looking her very best. Justin Carlsborough was a tall and classically handsome young man from a wealthy family, a third-year student much admired by the female students and considered by one and all to be a date well worth the catching. To her surprise and pique, his face remained cold and she guessed that nobody had told him that his date would be black. He greeted her formally, addressed most of his dinner-table conversation to the girl on his other side and, when the dancing began, danced with each of the other girls in rotation, pointedly ignoring Hal.

She was not doomed to be a wallflower, however. Her other neighbour at dinner had been another history student, already glimpsed in the corridors and even encountered over coffee. Gordon Hemmings was about Hal's height – rather more but for her heels – with a thin and intelligent face, lank brown hair and a slim but muscular build. He had been paired with a girl who seemed much more interested in one of the other men; indeed, a general post seemed to be happening quite spontaneously. He remained at Hal's side and soon invited her on to the floor. The dancing was ballroom rather than disco and they moved well together.

'That was a bad show,' he said severely. 'I apologize for my acquaintance. Being a distant relative of aristocracy doesn't do away with the need for manners.'

She forced herself to smile. 'People have been telling the aristocracy that since the dawn of civilization,' she said. 'It doesn't get through. Tell me, did the family money come from the slave trade?'

He hesitated and almost trod on her foot. 'I wouldn't know about that,' he said. 'It seems possible. I'm told that he had a rather unpleasant encounter with some coloured youths once and it may have set up a reaction.'

'I've been hassled by white youths before now,' Hal said. 'I don't take it out on the rest of you.'

'But then, you're more open-minded than he is. Just be assured that, as far as I'm concerned, you're a beautiful girl and you dance like a dream. You must let me see you back to your digs.'

Hal was aware of the unwritten rules. 'Shouldn't you be taking Louise home?' she asked.

'Look at her.'

Hal looked. There could be no doubt that Louise, a blonde programmer from one of the high-tech industries, was setting her cap at a post-graduate student in physics. The two were dancing so close as to attract shocked glances from the more straight-laced dancers.

'Any closer,' he said, 'and they'll be back to back. So, may I see you home?'

'Thank you,' she said. 'I'd like that.'

Gordon Hemmings escorted Hal to her digs and seemed quite satisfied with a quick peck on the lips.

Hal did not expect to hear from him again. She was not a fool and she had observed, from the sidelines, the social whirl. Attitudes among the white, male students were generally clear-cut. Some steered clear of coloured girls, knowing that they would never dare to introduce one to Mother. Others courted them in expectation of easy sex and a trophy to display. This left most of the girls with the choice between socializing with their own colour or, in the hope of ensnaring a more eligible husband, sleeping around. Neither of these options was attractive to Hal, although she could understand and sympathize.

To her surprise, Gordon phoned her two days later. They met for coffee, talked and laughed a lot and went to the cinema. It was soon clear that Gordon was treating her as a friend. Only after a month, during which they met as often as the demands of their studies permitted, did he assume any familiarities and even then he respected the line which she drew.

Examinations and the long vacation intervened, but they resumed their slow courtship and after another month he suggested, very respectfully, that perhaps they might give each other more pleasure in bed than at the cinema or the theatre.

Hal had expected this and had given some thought as to her probable reaction. She could not pretend, even to herself, that she was in love. She held back from admitting any such emotion, but she had come to hold Gordon in some affection. Their late-night farewells had become slowly but progressively more physical and she could recognize hungry responses from her own body. Moreover, it seemed to be a universal opinion that, for a woman, any subsequent affair would be much better than the first. The love of her life would arrive some day and she wanted to be ready for it.

There was no headlong rush into passion. They met for a drink in a quiet hotel lounge and then went to the flat that Gordon shared with two fellow students. Hal was curious rather than timid. She was touched to note that he had made careful preparations. By what was no doubt a long-standing agreement, his flatmates were out. There were soft lights and gentle music. There were even flowers beside the bed. Hal had made her own preparation with equal care. She was bathed and perfumed and dressed from the skin out in her very best. She had also made sure that her handbag contained the necessary supplies. She might be discarding her virginity but she was not going to become pregnant, and while she was almost certain that Gordon was clean and healthy, nobody had ever shot themselves by detouring around an unloaded gun, as her father had once told her in quite a different context.

Hal had been warned by her friends about the impetuosity of young men. Gordon was no sophisticate and she had no reason to believe that he was a skilful lover. But she found that he was patient and considerate. His foreplay seemed to last for ever. Any lingering doubts that Hal might have entertained were submerged by the response of her body which, while her mind was still insisting that the whole business was faintly ridiculous, responded with sensuous delight. When he entered her at last, his movements were leisurely and she sensed that he was restraining himself. As a result, her deflowering was less uncomfortable than it might have been and even proved mildly enjoyable. It ranked, she decided after her passion had cooled, among those events which she was glad to have experienced but was in no particular hurry to experience again.

It was therefore almost a relief when Gordon dropped out

of her life and was to be seen in patient pursuit of an assistant librarian in the Ashmolean. For him, conquest was the hobby and sex no more than a pleasant spin-off. She could have fallen in love with him eventually but, now that his feet of clay were revealed, she found that her heart was intact. She had been told that men were like that and now she knew it. She felt very cynical and worldly-wise.

During Hal's final year at Oxford, she began to worry about her options for a career. History was all very well. She had a talent for it. But what use were historians except to teach history to other budding historians? Perhaps she could use her degree as a stepping-stone into the civil service. Or there might be an opportunity for a grant for research into military history and a book or two. There must be some aspect that had not already been done to death, although none leaped immediately to her mind. When a vacuum demands something to fill it, it is hardly surprising when something is sucked into the vortex. In Hal's case, chance worked through the hackneyed medium of a collision in the cloisters. Hal, beginning to feel the pressure of imminent exams, was hurrying between a lecture and the library when, turning a sudden corner, she bumped into a man and scattered her textbooks on the paving.

The man, who she guessed to be in his early forties, was well dressed in a charcoal-grey suit, a tie which looked as if it belonged to some exclusive club or regiment, a discreetly striped shirt and shoes polished to a professional gloss. He was quick to apologize.

'It was my fault,' Hal said breathlessly. 'Tearing around as usual.'

The man, while giving due care to his trouser-knees, stooped to help her gather her books. As they stood up again, Hal's memory, triggered by the tie, suddenly performed one of its rare and sudden feats of recall. 'It's Major Bowman, isn't it?' she asked.

He regarded her curiously. 'It was,' he said. 'But that was several years ago. Colonel now. I think you should tell me how you know my name.'

Hal's memory was still working overtime. 'I know quite a lot more than that,' she said.

'How much more?'

'Let me see. It's Dennis or Desmond, I forget which. I believe you have the DSO. And you're in Intelligence.'

He waited, very much in command of the situation, for an explanation. He had dark-brown eyes, Hal noticed, and a distinguished streak of grey had appeared in his hair since her earlier sight of him. His voice was accentless in the way that is itself one of the accents of the upper social levels.

'I was brought up in and around Fergusson Barracks,' Hal said. 'My stepfather was the RSM and my mother ran the NAAFI. I've seen you before. You were walking with Colonel Hunter and talking about cricket. Somebody pointed you out to me. Word goes round.'

'I see. And you remembered?'

'Yes. I don't know why.'

His face crinkled into a smile and immediately he looked more human and less aloof. He chuckled. 'That puts me in my place. I had hoped that your memory was refreshed because you were coming to my talk tonight, but then I realized that you'd have got my present rank right if you'd seen the notice. So, my cover's blown, as we're generally believed to say.' He glanced down at the books that he was still holding. 'Tell me, what's your area of study?'

'British military history,' Hal said.

His interest sharpened. From being a man talking, perhaps rather patronizingly, with a beautiful coloured girl half his age, he became more formal. 'In that case, you should definitely come to my talk tonight.' He paused.

Hal, unwilling to admit that she had been too busy to look at the college notice-boards for several days, asked, 'Why?'

Colonel Bowman lowered his voice. 'Have you considered a career in Military Intelligence?' he asked.

'You want to recruit me as a spy?' Hal was glad that blushing never showed on her dark skin. 'Can you see me seducing African military dictators? Would I be sent to a special training camp to learn the arts of womanly wiles?'

He answered her question quite seriously. 'If there was ever any question of that, there would be quite a different channel of selection. But Intelligence isn't all MI5 and agents in the field – and those are usually recruited from people who are already in the right place at the right time. A little information arrives by that means, but very much more of it comes from aerial and satellite photography, embassies, radio and telephone traffic, the arms industry, well-disposed foreign nationals, even from media and guidebooks. Any such item of news on its own may be interesting or even mildly useful. But real Intelligence is putting it all together, collating and sifting it so that the whole becomes greater than the parts. That's how the real story behind all the little stories emerges.' He paused and waited for her reaction.

This was a whole new world of thought for Hal. She had recognized, at a low level of consciousness, that there had to be a human sausage-machine somewhere. Gleanings went in at one end and strategic information came out at the other. But what went on in between was a closely guarded mystery. Now it seemed that there were real people doing real jobs at real desks and machines, and it was being suggested that she become one of them.

'What would I have to do?' she asked.

'Nothing very alarming. Your education doesn't fit you for becoming a technician in computers or signals; you'd have to pick up a lot of expertise along the way. But those technicians are mostly civilians. You'd be expected to join the army. If you're accepted, opt for Intelligence. You'd attend the Standard Graduate Course at Sandhurst for nine months. Your time at university would count towards your seniority, so that you could expect to be promoted to captain before long.' The smile lit his face again. 'Perhaps you don't need to come along this evening unless you think of some questions to ask. You seem to have coaxed me into telling you most of what I intend to say tonight.'

It was all happening too quickly, and yet . . . yet she could see the mists blowing away from the future.

'I'll discuss it with my father,' she said.

# Five

At a secret location near Kermanshah, a very secret meeting was in progress.

There had been many such meetings and series of meetings in the past, but this time an unusual harmony of thought had brought unprecedented agreement. Some of the delegates present already had sensations of cold feet as they realized the momentous events that they had helped to set in train. Between the five Middle Eastern and three African countries (and one which, strictly speaking, should have been counted as Asian) an improbable alliance had been forged.

The chairman, president of one of the largest parties to the alliance, was smiling. It was the grin of a wolf that sees his quarry vulnerable at last. He had waited all his life for this day.

'It will be for our military advisers to prepare detailed plans and report back to us,' he said. 'That will not be tomorrow. It will not be a matter of days, perhaps not even months, but of years, because this time we must be prepared. We have seen what can happen when we depend on Allah alone. But the day will come. The West is already sick of being reviled and harassed at every turn, of being seen as the aggressor against Islam, while Islam is at boiling point against the satanic allies in the West. They have struck at our brethren too often when the quarrel was not theirs.

'There is one more step, which we should prepare immediately. When the day of jehad dawns at last we will need every advantage that we can steal. Our enemies must be distracted and divided and harassed by every means at our disposal, so that we have gained our objectives and

28

consolidated our victories before they can gather their forces. I propose that we give them such a distraction that their military efforts will be hampered at every turn. My Minister of Technology will explain.'

Abdul Bereshvah left his seat against the wall and came to stand at the foot of the table. He glanced benignly around the faces surrounding the huge carved table. The faces stared back at him dispassionately. Every style of dress was represented – Western suits, uniforms, robes. The ignorant fools, he thought, would not appreciate the enormity of the blow that he was about to propose, not until the blow landed, if then. The infidels would feel that their brains had been scooped out of their heads and replaced with dried camel dung. 'For this covert operation,' he said, 'we will need the services of a small number of trustworthy students in each of those countries likely to oppose us . . .'

# Six

Her degree exams over, her last parties attended and her farewells said, Hal quitted Oxford, with some regret, for the last time. She had enjoyed her time there, the lively company, the dignified townscape, the ordered life. Now her life was a blank canvas.

The first priority was thinking-time. Her parents' home was the logical place to pause. One base would be as good as another while she waited for her results and, if that was her decision, scanned the Posts Vacant pages. But first she wanted a word with her stepfather.

The cottage, in mid-summer, was almost too picture-postcard to be true, with roses round the door and house martins nesting under the eaves. It was becoming as much her home as the married quarters had ever been. Her modest accumulation of personal possessions had gone ahead of her by carrier. Hal got off the bus at the end of a lane where tall trees met overhead and finished the journey on foot. She greeted her mother quickly and escaped up the narrow stairs.

A quick dip into cartons and other containers sufficed to produce the basic essentials for unaccustomed leisure – old clothes, a favourite book and her fishing hat. She fetched her trout rod from the den and set off for the stillwater. She wanted to catch the former RSM away from home. There are times when a girl needs her mother, but this was going to be an occasion when the couple's views would certainly differ.

Her stepfather (as she still thought of him) was engaged in teaching a stout man to speycast a salmon line. He gave her a nod but resumed his struggle with poor co-ordination and a lack of understanding of elementary physics. Hal bought a ticket for the water and set up her rod but then settled down under a tree with her book and soon became absorbed. There had been little time for reading fiction at Oxford.

Some while later, a shadow fell on her book. She jumped up and kissed her stepfather on the cheek.

'Your fly isn't fishing until it's in the water,' he reminded her. It was one of his favourite sayings.

'There's nothing rising,' she retorted. 'And anyway, it's too bright for a dry fly. Can you spare a few nymphs?'

Her stepfather obligingly produced a box of pheasant-tail nymphs. Hal hooked several into the lambswool patch on her fishing waistcoat. They settled on a bench while she tied a cast of three.

'Dad,' she said. 'I want to talk.'

He glanced at his watch. 'I'm free for an hour,' he said.

Hal gave him the gist of what Colonel Bowman had said to her and in his talk. From her student-trained memory she quoted the colonel almost verbatim. 'What do you think?' she finished.

He looked across the bright water while he thought. A rainbow trout rose noisily, head-and-tail, but for once the splash and rings roused no response. 'For you,' he said at last, 'it would make a lot of sense. 'You're army from way back and you've got brains and education. But you're female. They won't let you fight.'

'I don't know that I'd want to fight anyway,' Hal said.

'But that's what an army's for,' he pointed out. 'There's no point having an army unless it's at least *prepared* to fight. You wouldn't be happy in a secondary role. But Intelligence . . . yes, I can see you being – what's the word?'

'Fulfilled?' Hal suggested.

'That's it. Fulfilled. Doing something valuable, on a level footing with the men. Using your education and brains. Firing knowledge instead of bullets. Listen, I've never been one to tell you what to do. But if you're asking for my advice, it's this: go for it, girl.'

'I'd pretty much decided that for myself,' Hal said. 'But there's something else. I don't think I want a commission.'

'Still?' said the former RSM. 'You said that before, but I

thought you were only making a point. Why ever not?'

'Can you see me, a black female, swanking around as an officer?'

'I can't see you swanking around. It's not your way. And the army doesn't allow discrimination on grounds of sex or colour these days. Remember what I told you once before – there can be an advantage in starting from a disadvantage.' He paused, trying to think of a metaphor to get the message home. 'A bullet mustn't fly too easily. It needs resistance for the powder to build pressure.'

Hal tucked a blood knot and drew it tight without looking up. For once, she was groping for the right words. She had to express what had been no more than a gut feeling. 'The army may not allow it, but that doesn't change what people are. What's more, I don't think I'd want to be one of that lot.'

'You've lost me. Why do you think I served them for all those years? Salt of the earth.'

'Toffee-nosed,' Hal said unhappily.

'A few, maybe. Less and less.'

Hal hooked her point nymph into the cork handle and put her rod aside. 'I thought you'd be the one who would understand,' she said unhappily. 'God knows I've heard you and your buddies talking between yourselves about officers often enough. You didn't seem to like them very much. And when I was little,' Hal said in a small voice, 'the officers were the ones who called me names. Not to my face, usually, but their children told me what they said about me. Those are the sort of people I'd have to mix with.'

'When you were little,' said her stepfather, 'you were a holy terror. You mixed with the boys and you led them into all sorts of mischief. I well remember the time when you and the adjutant's son – what was his name?'

'Tony Laverick,' said Hal.

'That's right. When you two were caught playing doctors and nurses. You let the regimental goat out of its pen more than once. You egged the Jorrocks boy on to moon at the NAAFI girls. And you pushed another boy's head through the railings so that they had to call REME to come and cut him out.'

'Those were happy days,' Hal said.

'For you perhaps. Not so much fun for those of us who had to pick up the pieces. Any child who got up to half the mischief you did would have been called all the names under the sun. The fact that you were black just gave them a handle to get hold of.'

'I don't know how you put up with me.'

'We loved you.'

'But you weren't my dad then.' There was a sudden silence between them.

He thought hard. 'I'm sorry if we gave you the wrong idea,' he said unhappily at last. 'I know what you mean. I remember how the talk used to go. But we were just blowing off steam. Call it sour grapes if you like. Men always bitch about those who have authority over them. But the officers had our loyalty, one hundred per cent. Try to understand. If somebody else, outside the regiment, had said a word against our officers he'd have had a fight on his hands. It was like the way men may speak of their children or their dogs, making a joke of the bad points . . . I'm not saying it very well, am I?'

'No,' Hal said, 'you're not. But you've helped me to make up my mind.'

'To go for a commission?'

'Not to go for a commission.'

Her father sighed. 'Maybe you'll make it to regimental sergeant-major, but I won't hold my breath. Your tender heart would stand in your way.'

'My heart isn't that damn tender,' Hal said. 'I don't know about you, but I'm going to fish.'

In due course Hal was notified that she had her degree, an upper second-class honours BA in British Military History of the Second Millennium. She enlisted immediately. The recruiting officer blinked when Hal insisted on enlisting under the abbreviated version of her first name, but he accepted it, and so it was as Private Hal Bathurst that she reported for basic training.

For the second time, Hal had to adjust to a major change of lifestyle, but this time the change was not for the better. She was issued with basic equipment – 'Combat 95' – barrack dress and Number Two for parades – trousers for workaday wear and a skirt for dress parades – and then left to sink or swim.

The camp was unlovely and utilitarian, a leftover from some earlier conflict, lurking on the edge of a bleak stretch of moorland. The huts were Spartan. Most were occupied by men, confused youngsters suddenly bereft of their accustomed backgrounds, but one long hut was given over to women recruits. Most had enlisted for the sake of secure and ordered employment not easily available in civilian life. Some were there because they were escaping from worse backgrounds. One or two might have made Civvy Street too hot to hold them.

Hal's military career might easily have begun with a black mark against her prospects.

The training, which was mostly in the field, she could take in her stride. It was aimed at developing fitness, and she was already fit. She was also steeped in army philosophy. Drill she accepted as the only way to teach a habit of immediate and disciplined response to orders. Spit and polish ensured that equipment was well maintained. She was well co-ordinated and she could already shoot. Map reading, signals and clerical skills came easily to her.

She could not accept barrack-room life as easily. Hal was unlucky. She was part of an intake in which rivalries embedded in age-old class hatred flared up. Bullying became rife. In this, a tough Yorkshire farm-girl named Hilda took the lead, followed by a small coterie of sycophants. Hilda was thickset, with a layer of fat over heavy bones. She had tight, blonde curls, a rosebud mouth and spots.

The more educated girls, some of them already earmarked for having officer training, were an automatic target for the bullying, but Hal, being both well-spoken and black, was the immediate focus. Her determination not to back down was obvious, so aggression was limited at first to snide remarks and petty persecutions. When it came to repartee, Hal could give as good as she got. She had learned in a hard school.

Then her kit began to disappear, but Hal helped herself, quite openly, to replacements from the kit of the obvious culprits. She told herself that she would endure, but if she ever became an NCO she would know what signs to watch for. There would be no bullying under her command.

Hilda chose an unwise moment to mount her first real attack. Hal was tired and fed up after a hard day. She returned from the shower, only too ready for her bed, to find that somebody had defecated between the blankets.

She looked around. Some of the girls were wide-eyed; some were conspicuously unaware of what was going on; some looked shocked, but Hilda was smugly triumphant and her hangers-on waited expectantly.

Hal felt a surge of fury but there was also a sense of relief. It was time that matters came to a head. If she couldn't handle this, then the army was too tough for her. She moved quickly and stood nose to nose with Hilda. 'You did that.'

Hilda smirked. 'I did not.'

'Tough,' said Hal. 'Because it has your smell, so you're the one who's going to eat it.'

That was enough, and more than enough. Hilda choked and grabbed at her. The farm-girl was strong but Hal could almost match her for strength, and her Oxford instructor had taught her to use her weight, strength and balance to best effect. Twice she slipped out of the other's clutches and sent her adversary tumbling. Hilda tried a roundhouse swing but Hal ducked under it and delivered a slap that made Hilda's head ring. Then Hilda made a lucky grab and caught Hal by the hair. Any other girl might have been dragged around the room but Hal, though her eyes were watering, was not beaten. She grabbed the other by an intimate and tender part of her anatomy and pinched with all her might.

Hilda squealed like an injured piglet. She released her grip but in the process raked her fingernails down Hal's face. Hal just managed to turn her head in time to save her eyes. They jumped apart.

Nobody moved to intervene. Voices were crying support for Hal and a few for Hilda. But it was time to call a halt before somebody got seriously hurt. Hal called on her earlier lessons in unarmed combat. As Hilda came boring in, Hal delivered a straight-fingered jab to the solar plexus. The fat girl's muscles had been toughened by her years on the farm but Hal had delivered the jab with her weight behind it, aiming for a point beyond the other girl's spine, just as her instructor at Oxford had taught her. Hilda folded towards her.

The sergeant in charge of the hut was on her way back from the NAAFI when she heard the din and broke into a trot. She found Hal seated on the floor with Hilda's head clamped between her knees. Hilda, kneeling, was also held in a double hammerlock. Her clothes were up and two of her former victims, at Hal's invitation, were laying into her bare backside, turn about, with webbing straps, to universal applause. Nobody loves a fallen bully.

The sergeant's voice could have been used to split logs and she knew how to get the most out of it. In very few seconds, she had the combatants apart and standing more or less to attention. Hal was already ashamed of her violence and un-decided whether to be penitent or defiant. Hilda, though, was not accustomed to retaliation. Unpractised at defeat, her mind had gone back to the last years in which she had suffered similar indignity. Knuckling her eyes and sobbing, she awaited the comforting that nobody would give her.

The sergeant was in a dilemma. Strictly, brawling in barracks should have been brought before an officer, but that the tension had been allowed to build up into such an incident would not have reflected well on her. A chorus of witnesses were vying to assure her where the blame lay and the evidence was only too ready to be seen and smelt. She looked severely upon the two sinners. There was a trace of blood in the scratches on Hal's face. Hilda's wounds were now hidden. The sergeant made her decision.

'By rights, this should be dealt with by the OC and end up on your conduct sheets. Any more nonsense from either of you,' she said, 'and that's where you go. But that would penalize you, Bathurst, and as for you, Settle, you've been a pain in the backside ever since you arrived. Just remember this: you'll neither of you make it in the army if you can't settle your differences without resorting to a punch-up.'

36

Hilda wiped her eyes with a solid forearm. 'You didn't see me fighting.'

'She started it,' said a voice.

'She messed in my bed,' Hal said stiffly. 'As far as I'm concerned, this is her bed from now on.'

Hilda wailed. What had been a joke on somebody else was a disaster when applied to herself. 'The sergeant said that that was my bed,' she said, pointing.

The sergeant had had more than enough of Hilda. The fat girl had been a thorn in her flesh since the first day of the intake. 'The sergeant said that that was your bed space. Right. You two.' The girls who had been wielding the straps had tried to melt into the throng but she singled them out. 'Swap the two beds over.'

The exchange of the lightweight beds was made in a few seconds. There were giggles and a few whispered comments.

The sergeant was tempted to press Hilda's humiliation a step or two further but it was evident that she was already a broken spirit. 'Bring the blankets and come with me,' she said, almost kindly. 'You're going to wash them out by hand. Tonight, you sleep in your sleeping bag.'

Hal and Hilda were excessively polite to each other for the remainder of their basic training. Hal even warned off a tough Glaswegian girl who decided that Hilda was now fit meat for bullying.

Hal's first posting was to Scotland, where she worked for a few months in the centre monitoring telephone and radio traffic. She was sent on a short course in decoding at GCHQ in Cheltenham and a longer course on computers. Then, under constant instruction, she was put to work interpreting aerial photographs and satellite imaging of areas unlikely to be of much interest to anybody.

If the frequent changes of company and places and the many journeys by train and army vehicle were unsettling, the work was always interesting. Her long acquaintance with military organization helped her to get by without putting a foot wrong and more than once she was able to give guidance to some other recruit who had fallen foul of the system. This must have been noticed, because she was soon awarded corporal's stripes.

Basic training had done little to correct Hal's deep-rooted mistrust of the officer class, and the officers themselves had not improved Hal's opinion of them by remaining remote and superior. Once at work, however, doing a specialist job under specialist officers, barriers were substantially lowered. Officers, both male and female, she discovered, were people. They were all different, as pertained throughout the human race. Some stood on their dignity while others were prepared to seek help when help was needed. Some were prepared to accept her as a fellow worker and human being and unbend over a cup of tea. None of them, she came to realize, was better educated than herself or more intelligent, just more fully trained and more willing to take on responsibility. Not all of them, even, were white. Her fellow rankers, by comparison, might have hearts of gold, but in other respects they fell short, their conversational level rarely attaining even the most modest intellectual level. Hal began to think about applying for a commission.

She was spared the effort. Eighteen months into her army service, she was summoned into the presence of her commanding officer, a woman lieutenant-colonel with metallic-grey hair, a formidable bark and a mouth tightly clenched against any admission of humanity. Hal would have wondered, once again, whether her sins had found her out, but on this occasion a quick search of her conscience assured her that there had been no sins worthy of the colonel's attention.

'Sit down,' said the colonel. This was almost unprecedented. Seeing her at close range for the first time, Hal realized that the colonel had kindly, grey eyes. She seated herself, making a conscious effort to be neither too stiff nor too relaxed.

The colonel glanced at some papers on her desk. 'You volunteered for Intelligence.'

'Yes,' Hal agreed.

'You gave the recruiting officer the impression that you had been unemployed since leaving school. No mention is made of further education, let alone at Oxford. I must admit that I've wondered about you. You're intelligent and disciplined, and your work is very good. Now it comes to my ears that you have a jolly good degree in military history. Well?'

Hal wondered what she was expected to say. 'That's true, ma'am,' she said at last.

The colonel showed irritation for a passing moment. 'I know it's true. I phoned. Why did you keep quiet about it? You could have gone straight for a commission.'

'That's why I kept quiet about it, ma'am,' Hal said. 'At that time, I couldn't see myself with a commission. My . . . my father was a warrant officer.'

'Your stepfather was RSM of the North Wessex and very well thought of,' the colonel said. 'That doesn't explain why you didn't want a commission. It can't have been lack of ambition. Was it your colour? Afraid of not fitting in?'

'Something like that, ma'am.' Hal gathered her courage. 'May I ask how you come to know so much about me?'

The colonel looked at her papers again. 'I don't see any harm in telling you that. I had a phone call from a Colonel Bowman. Do you know him?' The kindly eyes were watching Hal shrewdly.

'We met once,' Hal admitted. 'For a few minutes.' The colonel seemed to be wondering whether Colonel Bowman was seeking promotion for his black mistress.

'I see,' the colonel said. 'Well, I don't know how he came by his information and the question seems irrelevant.' She paused, and Hal suddenly realized that the friendly eyes were watching her sharply. 'You said "at that time". Do I understand that you've had second thoughts? Give me an honest answer, now.'

'I had begun to think about it,' Hal said slowly.

'And you're finding the prospect less intimidating?'

'A little.'

The colonel's eyes were on Hal, but Hal had the impression that they were not seeing her any more. 'I should tell you,' the colonel said at last, 'that the army has changed. No organization is perfect. There is still prejudice about class and colour, but it is being eliminated and merit is more and more being recognized. I don't think that you need have anything to fear. Can you accept that?'

'Yes, ma'am,' said Hal.

'Good. I'll put your name forward to be considered for a commission then.'

Hal went before the Regular Commissions Board at Westbury, endured three days of rigorous testing and passed with flying colours. The colonel sent for her to congratulate her. A month later, she was given a date for reporting at the Royal Military Academy, Sandhurst, and sent on leave.

It was the late winter, so there would be no angling except perhaps for grayling. Hal arrived home to find that her father, who could not bear to have a period of idleness in his year, was helping the gamekeeper on a nearby estate. She had to wait until evening before she could greet him. Then she had to kick her heels in the small sitting room with a gin and tonic in her hand while her mother, refusing all offers of help, worked in the kitchen and her father soaked away the day's weariness in a hot bath.

After they had eaten, she managed to manoeuvre her father into the sitting room. 'Did you go to see Colonel Bowman?' she asked bluntly.

He looked guilty but said, 'No, I did not.'

'You phoned him?'

'No.'

Hal took a seat on the arm of his chair and tapped him gently on his bald spot with her forefinger. 'Well, I don't see how else Colonel Bowman knew all about me and snitched to my colonel. So come on. Spill the beans. What did you do?'

'If you must know,' the former RSM said with dignity, 'I was invited to a regimental reunion and Colonel Bowman was there as a guest of the CO. He remembered me and he remembered you and he asked about you. He already knew you'd been up at Oxford so there wasn't any secret about your degree—'

'Which you boasted about until he was sick of the sound of it.'

'Which I boasted about until he was sick. Then he asked

what you were doing now. Was I supposed to make up some lie?' her father asked plaintively.

'No, I suppose not. I'll forgive you,' Hal said. 'But only just.'

'So what's happening about it?'

'I report to Sandhurst on the fifteenth.'

His usually disciplined face broke up into a smile and yet his mouth was trembling. 'I'm so proud of my little girl,' he whispered.

She jumped up. 'We'll have to have a drink on it,' she said. She turned to the drinks cupboard to give him time to wipe his eyes.

When she turned back, carrying a whisky for him, another gin and tonic for herself and a rum and peppermint to carry through for her mother, his mind had returned to its practical bent. 'If you'd gone for a commission straight from university,' he said, 'your time at Oxford would have counted towards your seniority. That's why you see such young captains and majors these days. But, coming up through the ranks, you've had the better grounding. You'll know what it's like to be a squaddy. You'll be the better officer for that.'

On her last evening at home, her father presented her with a cheque.

'You've never asked for money,' he said. 'You've managed on your army pay and I respect that. But you'll find life different as a junior officer. You'll be paid more – not a lot more and not enough. What you're paid won't be all yours to spend any more. You'll have to buy your own uniforms and there'll be mess bills to pay. This will help until you get established.'

The cheque seemed to be for a rather large sum. 'This won't leave you and Mum short?' she asked anxiously.

'Bless you, no,' he said. 'I've been saving for this day.'

'If I fluff the course, I'll pay you back.'

'That won't happen,' he said, laughing.

Hal was not so sure. Her cold feet were making an unwelcome return. From an ordered and established existence, with a known place in the scheme of things, she was making another dive off another deep end. She had moderated her first limited view of officers, seen from the lowly position of an Other Rank, as confident beings with arrogant voices, relaying their orders through a hierarchy of NCOs. Common sense suggested that these lordly people must once have been officer cadets, facing the challenge but full of the agony of self-doubt. She thought back to her youth. The army children had mingled freely and she had seen and listened to the officers off duty and off guard. Those had been just men and women like other officers whom she had encountered in Int-Corps, she decided. The training made most of the difference. If they could learn, so could she. But she had never been one to tempt fate. 'We'll see,' she said cautiously.

'So we will. They'll throw a lot of information at you. Learn it all. You never know when any piece of it will prove essential. But above all, learn the *system*. Study it. Learn to play it like a violin.'

Hal only nodded, but she was impressed. Her father had put into words what she had found intuitively for herself.

'One last thing,' her father said. 'You'll need your sense of humour, but don't let it run away with you. The army loves a joke but hates a joker.'

Next day, her father drove her to the railway station and insisted on carrying her brown issue suitcase to the train.

'Dad,' she said, 'if I make it—'

'You'll make it.'

'Please, listen. When I make it, I'd like to change my name. I want to be commissioned with your name. Brown. Is that all right?'

The former RSM swelled with pride. He was lost for words and left his reply too late. As the train pulled out, he saluted. It was against his training and tradition to salute in civilian clothes, but nothing less would have met the occasion.

# Seven

Sandhurst was not as much of a shock as Hal had feared. She had become used to sudden plunges into new company, but among the cadets were many familiar strengths and weaknesses. The selection process had produced a cross-section not unlike that at Oxford, but with a bias towards physical fitness and an ability to command and away, slightly, from raw intelligence. There were the same sudden friendships and personality clashes, the same rivalries and collaborations, the same snobbery and prejudices. But there was also a cleaning of the slate for fresh beginnings. Her green beret was changed for a blue-black one with the RMAS cap badge. Hal was sorry to lose her corporal's stripes, but they were all officer cadets now, no more and no less.

Hal, born black of mixed British parentage, was immune to feelings of colour prejudice. She had, as it were, a foot in both camps. She was aware of its existence, sometimes painfully so, but she was careful to treat people as people, letting friendship fall where it might and making no effort to choose the colour of her friends. Although the British Army prided itself on being free from such prejudice, few coloured cadets had arrived at Sandhurst from its ranks. On the other hand, friendly disposed powers of ex-colonial status sent their officer material for Sandhurst training, so that there was no shortage of black faces. She neither sought nor avoided their company.

Her room-mate was a willowy blonde from nearby in Berkshire. Susan Thyme was the daughter of an artillery major, now retired and teaching maths at Wellington. The two girls found an instant rapport based on nothing whatever except, perhaps, that as they went around together they drew male eyes to them. In khaki, they could have passed for negative and positive images of a single photograph and this somehow underlined the attractiveness of each.

Officer training was hard and demanding. For the first five weeks they were not allowed out at all, but even Sandhurst could not commandeer every minute of every day. Early in the course, they were seated in the shade of a spreading tree on a spring evening, enjoying the sunshine and watching the comings and goings of the other cadets.

Hal suddenly stiffened. A distant figure, pacing with confident strides and ignoring lesser mortals, had caught her eye. 'I think I see somebody I know from Oxford,' she said.

Susan read the distaste in Hal's voice. 'Somebody you didn't like very much. A woman, I presume.'

'A man, of sorts. The tall cadet talking to Captain Wynn.'

'Carlsborough,' said Susan, who had been quick to identify the better-looking men. While Hal had been acquainting herself with the layout and routines, Susan had been more interested in gathering information about their fellow cadets.

'That's right. I was taken on a blind date with him and he treated me like shit. I wonder how he comes to be here. He was all set to graduate from Oxford and go into the civil service.'

'He got involved in some scandal and got himself sent down,' Susan said. 'Something to do with drugs and a girl who nearly died. You're well out of that one. From what I hear, the civil service wouldn't touch him after that. He was sent for a long cruise, skippering Daddy's yacht around the Mediterranean, while his sins were forgotten and his folks pulled a lot of strings to get him through the Regular Commissions Board and accepted here. Anyway, thanks for the warning. Forget him. There would seem to be two other blokes heading our way. Not as good-looking and probably not as rich, but there's one of them at least who won't be bothered by any question of race.'

Hal looked. Two figures were walking in their direction with the determined but self-conscious strides of men who are still thinking out their pick-up lines and only too aware that they are inviting rejection.

'I've met the big one,' Hal said. 'He bought me coffee. I only spoke to him because I heard him quote from a poem in Swahili and I wanted a chance to practise. I think he fancies me.' The big one – and he was very big – was as black as Hal herself, but by tacit agreement skin colour was a subject usually avoided or ignored between them.

'Well, why wouldn't he?' Susan asked. 'And you could do worse. His uncle's the president of some African state. A complete bog-hole, they tell me, but a president is a president. When he goes home he'll probably start at brigadier and go on up from there.'

'My father's a president,' Hal said. 'But he's only president of an angling club, so I don't suppose it counts for much.'

'Not a lot,' Susan agreed.

The two men arrived. 'So we meet again,' the mountainous black man said jovially. His voice was a deep bass. 'I did not introduce myself. I am Simon Agulfo.'

'Hal Brown,' said Hal.

He reached for her hand. Hal took his and let him pull her to her feet. She introduced Susan.

The other man was looking at Hal with amusement. 'You don't remember me?' he asked.

Hal considered his broad build. His features were blunt but they were put together in a way which produced a face that was both friendly and likeable. What she could see of his hair was fair, inclined towards ginger. Something stirred in her memory but she still hesitated.

'Tony Laverick. I'm hurt. I'd have known you anywhere.'

'I don't suppose you would, really,' Hal said, laughing. 'You've grown about two feet, your voice has broken, you don't have gaps in your teeth any more and I can only see the stubbly fringe of your hair, so I could hardly be expected to recognize you before you spoke.' She turned to Simon Agulfo. 'Does he still believe everything anyone tells him?'

'Not a word! In his youth he was deceived by a woman and now he trusts nobody.' Simon laughed aloud and Hal joined in. The happy laugh of her childhood had turned into something warm and musical and it still gave her a pleasant

surprise whenever she heard it. Their laughter was infectious
and the other two laughed with them.

'Not true!' said Tony. 'I believe anything a beautiful woman
tells me. Nothing from anybody else.'

'In that case,' Susan said, 'you'll believe that I'm rich and
famous and a superlative lover.'

'Of course. I nearly made the British Olympic team as a
lover myself.'

'I like this boy,' Susan said.

'You two will have many years to catch up on,' said Simon.
'I suggest a drink. Very much my treat.'

He helped Susan to her feet and the four set off, very careful
to behave with the utmost propriety. Evaluating eyes were
always on them.

The four fell into the habit of going around together. As a
foursome they found many tastes in common. Their precious
leisure time was filled with jaunts and jokes. If Simon's humour
was sometimes a little heavy-handed, he had – courtesy of
his uncle, the president – an expensive car, which went a long
way towards compensating, although the use of cars by cadets
was strictly limited to Sundays. The car, an Alfa Romeo, had
a radiator grille that resembled a mouth puckered for a kiss,
which Susan said privately was probably what had attracted
him to the model in the first place. He was never short of
money and, without any trace of ostentation, he managed to
underwrite, as his share of the common expenses, any sums
that might have embarrassed the pockets of the others.

The physical content of the course was exhausting, far more
severe than basic training had been, but there were also more
academic subjects to provide relief. For some subject-matter
the cadets were grouped according to their regimental desti-
nations; for others, men and women were separated; but a
basic understanding of infantry and other tactics was deemed
necessary for all. Hal was to remember one paper tactical
exercise. The cadets were ordered to pair off and they were
set a problem. They were furnished with a map. One of each
pair was to prepare a plan for the defence of a small hill in

a narrow valley; the other was to prepare a plan of attack. The two plans would be compared and judgement delivered.

It was generally assumed among their fellows that romance was in the air and that Hal was paired with Simon and Susan with Tony. It was a rational assumption, but a false one. Sexual tension was inevitably sometimes present, but on the whole relationships were near platonic. Simon Agulfo was heavily flirtatious towards both girls. Hal, however, felt no more than a mild liking for him but instead was conscious of an affection – part nostalgic and part sisterly, she told herself – for Tony. Susan seemed to have difficulty conversing with any man without exuding pheromones and her presence was usually enough to make Tony retire into his shell.

That assumption, however, may also have been adopted by the staff because, when Hal and Simon agreed to become a team, the officer in charge of the exercise made them change their pairings. Hal was paired with Tony and Susan with Simon. The men were designated the attackers, a decision that the girls privately considered sexist.

In the subsequent debriefing, the results were clear. Susan had prepared a defence against a frontal assault up the valley but Simon had used a series of defiles in the surrounding hills to outflank and enfilade her defences. Susan was not greatly concerned; she was destined for Signals and the likelihood of her ever being called on to command a company in action was acknowledged, even by the staff, to be remote. Tony had mounted a similar but more subtle attack, but Hal, making use of her earlier training in Intelligence Preparation of the Battlefield, and after careful study of the map, had moved her troops from the hill to a more defensible position overlooking both the hill and the defile. This, it appeared, was the solution favoured by the staff.

The four gathered for a pre-dinner drink in the bar and settled at a corner table. 'I can lose gracefully,' Tony said, 'but I don't see why I should have to. Short of a squadron of helicopters, there wasn't any alternative for the attacking force.'

Hal produced a pen and began a quick sketch of the map on a paper napkin. 'Maybe not,' she said. 'But you wouldn't have been ambushed if you had taken more care. It was obvious from the contours that if you'd sent a party up this gully *here*, not more than half a kilometre, they'd have been able to see what I was up to.' She had placed a section with light machine guns and an 81mm mortar in position to wipe out any such scouting party, but she decided not to mention that piece of forethought. It might prove decisive next time around.

Hal managed to avoid any contact with Justin Carlsborough until one evening later in the course, when she was almost the last to enter the large dining hall, to find that the only vacant seat was at his side.

He glanced round as she seated herself. He lifted his rather prominent nose at the sight of a coloured girl joining him. Then his eyes sharpened as recognition dawned. 'What the hell are you after?' he asked quietly. 'They serve no soul food here.'

'Speaking to me at last, are you?' she retorted. 'That was a silly sort of question. After all, I know exactly what you're doing here.' After a pause, she could not resist adding, 'And why.'

She saw his jaw muscles tighten. 'Well, you can stop following me around,' he said in a furious whisper. 'I am not interested in black tail.'

She kept her temper but declined to keep her own voice down. 'And I am not interested in conceited, honky rejects,' she said. Somebody on the other side of the table sniggered.

He swore at her under his breath and turned away. For the rest of the meal he made forced conversation with the man on his other side.

After dinner, Hal intercepted Susan and told her about the exchange. 'You know all about everybody,' she said. 'What's got into that bastard? I never did him any harm.'

Susan shrugged. 'I believe that he was brought up some-where in East Africa,' she said.

'He probably had his bum wiped by a black ayah and he's never got over the indignity of it.'

'Worse than that,' Susan said. She lowered her voice. 'I heard that he caught a nasty disease from a black girl once. And ayahs were in India. The word's Hindustani or Urdu or something.'

'Whatever,' Hal said. 'Anyway, he needn't think that he can take it out on me.'

The general assumption that Hal and Simon, if not already in the throes of an affair, were heading in that direction, seemed to be held by Simon himself. From occasional nuances in his conversation, she gathered that he had a fiancée, of his own choosing, back in Africa and she was fairly sure that he spent occasional evenings in nearby towns, pursuing the local girls. But his manner towards Hal became progressively more flirtatious and proprietary.

Hal tried to stave off any more direct approach without hurting his feelings, but her hints were ignored. He persuaded her one evening to join him for a walk in the Berkshire countryside on the pretext of learning something about British wildlife. They stood together on a hilltop and admired the view. They were in civilian clothes and Hal thought privately that his shirt was the brightest object in sight.

'We have a weekend pass to come,' he said. 'Will you be going home?'

Hal had already decided against the journey. If she decided to stick to public transport rather than bother her father (who was inclined to curse other drivers for their lack of discipline and to insist on his right of way) she would have arrived home with barely time to turn around and start back. 'Perhaps,' she said cautiously.

'I would like you to accept this.' He produced a small box. 'I thought that we might go to a motel that I know. Small and discreet, but very comfortable.'

She had enjoyed his company but she was not attracted to him romantically or, she thought, sexually, and she was not flattered by his easy assumption that she would make herself available. She thought quickly, searching for a polite form of refusal. 'I don't think that I'm ready for any sort of relationship,' she said. She was about to return the box but curiosity made her open it first. Coiled inside was a necklace of small-to medium-sized pearls – probably cultured, she was not expert enough to tell the difference, but a valuable gift all the same. She snapped the box shut and tried to hand it back. 'Thank you very much,' she said, 'but no thank you.'

He smiled, showing teeth as white as hers. He seemed neither hurt nor abashed. 'Keep it anyway,' he said. 'You may change your mind.'

'I don't think so,' she said. She pushed the box into his hand and turned away.

He caught up with her. She was aware of an awkward silence. To break it, she said, 'I like your shirt.'

He took it off. His barrel chest was heavily padded with muscle. 'I give it to you,' he said. 'I like your dress.'

'You would never fit into it,' she said. He boomed with laughter and resumed his shirt. Hal was suddenly aware of the emptiness of the countryside and she walked faster until they reached the road again.

It was soon evident that Simon was not perturbed by the rejection. That evening, Susan tackled Hal. 'Simon's invited me to go away for the weekend,' she said.

Hal decided to proceed carefully. 'And what did you say?'

'I told him that I'd let him know tomorrow. Hal, would you mind if I took him up on it?'

'Not in the least. Simon means nothing in my young life. But, Sue . . . Be careful.'

Susan laughed. 'It's all right, Grandma. I do know about the birds and bees.'

'So I would hope,' Hal said. 'But I wasn't thinking about babies and things. It wouldn't do your chances of a commission much good if they got to think that you were easy meat.'

'Probably not,' Sue acknowledged. 'But we'd be discreet. I'm not planning to fall for him – that wouldn't be on at all. But it's been work, work, work, and I'm overdue for a little fun. And, Hal, he's given me the loveliest present. Pearls.'

Hal was piqued. The necklace had been hers for a few seconds. 'A necklace?' she asked.

Susan shook her head. 'A bracelet.'

'A diamond cap badge might have been more suitable.'

'That would certainly make some eyes pop.' Susan laughed and then sobered. She sat down on Hal's bed. 'We certainly won't make any babies. Hal, is it true what they say about coloured men?'

'I have no more idea than you have,' Hal said.

'That was tactless of me, wasn't it?' She paused and took a breath. 'Hal, do you mind being . . .'

'Black?'

'I was going to say coloured.'

'But I'm not coloured,' Hal said gently. 'Coloured means red, green or blue. I don't think about it very much, but when I see my hands or look in the mirror, what I see isn't even brown, it's black and there's not much point being mealy-mouthed about it. And black means no colour at all, if you think about it.

'To answer your question, no, I don't mind a lot. It's only pigment and it doesn't really mean a thing unless you want it to, except that I can go out in the sun when you have to smear yourself with sunblock. It's a nuisance when it gets me hassled by some racist yob, or if some ignorant prat like Carlsborough thinks that it gives him the right to look down on me, or if . . . some other man thinks that he can order me to jump into bed with him. But I'm quite capable of defending myself, and if it comes to a slanging match I can give as good as I get. On the whole, no, I don't mind. I know that I'm me and I know what I am and if somebody else can't take me for what I am, then that's their fault and not mine.'

'Well, I think that's very well balanced of you,' Susan said.

'I have to be balanced about it. My only alternative is to get a bloody great chip on my shoulder.'

'Instead of pips?'

Hal laughed. 'Exactly,' she said. But deep inside her was a knowledge that she never brought out into the light of day. She tried hard to pretend that it did not exist. But once her reservations had been overcome and she had agreed to go for a commission, ambition had raised its head again. Yet she knew that her prospects of promotion would be finite – not because of any policy or regulation but because, when promotions were on the wind, there would be an unspoken, unconscious black mark against her name, deriving from the certainty that a proportion of whites, even of white women, would have an instinctive reaction against accepting orders from one of her colour.

She sighed. Time enough to worry about that when it happened.

Susan left for her heavy date, walking the first half-mile rather than getting into Simon Agulfo's car on the threshold of the Royal Military Academy. Hal spent a lazy Saturday afternoon, but her muscles were tuned to physical activity and she found herself restless. In the evening she went in search of an opponent for a few games of squash.

Susan reappeared in time for Sunday lunch, looking dreamily pleased with herself.

'You've had a good time?' Hal asked carefully.

Susan was more outspoken. 'Great. Which do you want first, the good or the bad?'

Hal laughed her warm chuckle. 'Let's get the bad over with.'

Sue stretched and made a face. 'Our friend is not one of your gentle, considerate lovers. His view is that if a thing's worth doing, it's worth doing violently.'

'I'm not terribly surprised. The good?'

'Tireless. And it's true what they say about black men. You should try it some time. God has been good to him.'

Hal, though less experienced, knew what she meant. She admired the pearl bracelet without envying it.

She was fetched out of a lecture on military law next morning and sent to the small office occupied by her company commander, a young major from one of the Guards regiments. The company commander was clearly embarrassed.

'You'd better sit down,' he said. This was unusual and he recognized Hal's surprise and alarm. 'Nobody's died,' he said quickly, 'and this is not a disciplinary matter – more of a fatherly talk. It's been reported that you went to a motel on Saturday night with a fellow cadet, and a foreign national at that. No, hear me out,' he said as Hal began to protest. 'What a cadet does in his or her spare time, provided it is done without scandal, is their own business. You are an adult, even if a young one, and presumably know what you're doing. But you in particular are supposed to be destined for Intelligence work, and any hint that you might be susceptible to seduction or blackmail might be very damaging to your prospects.'

Hal could feel her blood pressure rising. She rose to her feet. 'I would prefer to stand for the moment,' she said. 'Let me assure you, sir, that I did not leave here on Saturday night.'

The company commander frowned. 'So far, I have only been offering you a word of advice. Better, perhaps, that we don't take it any further. These things can so easily get on to the record.'

That was all very well, but Hal was sure that a note would be made in her file, to follow her throughout her career and cause a further reduction in her promotion prospects. 'I'll take it as far as anyone wants,' she said slowly and distinctly. 'I can guess who put the poison in. Carlsborough. Am I right, sir?' She got no answer. 'This is the purest spite. For some reason, he's had it in for me ever since we first met at Oxford. On Saturday evening, I played squash with the chaplain and after that we went for a game of chess. I was with him until after eleven. Rather late to be setting out for a night of dalliance, wouldn't you say?'

The major sat very still. 'You'd better wait here,' he said at last.

Hal resumed her chair. She waited, alone, for nearly an hour. Her blood pressure fell, along with her spirits. She was looking out of the window when the major returned, bringing with him Justin Carlsborough.

The cadet was looking unhappy. He stood to attention and looked at the wall above Hal's head. 'I hope,' said the major, 'that we can dispose of this matter before anyone gets hurt. Otherwise there will undoubtedly be tears before bedtime. Go ahead.'

'It seems that I owe you an apology,' Carlsborough said stiffly. 'On Sunday morning, I heard a car and a woman's voice. I looked out. Cadet Agulfo was locking his car. The woman was already out of sight. I jumped to the conclusion that the voice I had heard was yours.' This was said woodenly, as though learned by heart, but there was fresh venom in his voice as he added, 'Knowing that the two of you have been inseparable.'

The major hesitated and then asked, 'Do you accept that

apology?' His tone was doubtful as if, in Hal's shoes, he might have had reservations.

'I didn't hear an actual apology,' Hal said.

'I apologize,' Carlsborough said. The words seemed to be squeezed out of him.

Hal, in her turn, also hesitated. She wanted to make a formal complaint that would result in Carlsborough being dragged before the CO. But any such malice would undoubtedly rebound against herself. 'Yes.' The word came out as a whisper. 'I accept the apology.'

'Very well. This will not go on either of your records.' The major looked up at the ceiling, choosing his words carefully. 'The army does not appreciate malicious gossip. Any further examples will certainly be noticed and action taken. And, Cadet Brown, you may care to note, for purposes of your career in Intelligence, what can come of drawing unjustified conclusions from inadequate data. You may both go.'

Outside the office door, Justin Carlsborough strode off without another word or glance.


On their last morning at Sandhurst, Hal met Simon Agulfo. They had remained on friendly but outwardly platonic terms even during Simon's short affair with Susan, although there was sometimes a hot gleam in his eye when their eyes met. He intercepted Hal as they walked to the parade ground for the last time, each very stiff in new Number One Ceremonial dress.

'So this is farewell,' she said lightly.

'It is. And I would like you to take this.' He tried to put the box with the pearl necklace into her hand.

Hal put her hands behind her back. 'I can't take it.'

He assumed a hurt look. 'I gave it to you as a friend.'

'And I'm declining it as a friend,' Hal said firmly. She was in no doubt that the necklace had been given in expectation of favours that had not been forthcoming and she was not one to welsh on a debt.

Hal's parents, beaming with pride, attended the passing-out parade. The ceremony over, Hal's mother kissed her fondly, but when Hal offered her cheek to her father he hesitated and tried to settle for a long handshake. Warrant officers – in his strict view, even retired warrant officers – did not kiss commissioned officers in public. Then he threw dignity to the winds and clasped her to him. Hal was startled to realize that his face was wet with tears.

Later, Hal went around saying goodbye to her friends. She found Sue and Simon together and waited discreetly while they parted. Neither seemed heartbroken; her own goodbye to Susan seemed to hold more genuine emotion. Simon waited nearby to gain her attention. 'I shall remember you always,' he said.

'And I shall remember you,' Hal said politely.

'I hope so. And any gift that I give remains given. That necklace will always be yours, wherever it is.'

'That's a beautiful thought,' Hal said.

'And a true one. I shall think of you often.'

They wished each other luck.

Hal and Tony had still to say their farewells. Tony was clearly holding something back. In the end he only gave her a quick peck on the cheek, mumbled a few words and turned away. Throughout the course, Hal had been aware of a tension between them, warm and comforting but impossible to pin down. At first, she had put it down to friendship. Then she had wondered whether it was sexual attraction. Tony was not an obvious stud, reeking of testosterone. His appearance and manner were both definitely 'boy next door' rather than 'rampant stallion'. But Hal was experienced enough to know that she attracted men. Could a physical desire for her on Tony's part be raising an echo in her? But no. The light in his eyes was not pure lust. Affection, then, and nothing more. They were embarking on their careers and heading in different directions, he to the North Wessex Regiment and she to Intelligence. An entanglement at this stage would, at best, be impractical.

When Hal unpacked her cases that evening at home, she found the necklace, in its box, tucked into her pyjamas.

# Eight

After her first, impulsive gesture, Hal had had second thoughts about a change of name. A black girl named Brown would be a cliché, inviting infinite racial humour. But her father had been so proud and pleased at the suggestion that she had no heart to disappoint him, so she had gone through the surprisingly simple processes of a name change by deed poll.

As a graduate she was not required to serve as a second lieutenant, so it was Lieutenant Hal Brown, very smart in her brand new uniform, who was posted straight from Sandhurst to the Intelligence Training School in Kent. Her previous experience made sure that she had little trouble with the technical subjects and she absorbed the human parts of the training without effort.

She was sent to Cheshire, to a unit that specialized in the sifting of messages intercepted by radio, but her fluency in Swahili and her almost equal acquaintance with Arabic were soon noticed, and Lt Brown was posted to the Ministry of Defence in London.

Her four years in London were a revelation to Hal. Hitherto, she had considered herself to be a country girl, but London – expensive, gritty and odorous, hostile and friendly by turns, packed with swirling crowds, offering tawdry entertainment but backed by age-old culture of a high order – absorbed her as though she had been born beneath the statue of Eros. She merged into the multinational melting pot, but she avoided being drawn into any clique of similar colour to her own. Her good looks, her rich and happy laugh – along with a sense of style backed by the remainder of the ex-RSM's nest egg – made her more than acceptable among her many colleagues, most of whom already had a circle of civilian friends. Her leisure time became filled with dining, dancing and the theatre, and she was carried off to Henley, Wimbledon and Twickenham. To prevent this sybaritic life removing the physical edge that she valued, she played furious games of squash several times a week and continued to undergo instruction in self-defence and unarmed combat. If, along the way, she looked kindly on a suitor, that is none of our business. As she had been advised by her company commander at Sandhurst, she was discreet and careful and she neither inflicted nor suffered any emotional damage.

She took to intelligence work like a duck to water. Her languages ensured that she became a member of a section comprising both civilian and services staff, sifting and collating the intelligence deriving from a corner of Africa. Other staff could read written Swahili or Arabic, but her familiarity with them as spoken languages was, at first, a disadvantage because she was mainly employed as an interpreter of recorded phone calls and broadcasts. However, her knack of managing people while, in her father's words, 'playing the system like a violin', singled her out. She soon had her share – and more – of collating information, drawing conclusions and writing clear reports.

Still benefiting from her degree, she became a captain four years after leaving Sandhurst. Her father's only regret, when he heard of her promotion, was that he was by now too old to turn handsprings. Then, in her fourth year at the MoD, the leader of her section was transferred to confidential duties in some highly secret destination. There were others with longer service than Hal's, but meritocracy was the mood of the day and Hal had, in effect, been acting as his deputy. She stepped into his shoes, as a Staff Officer Grade 3, with a general brief for Africa and special responsibility for her own small area.

The usual peacetime complacency was noticeably absent. There were ominous stirrings in the Middle East and warning messages were coming out of Africa. Hal's superior, a grizzled major with ulcers and a nervous tic, was called almost daily to brief a committee of top brass who were making the final evaluation and advising the Government on the intelligence that was flooding in and almost overpowering the system.

Hal was puzzling over a badly worded analysis of some satellite images while wrestling with a computer that seemed determined to misunderstand what was required of it, when a colleague made a sudden entry.

'Hey, Pollyanna,' he said urgently.

Hal sighed, losing the thread. 'What is it, Honky?' she asked wearily. The two were on such terms that they could so address each other without offence being taken on either side.

'Where's your galloping major?'

'His wife just phoned,' Hal said. 'He's been taken to hospital. One of his ulcers went pop.'

'God! The Chiefs of General Staff are expecting him.'

'When?'

The captain whom she had addressed as Honky looked at his watch. 'About five minutes ago. You'd better go and stand in for him. M of D, main building, third floor.'

'Not this chicken,' Hal said. 'You go.'

'I wouldn't do. Not pretty enough. Besides, they want to discuss your report on Liboon and Maveria. Not my scene, thank God!'

'How about Staff Officer One?'

'I've already looked. He must be hiding in a lavatory somewhere.'

Hal said something rude, but confining herself to Swahili in deference to the other's youth and innocence. She looked quickly into the only available mirror, but she was uniformed and tidy. Gathering up a file, she bolted out of the building and was lucky enough to find a taxi. Five minutes brought her to the huge neoclassical building in Whitehall. She showed her pass and was escorted via a lift to the third floor. There she waited under the eyes of a secretary and a guard for more than an hour while, for lack of her presence, some other report was considered. Then the double doors opened and a colonel from the Iran section emerged. He looked drained.

Hal was summoned. She wanted to run or go to the lavatory, or even jump out of the window, but she gathered her nerve and walked with assumed confidence through the double doors. The Chiefs of General Staff, functioning as the Joint Planning Staff, seemed at first to be comprised of impressive older gentlemen gleaming with gold braid and medals, all scowling horribly. But when her first panic subsided she realized that there were no more than a dozen or so seated around a large, U-shaped table, in modest uniforms bearing no more than the insignia of their very senior ranks, and any signs of impatience were quickly replaced by mild curiosity at the unexpected apparition. Several junior officers were seated in the background, taking notes. Hal was comforted to see one or two familiar faces, even former dancing partners, among them.

There was a smaller table with a chair in the middle of the U. Hal placed her file on the table and remained standing.

The admiral in the higher-backed chair placed centrally to the table raised bushy eyebrows at her. Hal had seen his image on the TV news the previous day. 'You are Captain . . .'

'Brown,' said Hal. It came out as a squeak.

'You're H. Brown, the author of the report on Liboon and Maveria?' His voice expressed surprise, bordering on incredulity. 'Where's Major Fisk?'

'In hospital, sir. One of his ulcers has perforated.'

'Oh. Please, sit.' Each member of the committee seemed to have a copy of Hal's report before him. The admiral tapped his copy. 'This seems to be a very thorough report, but I doubt if any of us have had time to digest it beyond reading the summary. Take us through it in your own words.'

'And begin at the beginning,' said a dyspeptic-looking man in khaki with a general's red flashes. 'I only have a vague idea of the geography and none at all of the politics.'

'There's a map on the last page,' Hal said helpfully. She moistened her lips. 'Liboon and Maveria are on the north-east coast of Africa, with Maveria to the north. Maveria was a British colony prior to independence in 1952 and is now a protectorate. The two countries, Maveria and Liboon, have been one several times in the past. Liboon, which is substantially the larger, has always claimed sovereignty over Maveria, but not on any good political grounds. Even their ethnic origins are different.' Hal glanced round the faces and saw that they were beginning to lose patience. She decided to cut a long story very short. 'The motivation is that Liboon's coastline is all cliffs and rocks, which has always placed their economy at a disadvantage. Maveria, on the other hand, has a good natural harbour. Maveria also has some valuable mineral resources.

'Over recent months there have been signs that Liboon is planning an armed incursion. They were expanding their army by recruitment and training and buying arms, principally from us, but through South Africa. We have been hearing for some time that the mood of the country was expectant. More recently there has been movement of men and equipment to camps near the border.

'That border is formed by the Barawat River, sometimes called the Green Nile, which has cut itself a deep gorge along the whole frontier. There is only one crossing, by a bridge built with British and French help before the rise of the present military dictatorship in Liboon. For the first time in years, there has been some repair work to the bridge and to the road on the Liboon side of the gorge.

'As I said, Maveria is a British protectorate, but the garrison there has been somewhat run down. The CO is a brigadier, but in fact the garrison has been reduced substantially below brigade strength. The Liboonese army outnumbers it heavily and both sides know it.

'The conclusion drawn in the report is that Liboon is waiting to see what develops in the Middle East. If war flares up, they will walk in, expecting the world to be too distracted by other events to pay much attention.'

'That might not do them much good in the long term,' said a man in the lighter blue of the RAF. 'They must know that, even if we didn't have the resources to spare to fight another war at the time, we'd certainly come after them when the other ructions had settled down.'

'That's hardly a fair question to put to the captain,' the admiral said.

Hal was shedding her awe of the assembled brass. After all, they were only men. They even looked benevolent, not at all the types to eat a young, female, black captain. 'If I may, sir,' she said, 'I'd like to comment on it. That aspect has been the subject of some discussion. Also, we were lucky; we intercepted and recorded part of a phone call between the Maverian president and his chief of staff. Our view, borne out by as much of the phone call as I translated, is this: they would expect us to be tired and weakened after such a conflict and ready to settle for peace at any price. But alternatively, if they can just occupy Maveria for a few years of propaganda, ethnic cleansing and organization, they could allow democracy to return to Maveria, knowing that the Maverians would by then show a majority in favour of rejoining Liboon.'

Another navy man leaned forward. Hal tried to count his rings but lost count. 'You translated the phone call? You understand Swahili?'

'Some, sir,' said Hal. 'But the phone call was in Arabic.'

'If I said to you *"Habari ya asubuhi"*, how would you reply?'

Hal relaxed and even smiled. She glanced at the clock above the chairman's head. 'It's after midday,' she said, 'so I would reply *"Habari ya mchana"*. "Good afternoon."'

The admiral asked, 'Has there been any communication between President Acori of Liboon and any of the Arab leaders?'

'None that we've intercepted,' Hal said.

The admiral glanced round the table. 'Very well, Captain Brown. That will be all.'

Hal walked, six inches clear of the floor, out through the ante-room, past a major and a colonel, each of whom was sweating. She favoured them both with a friendly nod. A bubble of relief was expanding inside her.

Back in the committee room a brigadier spoke up. 'I take it, Admiral, that the point of your last question was whether the Liboonese were put up to it as a diversionary tactic?'

'Exactly,' the admiral said. 'A bluff. Perhaps being promised support as a reward. But, so far, the Liboonese preparations seem too secretive to be intended as a diversion. Captain Brown, I may say, is a very capable young woman. I made time to read her report. A very thorough document. It's fat, not because of verbosity but because she has a subtle military mind, most unusual in a woman, and she seems to have covered every eventuality. We should bear her name in mind. It may be necessary to send an adviser to Maveria.'

'Brigadier Wincaster would never accept advice from a woman,' said one of the generals.

'An Arabic- and Swahili-speaking woman who could pass for a native?'

'I don't know,' said the general. 'He's not the man he was. Frankly, the post no longer merits somebody of his rank, but he was left there to wait for retirement because nobody wanted to find a job for him at home.'

'If we don't reinforce him, he's going to be overrun,' said the brigadier.

'If all goes the way it's heading,' said the admiral, 'we won't be able to spare any resources to fight a second and smaller war. I'd prefer that we pulled out of Maveria for the moment, but the public – and parliament – would scream to high heaven. Wincaster will just have to do the best he can. We can top up his supplies by airdrop and that's about the end of it. And that, I may say, is the PM's view and I believe that he has cabinet backing.'

'Wouldn't we be putting that young woman into serious danger if we sent her there?' somebody asked.

'She's a soldier. She knows the risks. If she was caught it might go hard with her. But, in point of fact, if Maveria's taken, a black woman who speaks both Arabic and Swahili has more chance of evading capture than anyone else. And now,' said the admiral, 'can we leave this side issue and get back to the main subject of our remit?'

# Nine

In the biggest hotel in the Caspian Sea resort of Rasht, an entire hotel had been taken over at short notice, for the sake of security, for the meeting.

'At last,' said the chairman, 'all is ready. Agreed?'

Around the table heads nodded.

'Very well. They have found our demands unacceptable, which is as we intended. In the eyes of the world, we now have every reason to make our move.'

'We have given the Western infidels all the warning they could need,' said a sallow man in a khaki suit. 'They will be ready.'

'In the process, we have sown dissent among them.' The chairman paused. How to explain to this peasant the long and subtle manoeuvring that had gone before? Better, perhaps, not to dwell on the part played by covert warfare. 'Terrorism', the infidel called it, but one man's terrorist was another's freedom fighter. 'Once,' he said, 'we struck without warning, and look what we brought on ourselves. Desert Storm and one of our number standing alone. Later, the anti-Islam alliance struck first. Afghanistan. Iraq. They continue to vanquish us, one at a time.

'This time, they must know that we all stand together. Some of our enemies will stand back, from fear or for economic advantage. And they know nothing about our secret, Operation Switch, the switchblade knife aimed at the soft underbellies of their armies. Our agents already have the numbers they need and they have the means to find the passwords. So now we move. Allow three days for all forces to be fully briefed and in position. Yes?'

The heads nodded again.

'Then it is agreed. At dawn on the morning of the third day, we move.'

'And Operation Switch?' somebody asked.

'That must not begin too soon or they will have time to revert to the old ways. We wait until it will hurt them most, when they are fully committed. Tell all our helpers in the West to begin now. Plant the seed, but it is not to flower until the last day of this month, at noon, our time.'

The day dawned and the alliance of Arab nations moved suddenly into battle. Israel came under heavy attack and fought back furiously. Some of the participants had been eyeing their neighbours' wealth or assets and went after them under the guise of a Holy War or whatever other pretext came most readily to hand. Others were merely paying off old scores. A few believed that they were serving the Prophet.

Among the Western nations, indignation was loudly expressed. But this was not NATO territory, so NATO could not move. The UN debated the matter and would clearly continue to do so for months, if not years. But Britain and America had been forewarned and had already decided to honour one treaty obligation or another. In all, a handful of nations was prepared to stem the tide. Others promised support but, fearful of losing their sources of oil, contented themselves with cheering from the sidelines or offering the use of bases on favourable terms. Russia, while pontificating about diplomatic solutions, seized the opportunity to walk back into one of her breakaway republics.

The west still had friends among the Arabs. Brother does not usually fight brother, but footholds were offered along with oil and, surreptitiously, finance.

The suddenness of these counter-moves surprised the Arab alliance, which had counted on the usual long period of debate and confusion. They hesitated, waiting for their hidden master stroke to take effect. There was some furious fighting, notably around the Golan Heights, but, in the main, army faced army, each manoeuvring to counter its opponent's moves in a ponderous formation dance. There was some exchange of shellfire, but close contact was limited to accidental encounters by occasional patrols.

It was a time of waiting.

# Ten

Hal and two colleagues were told to make ready for overseas deployment. They would function in the field as intelligence advisers, interpreting information as it was obtained, faster than waiting for London to process it, and being available to answer questions.

Kitted out for warmer climates and inoculated against every disease and parasite to be met with between Bombay, Rome and Cape Town, they were flown to Athens and booked into a hotel while they waited to be told which particular front would be the destiny of each of them. While they waited for the high command to make up its mind they went sightseeing and visited the shops. Because of the possible terrorist activity, they went in civvies. Hal, in her Armani suit, attracted some curious but not unfriendly looks.

On the first evening, Hal dined in the hotel. She was unfortunate in being served by the only waiter whose command of English lay between poor and non-existent. Hal's modern Greek was no better and, although she had absorbed a minimum of ancient Greek from her headmistress, it seemed that the Greek language had suffered a great sea change since the days of Plato and Aristophanes. She managed a satisfactory main course (of *kotopoulo*, had she but known it) by pointing at what a nearby diner was eating and making affirmative noises. Her neighbour, however, had left the dining room without taking a dessert and Hal was straining for a translation of *loukoumades* when she was relieved to be interrupted by another hotel employee, this time with excellent English. A visitor, she was told, awaited her in the hotel's lobby.

The visitor was a distinguished-looking man, English to judge by his clothes, nursing a fat briefcase. She had to look twice before she recognized him. The streak of grey in his hair had turned white, but otherwise he was the same.

'Colonel Bowman?'

'Captain Brown. We need to talk privately.'

'My room?'

'Let's make it mine. I'm not expecting anybody to be interested in our talk, but one never knows. You've been here for some hours and I've only just booked in.'

They took the lift and Hal was admitted to a room identical to her own. There were several cartons stacked neatly in a corner. Colonel Bowman glanced into the wardrobe and the bathroom before inviting Hal to take one of the two chairs. His caution seemed to be a matter of habit rather than necessity.

'Now,' he said, 'do you know what you're doing here?'

'We're waiting for orders.'

'No more than that?'

'No, sir.'

'Good. Somebody's learned discretion at last. But you won't be going with the others. I'll explain. The Joint Planning Staff was – or were – impressed by your report on Liboon and Maveria. As a matter of fact, so was I. And events there are working out almost exactly as you forecast. The Liboonese army has begun to cross the border. The garrison will soon have to defend itself.

'All our other resources are committed to the bigger conflict. We are having difficulty meeting our obligations to the alliance. We simply cannot divert troops to fight another and smaller war. However, your report pointed out, quite rightly, that the border is marked by the Barawat River, which has carved a deep gorge for itself and is spanned by a single bridge. Until Liboon crossed the border, we couldn't carry out an air strike without being accused of an unprovoked attack on a friendly power. Very sensibly, the Liboonese began their troop movements under cover of darkness. We were able to keep track of their movements by means of thermal images from satellites. At dawn this morning, the satellite images showed a force across the border and, by good luck, an Australian aircraft carrier was within range. An immediate air strike destroyed the bridge. On the way back, they caught the Liboonese air force on the ground and shot it up, all five planes of it.

'As you know, the Barawat River, also known as the Green Nile, makes a formidable barrier.' Hal nodded. The river had precipitous sides and was infested with crocodiles. 'The Liboonese army in Maveria will find reinforcements and even supplies very difficult to come by. That much we could do.

'From the satellite images, it's clear that a substantial part of the Liboonese army crossed the border before the air strike. But, as I said, we can't let a side issue like Maveria distract us from the main conflict. So Brigadier Wincaster is going to be outnumbered, but he will have to manage as best he can until we can spare the men and equipment to back him up. He will need all the skills he can muster. You know the background and you're familiar with both languages. You're the obvious person to go in as intelligence adviser.'

Hal found that her mouth had gone dry. She had been given an exceptional education in warfare – in theory and on paper. This would be her first encounter with the reality of people killing people. 'Do we know the strength of the Liboonese in Maveria?' she asked huskily.

'You'll be fed the figures as we get them.'

He waited. This was the moment at which she might jib at the assignment. He braced himself, preparing to point out, as gently as he could, that orders were not open to debate.

But Hal's mind had been racing ahead. 'Do I get a new communications kit?' she asked. 'If they've been planning their move for some time, they'll have been preparing to jam normal radio frequencies.'

The colonel nodded approvingly. He gestured towards the cardboard cartons. 'You'll find a new-style digital encryption and satellite radio telephone there. You'll have your own radio and your own radio contact, a Signals section based in Nairobi. You'll almost certainly have to be your own signaller.'

'That seems a little unusual, sir,' Hal said cautiously.

'It is unusual. Normally you would work through the garrison's own Signals section. But these are exceptional circumstances. I had better warn you that you may have a problem with Brigadier Wincaster. This is in confidence. He has served his country well – an MC, a DSO, a successful command in the Falklands and another in Ireland – but he's a soldier of the old school. What was it that Admiral Wemyss is supposed to have said about intelligence?'

'"Uncertain information from questionable people",' Hal said.

'Right. Perhaps the brigadier doesn't go quite as far as that, although he certainly inclines in that direction. He has his own intelligence officer but he keeps him on a very short lead.'

Hal's anxiety increased. 'Then am I really the right person to send?' she asked.

'We rather hope that somebody so completely outside his normal experience may get through to him where more familiar approaches might be brushed aside. But your function goes a little deeper than that.' Colonel Bowman leaned forward and instinctively lowered his voice further. 'The garrison in Maveria hardly merited an officer of his rank after the establishment was scaled down, but there have been suspicions that he may not be quite the man he was. His early service was eccentric but inspired. His men would have followed him through hell and sometimes did so. But, not to put too fine a point on it, there are signs suggesting premature senility. However, he had friends in high places and he was left in Maveria to await retirement at the proper time. He's ruled the garrison with the proverbial rod of iron. Recently we've come to suspect that no signal leaves Maveria without his personal approval. There was a very guarded letter from the medical officer – guarded, I suppose, in case it came to the brigadier's attention – suggesting that Wincaster might be overdue for a medical and hinting at an unfavourable outcome. This is all very nebulous and uncertain, but if it's going the way we suspect, we cannot leave such a volatile and unpredictable character in the middle of the developing situation.

'We want you, therefore, to pursue another objective. Keep your ear to the ground. Form your own opinion. Consult the medical officer. But, above all, listen to what the men are saying, they'll know better than anybody. If, from all this, you conclude that the brigadier's fitness to command has been impaired and that none of his staff is being given an opportunity to comment on the fact, send a code phrase which we'll agree in a minute and he will be on leave in Britain and replaced within a day or two. I know that this is putting an unfair burden on your shoulders, but at least I can promise that there will be no repercussions. Will you do it?'

'Looking at it one way,' Hal said, 'you're asking me to betray a senior officer. On the other hand, I can see the necessity. Reluctantly, I suppose I'll have to do it.'

'Good for you! I suggest the code phrase "Prospects are not good". If we get that from you, we'll know that all's not well. And the brigadier would be unlikely to listen to anyone below the rank of major, so up you go, as of now. I have your crowns in my bag.'

'Local? Acting?'

'Heavens, no! The old boy would see through a local or acting rank immediately and the objective is to get him to trust you. He certainly won't listen to anybody below major. You're just about due your substantive promotion, so we're bringing it forward a few months.'

Hal was pleased and yet in a way she regretted the promotion. Policy notwithstanding, there would be infinite barriers between someone of her race and colour and the rank of colonel, so major was as high as she could reasonably expect to go. She was sad to have reached the pinnacle of her career with so much of it still to come. 'My father will be delighted,' she said at last.

'The ex-RSM? I'm sure he will.'

'That must make me one of the youngest majors in the British Army,' Hal said.

'Possibly. Promotions tend to be rapid in time of war. And now that we've got that out of the way, we have several hours before your flight. I'll hand over the travel and briefing documents and after that we'd better familiarize you with and let you sign for all the equipment we're sending with you. I hope you'll be as impressed as I was. You won't be able to receive satellite images direct, but we can interpret them for you or we can beam them to you and you can print them out for yourself. Brigadier Wincaster may want to see for himself.'

'I'll want thermal images,' Hal said.

'You shall have them.'

Two hours later he saw Hal and the cartons into a taxi and watched it move out of sight. Then he sighed and went back into the hotel. The part of his job that he liked least was the need to send people on postings from which they would be lucky to return in the same state as when they went. He hoped that he was not going to be the one to take bad news to her father.

# Eleven

Hal was flown in a military aircraft to an airstrip somewhere in Kenya. The runway was outlined by flares. She descended sleepily from the plane, which took off again immediately and vanished among the stars. Even in the small hours, the heat and smell of Africa wrapped around her. This, she told herself, was the country of some of her remoter ancestors. She opened her mind to it, but she could not sense an immediate rapport.

An uncommunicative man in a khaki suit without insignia loaded her cases and cartons into an open Land Rover and drove her by way of unmade roads to the side of a large body of water. Here a small amphibian was waiting beside a wooden dock, a former British Army Air Corps Beaver left behind, so the pilot explained. She was the sole passenger.

They took off in moonlight. Dawn came up as they crossed a range of broken hills. As on the previous flight, Hal – despite the distinctive racket of the big radial engine – had fallen into a light sleep, but the turbulence over the hills snapped her awake and she realized that she was being given her first sight of Maveria – from a considerable height, in deference to the possibility of gunfire from below. She recognized most of the topographical features from her study of the maps. Maveria, she knew, was an approximate rectangle. It had been described as being 'about the size of Wales' but, while that might be true of Maveria within its geographical boundaries, much of the land was taken up by barren foothills and by swampland. There were even areas where the forest became jungle. To her right she could see the deep gorge of the Barawat River, which formed the short south-eastern border with Liboon. Far ahead, the sea that bounded the country to the north-east was coming into sight. They had just crossed the hills, overspill from the Somali highlands, in which were hidden the south-west and north-west borders.

Hal looked down, searching for any sign of the invaders, but much of the country was wooded – thinly, and mostly with acacia trees, but it could have been enough to hide an army. She was rewarded with the sight of elephants at a waterhole, looking as small as fleas on a blanket. There were scattered small villages of beehive huts and the occasional sign of cultivation, although the locals were mostly cattle herders. There was what seemed to be ample grassland, but she knew that some of it comprised areas of reedy bog, fed by the water shed from the highlands.

They had begun to descend. The coast was clearly visible, and a town that would have to be Pembaka, the capital and indeed the only township of any substance. Conversation was only possible with the use of microphones and headsets but she made fumbling use of the equipment and managed to ask the pilot to circle.

A second river, the Urma, descended from the hills to the east and, its course being turned by a rocky ridge running along the coast, reached the sea beyond Pembaka after a lengthy journey running roughly parallel to the coast. Pembaka was built on the ridge at the nearest point to the harbour. A few miles upstream she could see the glint of water from a lake or reservoir.

The town had once been a slavers' headquarters. The centre of the slave trade, she knew, had moved there after Sultan Barghash of Zanzibar was forced to outlaw it in 1873. Thus there had been ample funds and cheap labour available and a need for defence against marauders. Apart from a small, straggling suburb above the large harbour, which had begun as a natural bay and had been accorded the added shelter of a sea wall, the town was enclosed within a high wall, several metres thick. The town was a widespread huddle of flat-roofed white buildings with palm-tree tops making green featherings above the white. There was a slender minaret near one corner. The harbour seemed to be empty except for a single, dhow-like fishing boat.

A few kilometres south of the town, at the flattest part of the same ridge and connected to the town by a tarmac road, a neat layout of buildings and a rectangle of beaten-earth parade ground all within a perimeter fence marked the position of the British barracks, but Hal could see no sign of human activity. Could the garrison have been overrun already? The pilot made a lower pass over the town. She could see several figures in what seemed to be British uniforms. But the Liboonese could hardly have arrived already, and anyway, the faces that glanced up at them were predominately white. So the brigadier had withdrawn from the original barracks into what was clearly a more defensible position. Perhaps the old chap was not so senile after all.

The Beaver circled once more on a downward spiral, touched down in a rainbow of spray and taxied noisily across the harbour towards the town. The engine died, leaving behind a hissing silence. The pilot hopped nimbly down on to one of the floats and dropped a small anchor. The plane swung slowly and settled to the light breeze. Salt-laden air, already warm but deliciously fresh, flooded in.

A large canoe was already on its way from the wooden dock, paddled by four Africans but also bearing a corporal and a private in British uniforms with the flashes of the North Wessex Regiment. Hal began to feel a little less cast adrift.

'Morning, miss,' said the corporal cheerfully. 'Ma'am, I should say. Corporal Jenkins, at your service. And this is Private Gordon.' The two men stood up to salute, rocking the narrow canoe in the water to the consternation of the paddlers. 'Much kit to come ashore?'

Hal returned the salute. 'Quite a bit,' she said. 'See for yourself.'

With the aid of the pilot, all Hal's luggage was transferred to the canoe. When she stepped across the narrow gap from the float to the canoe, one of the paddlers reached up a hand to steady her.

'*Asante sana*,' Hal said, seating herself carefully, and then, '*Shukran gazeelan*.' The paddler grinned and made a reply. The men dug their paddles in and the canoe, now sitting much deeper in the water, moved sluggishly shore-ward.

'What was that about, miss . . . ma'am?' the corporal asked.

Hal decided to satisfy his curiosity. 'I thanked him in Swahili for his help,' she said. 'He didn't seem to understand and I remembered that Swahili is only spoken about as far north as Liboon. They all have their native dialects but the common language here would be Arabic, so I said it again in that.'

'And what did he say, ma'am?'

'I wouldn't repeat it, but it was probably meant as a compliment.'

'You speak English, Arabic *and* Swahili, Mum?' said the private, who seemed to have made up his own mind how to address a black and beautiful officer. He had a strong Scots accent. 'Yon's winnerfae. I can only scrieve English.'

'You can't even *speak* English, Gordon,' said the corporal. 'And don't speak at all until the officer speaks to you. Sergeant-Major Hindley's looking forward to meeting you again, ma'am,' he added. Evidently the inhibition did not, in his mind, apply to NCOs. 'He's been talking about it ever since the signal came in.'

The name Hindley rang only a very faint bell in Hal's mind, and she had no recollection of a warrant officer of that name. 'I expect that I shall be happy to see him again,' she said vaguely.

The canoe bumped gently against the dock. Corporal Jenkins whistled and three more Africans materialized and were loaded with Hal's luggage. Hal thanked the paddlers in Arabic. She had never witnessed her own shining smile but the paddlers returned their own echoes of it.

The way up to the town was steep. Hal had hoped for a jeep, but several short flights of steps were set into the unmade footpath. She saw a handcart being manhandled upwards but her cartons were carried easily by the men. The path climbed between houses, a mixture of constructions in mud, thatch and various corrugated materials. A few black faces watched her curiously. Her senses were assaulted by unfamiliar colours and smells but the place was not the noisy and teeming suburb that she had expected.

'Where have all the people gone?' she asked Corporal Jenkins.

'Most of 'em took fright and went off in the fishing boats, ma'am, as soon as we got news that the Liboonese were crossing the Barawat.'

The full heat of the day was still to come, but the sun was on Hal's back and the climb was steep. By the time they arrived at the seaward gateway in the massive wall she was sweating in a way that she considered unladylike and probably un-officer-like as well. The two great wooden doors stood open and the pair of sentries on duty saluted smartly. Inside the gateway was a small square. Beyond, the nearer part of the town seemed to be comprised mostly of larger and more substantial houses.

As they passed into a welcome pool of shade, a figure hurried out of one of the houses, stopped abruptly and, while saluting, beamed.

Hal acknowledged the salute. 'Tony?' she said. 'Tony Laverick?'

Captain Tony Laverick's beam widened. 'The same,' he said. He was tanned and he seemed to have filled out, but otherwise he was unchanged. 'I meant to greet you down at the dockside but the Old Man was still dishing out orders. Well, look at you. And a major, yet!' They shook hands formally. 'By God! It's good to see you!'

'You too,' Hal said, conscious that it was true. Tony's presence transformed Maveria from a strange and hostile environment to somewhere not so very far from home.

'You do seem to keep popping up in my life,' Tony said. 'And very welcome you are. But we knew that it had to be you when the signal came in. Well, how many Hal Browns can there be in Int-Corps? The Old Man wants to see you,' he finished.

'He can wait. I suppose he knows I'm here. He must have seen or heard the plane come over.'

'Must have done,' Tony agreed.

'As soon as I've seen my chattels disposed of and had a wash – I suppose a shower's out of the question?'

'A cold shower is no problem,' Tony said. 'Hot or warm requires notice.'

'A cold wash then and tidied myself up a bit, I'll go and make my number. I suppose he wouldn't wait while I catch a little sleep?'

'Waiting is not something that he does with any enthusiasm.'

'So where do I work and where do I sleep?'

'Not far. This way.' Tony led the small party into the mouth of an alley. 'One thing, we're not too short of accommodation. Most of the locals did a bunk as soon as there was any sign of an invasion. The last time the Liboonese had power here they made a meal of it, from what I can gather, and when, with a little help from ourselves, they were finally booted out, the Maverians helped them on their way at bayonet-point. That was yonks ago, but both sides have long tribal memories. Here we are. You share this house with Signals and the sleeping quarters for the women officers. By the way, you'll never guess who the Signals officer is.'

Hal could only think of one Signals officer who Tony would have referred to in those terms. 'Not Susan Thyme?'

'That's just who. Small world! Well, perhaps not. But a small army, and getting smaller all the time. There are several old friends of yours here, plus one who you mayn't be so happy to see again. Justin Carlsborough.'

'You're right, I won't be too happy.'

'Nor will he when he sees that you outrank him.' Tony led them inside and threw open the door to a small room furnished with a chair and a trestle table. 'Your office. Tell us what else you want and we'll see what we can do. You sleep in the next room.'

'And the sooner the better. I've been travelling all night.'

'It's a hard life in Int-Corps. The bathroom's beyond your sleeping quarters.'

Hal saw her precious boxes safely in place. Private Gordon was left on guard. Tony made to leave.

'Don't go yet,' Hal said. 'I haven't time to change, and anyway my other uniform will look like a crumpled oak leaf by now. Show me my room and tell me about the brigadier while I tidy myself up.'

Hal's sleeping quarters proved to be a tiny cubicle with a camp bed, a locker and some hooks behind the door, but at least there was a crate doing duty as a washstand, with a basin and a jug of water, still almost cold. She washed quickly and was immediately more awake. There was electric light, she noticed, but a torch had been provided for emergencies.

'The brigadier's a bit of a stickler,' Tony said. 'Things have to be done his way, or else. He doesn't allow women in the mess, I should warn you. Not even majors, unless he's going to make an exception.'

Hal paused, hairbrush in hand. 'How in God's name can he get away with such a piece of blatant discrimination?'

Tony shrugged. 'He can't, but he does. The trouble is that all the longer-serving officers, which means the more senior ones, remember him in the great days. I'm told that he was quite a leader – eccentric, autocratic, but sometimes almost brilliant. The brigade did two years in Ireland and his tactics kept most of them alive. They remember that and they're still trying to convince themselves that he's only becoming even more eccentric. So he can get away with a lot, but even while I've known him he's passed from eccentric to loopy. To be frank, he's a bit of a loose cannon. You'll see.'

Hal was indignant, but, she reminded herself, the last word would almost certainly be hers. Even by declaring field conditions, the segregation of male and female officers – and to the disadvantage of the latter – would be impossible to justify in the current climate. But she was becoming more concerned about her hunger pangs than about the brigadier's mental state. 'While I'm waiting to see, where – if at all – do I eat?'

'I'll show you. First, we'd better get you to the Old Man. Frankly, I don't know what he's going to make of you.'

'He doesn't have to make anything of me,' Hal said. She began to brush the dust of travel from her uniform, paying special attention to her brand new crowns. 'He just has to listen.'

'Listening is something else he doesn't do very well,' Tony said. 'As far as he's concerned, democracy begins and ends in a strategy meeting with his senior officers, majors and upwards. There's one tonight in the mess. We serfs are excluded. He has me acting as his aide-de-camp as well as his intelligence officer—'

'Brigadiers don't have ADCs,' Hal pointed out.

'Don't tell me, tell him. But even I don't get to attend. It's probably just as well. They usually finish by boozing half the night away, and I don't think my health or my pay could take the strain.'

Hal paused in the act of changing her shoes. 'Majors and up? Does that include me?'

'I doubt it very much,' Tony said. 'He does make one or two very occasional exceptions, but those are—' He stopped in mid-sentence.

'His favourites?'

Tony bit his lip without replying. Hal gave him full marks for loyalty.

Hal very much wanted a tepid bath, a complete change of clothes, some properly cooked food and a deep, horizontal sleep. Her mirror assured her that she looked ten years older than her true age, but passable for all that. Perhaps an appearance of maturity would help to impress the brigadier. 'Should I slap on some make-up?' she asked.

'No way! The Old Man disapproves of women painting their faces. Come on. He'll blame me for any delays. No, one thing more. Did they issue you with a handgun?'

'A brand new Glock,' Hal said. 'More ladylike. Smaller and more lethal than the nine-mil Browning.'

'Well, you'd better buckle it on. He expects his officers to go armed while the emergency lasts.'

Hal sighed, extracted the pistol and its holster from the luggage and strapped it on. Immediately, she felt lopsided from the unaccustomed weight. 'Should I load it?'

'God, no! Susan had a full magazine in hers once. Nothing up the spout, but he made it clear that he expects women and live ammunition to be kept a long way apart.'

'I can live with that,' Hal said. 'Is Susan around just now?'

'I doubt it. And we don't have time to go and find her. I remember how you two can talk when you get together. Do come on!'

'All right. If there's nothing else,' she said, 'let's go.'

They emerged, blinking, into strong sunlight. The paving was hot underfoot but a cooling breeze was blowing from seaward. Tony led her back the way they had come. 'The brigadier took over the hotel for himself and the officers' mess. It's quite a good hotel.'

'Could this place ever really support a decent hotel?'

'There was a nice little tourist industry developing before this trouble blew up. The scuba-diving on the coral reef is some of the best, and palaeontologists have been poking around and finding fossils that have set their little world alight – Neanderthals and Cro-Magnon men apparently living simultaneously and perhaps even cohabiting. The mining engineers are still here but the brigadier kicked them out of the hotel. They took over another of the merchants' houses. The aristocracy and plutocracy were over the hills and far away before anyone else and are believed to be in Switzerland. Civil government is represented by the prime minister, who seems also to be everything else, and a token council of elders who dance to his tune. A very useful old boy. You must meet him. He was offered several chances to get out but he wouldn't go. He says that he can trust us to deal with what he thinks of as a bunch of illiterate savages, just as we did once before. Here we are.'

A sentry saluted them smartly as they entered the hotel, which stood just inside the gates in the great wall. When they passed it earlier, Hal had taken the plain and almost windowless structure for some sort of civic building, possibly the jail, but now she saw that the interior was luxuriously furnished. Most of the rooms had windows on to an interior courtyard shaded with vines, but the pleasant coolness and a faint muttering and stirring in the air suggested air conditioning. Hal could feel the perspiration drying on her back.

The public rooms on the ground floor, now silent, had evidently been retained as the officers' mess. Tony led her up the main staircase. On the broad landing, a desk had been installed and a dark-skinned girl in uniform with sergeant's stripes, who seemed to be present as secretary and receptionist, jumped up and saluted.

'This is Mamie,' Tony said. 'Chief clerk to Brigade HQ.'

Hal had lost the habit of shaking hands. She acknowledged the salute and smiled.

'If you're Major Brown, you better go in quick,' Mamie

said. 'He's axed me twice where you got to.'

'Relax, Mamie . . . *Nos morituri*.' Tony knocked on a substantial teak door. A voice from within yapped like a terrier. Tony made a face, opened the door, saluted and announced formally, 'Major Brown, sir.'

Hal stepped inside and made her own salute. The room had evidently been one of the public rooms. A huge desk, evidently made by local craftsmen from some kind of red hardwood, was almost lost in the middle of the floor. The desk was strewn with files and loose papers. Behind it sat the brigadier. Judging from the respect which he seemed to inspire in those around him, Hal had expected a large man, a towering monster, but the brigadier was smaller than average, thin and rather hollow-chested. His scalp was largely bald and freckled above a face which time and foreign service had wasted away, leaving only a hooked nose, a thin mouth, leathery skin and beady little eyes that looked momentarily surprised at Hal's appearance.

The brigadier neither acknowledged their salutes nor invited Hal to sit down, or even to stand at ease. A handshake, it seemed, would have been unthinkable. She remained stiffly to attention. 'Major Brown,' he said. 'So you've arrived safely. My ADC – Captain Laverick – has shown you your quarters?'

'Yes, sir.'

'That's all right, then. He can show you around. He also acts as my intelligence officer, so any information you come up with you can give to him.' The brigadier paused, but evidently decided that he had said all there was to say about Hal's duties. 'No doubt he's told you that women are not permitted in the mess except on guest nights.'

Hal swallowed. 'With all respect, Brigadier Wincaster,' she said, 'I would like to point out that I am a properly commissioned officer.'

The brigadier glared at her. 'I am aware of that. I am also aware that you are a woman. If I'm wrong about that, you can show me. No? That's all, then. Dismissed.'

To lose your temper with a brigadier is not a good career move. Hot-faced, Hal saluted again, turned about and beat a retreat.

Not a word was spoken until they were in the square. 'Well, now you know,' Tony said quietly.

'Where do I eat if I'm not admitted to the mess?' Hal asked.

'We've taken over a room for the women officers to dine in. It's in the same house as the warrant officers' mess – there are only three of you anyway. We junior officers share it when we're excluded, as tonight. One or two of the warrant officers are longing to see you again. Shall we go and have a beer, or coffee, and give them a chance to intercept you?'

'Could we talk there privately?'

'Maybe, maybe not,' Tony said. 'Walk first, then, and sustenance later. This is the main drag, linking the only two gates. On our left, the house belonging to the most prosperous merchant, presently the WOs' mess. In the shaded part of the courtyard, one jeep.'

Hal had resigned herself to walking, so it was a relief to get into the passenger seat of an open Land Rover. She forgot her hunger for the moment. They progressed up the cobbled main street, returning salutes, while Tony pointed out the principal buildings. The heat seemed to grow more oppressive until she realized that by proceeding downwind they were losing the benefit of the breeze. The town was larger than she had thought when looking down on it from the air. As they approached the landward gateway in the big wall, Hal saw helmeted heads above the ramparts.

Tony drove out through the gate and parked in the shade of the wall. The cobbles gave way to a tarmac road, which stretched away along the ridge between two rows of palm trees and in the direction of the presumably abandoned camp. The road departed from a straight line in order to find a level route between undulations and rocky outcrops.

'This is the only safe and comfortable walking for miles around,' Tony said. 'Come on.'

The palms had been planted in a mown, level strip each side of the road. Beyond was rough ground and wild growth. 'We walk in the shade of the palms,' Tony said. 'That way, we get the shade and the breeze. Just watch out for snakes.'

'Snakes?' Hal said.

'Puff adders. They won't attack unless you step on them, but their bite's lethal. The palm trees are safe enough, but if you have to go among bushes and trees with low branches, watch out. Mambas. Egyptian cobras. Nasty. Don't ever go off the beaten track without making sure that you can get to the nearest source of antivenom damn quick.'

'I won't,' Hal said with feeling. On the other side of the road, the undergrowth had been cut back as far as the brink of the ridge, where the ground fell abruptly to the Urma River. At one gap, they could see the river and across it to the wooded bank on the far side, a kilometre away. A muddy island in the middle divided the steady current and supported a few trees which looked to Hal like mangroves.

Every hundred metres or so, a slit trench had been dug and was manned by a brace of unhappy-looking soldiers. 'What about those chaps?' Hal enquired. 'Aren't they in danger from snakes?'

Tony chuckled. 'There was a snake popped into one of the trenches yesterday. It turned out to be non-venomous, but the men didn't know that. They were out and running in half a millisecond. The brigadier's expecting those men to be brought up in front of him for deserting their posts, but their sergeant won't do it. He said that he'd have been way ahead of them, and quite right too if you ask me. The brigadier will have forgotten all about it by tomorrow.'

They had passed beyond the range of any possible ears. 'If you're acting as his ADC as well as his intelligence officer, can you really spare the time to be showing me around?'

'I've got plenty of time,' Tony said. 'I'm just a glorified errand boy and a sop to his vanity. I pass on what intelligence comes over the air and listen to what the natives tell N'koma, the Prime Minister. The brigadier doesn't delegate. He believes in doing everything himself. "If you want a job done right" and all that sort of thing.'

'And as his intelligence officer,' Hal said lightly, 'do you still believe everything you're told?'

'You cured me of that a long time ago.'

'Robbed of your illusions by a woman? It's an old, old story but I don't really believe I was guilty. Between you and me,' Hal said, 'he's more than a bit loopy, isn't he? No women officers in the officers' mess? You can't get away with that in today's climate.'

'He doesn't believe in today's climate.'

'And this all looks a bit 1940s.' Hal pointed towards the slit trenches.

Tony stopped. 'Between you and me, yes. The NCOs all think so but they're too loyal to say it out loud. They've served with him. He's not only been successful, he's always succeeded with minimal casualties among his own men, which is the test of a good officer. Most of the ORs wouldn't know the difference – they're young and inexperienced. Don't misunderstand me. At times, and about some things, he's so rational that you overlook areas in which he's gone batty. You begin to wonder whether he's right and you're losing your own marbles.' Tony sighed. 'He's been a great man in his day and he deserves an honourable retirement. He deserves to be retired before he ruins it all and throws away a lot of lives by dropping some major clanger. He's been going downhill ever since I got here. He seems to be living in the past.'

'That's what I meant,' Hal said. 'And I'll tell you something else. His strategy's too defensive. Is he preparing for a siege?'

'You've put your finger on the button. He is. He's been stockpiling food and ammunition. He reckons the walls will keep anybody out.'

Hal experience a sinking feeling. 'For a time,' she said. 'But time is on the other side. Can't he see that? Time will give the enemy the chance to reinforce, to mine the walls, to starve us out, or even to build trebuchets.'

'What on earth are those?'

'Siege engines, powered by counterweights and capable of throwing large stones with great force. Edward the First flattened parts of Stirling Castle with one, so I've no doubt that they could breach these walls.'

'Let's hope,' Tony said, 'that the Liboonese aren't as steeped in history as you are.'

'We'll go back in a minute and try to find out what kind

of force they managed to get over the bridges before they
were bombed—'

'About four thousand men, Mr N'koma reckons. He's got
his ear very close to the ground.'

'And we've got. . .' Hal waited. She hoped very much that
the figures she had seen were wrong and that the garrison
included a few thousand troops which had somehow been
overlooked. But she was to be disappointed.

'We're supposed to be at brigade strength but they've drawn
off a lot of men to meet the emergency in the Middle East.
We're down to about nine hundred Brits, mostly the young
and innocent, and a company of Africans from the local militia.
And that's counting all the cooks and bottle-washers.'

'If we hang about here, waiting to be attacked,' Hal said,
'the Liboonese will repair the bridges or figure out some other
way to reinforce their army on this side and a siege won't hold
out for very long. History's full of examples of commanders
who waited for disaster to come to them instead of going out
to meet it. Or who waited too long for relief that never arrived
– like Townsend in Mesopotamia. We should be proactive.'

'Doing what?'

Hal lifted her arms in a gesture of impotence. 'I don't know.
Something clever. I'm supposed to be here as an adviser. I'll
try to think of something.'

'Well, I don't know what we'll do with it if you *do* get an idea.
He won't listen to advice from anybody, especially a woman.'

'Especially a black woman? Don't answer. Perhaps if I
painted myself green and announced that I'd newly arrived
from Mars, I might get a better hearing. Let's get back.' She
dabbed her forehead. She was beginning to acclimatize.
Perhaps her colour helped.

They returned through the town by a different route, threading
through lanes and alleys only just wide enough for the Land
Rover to pass, shaded by vines and creepers trained overhead. It was cooler heading into the breeze. An unexpected
open square fronted the mosque. Soldiers backed, saluting,
into doorways to let them past. Tony pointed out messes,

cookhouses, offices, billets and the workshops, adapted from civilian to military use with all of the army's talent for rapid improvisation.

He returned the vehicle to its courtyard parking space. 'Lunchtime,' he said. 'Are you ready for a noggin?'

Hal was thirsty and very hungry, but she was prey to a feeling that the situation had slipped out of gear and that she, at least, was going to play her part in setting it to rights. 'I want to find Susan first,' she said.

Tony was as obliging as ever. 'Right you are,' he said cheerfully.

Private Gordon was still guarding Hal's equipment. 'Another few minutes,' she told him.

'That's OK, Mum.'

They found the Brigade Signals Platoon on the top floor of the building. Windows were open to counter the heat of the sun on the roof and an electric fan was aiding the natural flow of air. Papers were weighed down with souvenirs of fossil rocks. Trestle tables were littered with equipment at which a sergeant and three privates were at work. Susan Thyme, in uniform with lieutenant's pips, was presiding. The atmosphere was efficient but easy-going. Tony watched benignly as the two women exchanged salutes, then handshakes and then, throwing dignity to the winds, hugs.

'It's great to see you, too,' Hal said, 'but we can catch up over lunch. First, business. I've brought a stack of the very latest SATCOM kit. I was given a ten-minute briefing on it but half the time my mind went blank. Can you manage to fit it together? I could do it, but it would take me a week.'

'Not personally, no,' Susan said. 'But Sergeant Wilkes has a degree in electronics. He should manage to puzzle it out. Right, Sergeant?'

'I wouldn't be at all surprised, ma'am,' said the sergeant.

'Come and fetch it,' Hal said. 'Work your magic. Just one embargo. There's new digital encryption gubbins in there and an owner's manual. They're to be considered as secret as anything can possibly be and the new kit is not to be used until I say so. No point letting the enemy start trying to jam them before we have to.'

'Are they really that far advanced technically, ma'am?' the sergeant asked.

'We don't know. Why take chances?'

'I can't quarrel with that, ma'am,' the sergeant said.

'Have you unscrambled their traffic?'

'They're only using versions of old British ciphers,' Susan said. 'We seem to have sold them SLIDEX and GRIDDLE. We listen all the time. We record them and then a Swahili speaker among the local sergeants comes in and interprets them. They use a lot of code words and phrases but we can usually figure them out.'

Private Gordon was relieved. They left Susan supervising the transfer of Hal's cartons upstairs but promising to join them shortly.

In accordance with custom, the WOs had done well for themselves. A spacious house had been hurriedly but comfortably adapted for their use. Hal could see into the largest room. There was an air of expectation and earnest talk – of the fight to come, Hal was sure of it.

'We can eat out on the terrace,' Tony said. 'Officers and warrant officers pretend not to see each other. The bar's through there. I don't see a waiter. We'll have to stop in the hall and order at the hatch. Have a seat. What will you take?'

'A gin and tonic.'

Tony shook his head. 'You need a long drink, to replace the – um – evaporated fluids.'

Hal hid a smile. Tony had been reared in the convention that ladies never sweat. 'A beer, then,' she suggested. She lowered herself modestly into one of the low couches in the hall.

As soon as Tony had turned a corner to visit the hatch, one of the men emerged from the room and approached. His grin went from ear to ear.

Hal had been given a clue by Corporal Jenkins's earlier remark. Her memory clicked. 'Hindley,' she said. 'You were a corporal when you used to let me ride on the colonel's horse, but I see you're a sergeant-major now. Many congratulations.'

'And you're a major!' The grin tried to widen but failed. 'Your dad will be proud. How is the old chap?'

'Enjoying his retirement. And how's your wife? Ruby, wasn't it?'

'Still is, ma'am.' He hesitated. 'She's very well, managing a pub, ready for when I pick up my pension. May I join you, just for a minute?'

'Yes, of course. Tell me, how are things here?' She kept her voice light but she waited anxiously for his reply.

Sergeant-Major Hindley seated himself carefully beside Hal, leaned towards her and lowered his voice. His face, as she remembered it, was always cheerful and open but he was looking worried. 'Is it true you're here as an adviser?' he asked.

'Quite true.'

'I shouldn't be saying anything, ma'am. I've served under the brigadier. I owe him. But somebody's got to speak up. In confidence, like.'

'Please tell me what you think,' Hal said. 'Nothing that you say to me will go any further.'

Hindley nodded sadly. 'I don't know if you can get through to the brigadier, and it's not my place to say this, but there's a bad feel to this business. If we've got to wait for the enemy to come to us, which may be right or may be wrong, we're not doing it properly. Slit trenches just outside the walls, right where the enemy'd expect them and wide open for mortar fire. There's not a thing to stop the enemy getting within mortar range. We've warned our officers and I know the adjutant's tried to speak to him, but he won't listen, ma'am. What worked in the Falklands may not work here.'

'I'm really only here to advise on intelligence,' Hal said, 'and I've only had time for a quick look around, but I'll see what I can do. If I sent him an appreciation of the latest intelligence in the morning and tacked on a brief set of suggestions...'

'I don't know, ma'am. I really don't. But he won't pay attention to anybody else.' Sergeant-Major Hindley made a gesture that was almost despairing. 'I've been under Brigadier Wincaster for most of my service. Ireland, Cyprus – yes, and the Falklands. He was only a colonel then, but I trusted my life to him and he didn't let me down. In those days you could speak to the officers and they'd speak to him and he'd listen and then make up his own mind. But now, he seems to have lost his grasp. He just isn't the same man. He was handing down orders yesterday and I looked into his eyes. I didn't recognize the man who was looking back at me. Do you know what I mean?'

'I know exactly what you mean.'

'Maybe somebody as different as you . . .'

'I'll try,' Hal said. 'But I wouldn't count on it. I met him this morning and he made it clear that I'm as dust beneath his chariot wheels. But I'll try.'

'You do that, ma'am.' He got to his feet and threw another salute. His voice, which had sunk almost to a whisper, regained its parade-ground strength. 'Good to see you again, ma'am.'

'Good to see you, Sergeant-Major.'

He turned away as Tony came back with the beers. Susan joined them a few minutes later and they took lunch, smartly served by an African orderly, on a shaded terrace behind the house.

Back at the Signals Platoon, Hal could hardly keep her eyes open. She came alert again as she saw the tidy set-up arranged by Sergeant Wilkes. The sergeant was aglow with enthusiasm over the new toys.

Hal seated herself at Susan's desk and opened the brief-case she had been given in Athens. She started jotting on a pad. 'Send this now,' she said. 'The SATCOM special wavelength. These are just previously agreed code words and phrases, so they wouldn't mean anything to the other side. There's no need for encryption.'

Susan looked unhappy. 'I'm not supposed to send anything without the brigadier's prior approval,' she said.

'Then stand aside and I'll send it myself. *Absolom* means that I'm asking for an immediate, up-to-date sitrep. *Doncaster* means that they're to send me a full set of the latest satellite images, including thermal images, as at oh-seven-hundred our time tomorrow, so somebody had better be on the ball by then.'

'What about *Prospects are not good*?' Susan asked.

Hal hoped that she might be forgiven. 'That's just to report my safe arrival,' she said. 'If you're not happy about it, move over and I'll send it myself. This is my equipment and I have my orders.'

'Well, all right,' Susan said unhappily. 'We'll send it. But you realize I'll have to lay a copy, complete with interpretation, on the brigadier's desk in the morning and he'll probably have both our heads.'

'And mine,' Tony said.

'I'll carry the can,' Hal said. She was fairly confident that the brigadier would not be around to vent his wrath on them for very long. 'You'll be all right, Tony. You aren't even here. I can't think where you've got to.'

The situation report must have been ready and waiting, updated. It came back within ten minutes of the transmission. Hal skimmed through it quickly. 'Much as we thought,' she told Tony. 'Four or five infantry battalions. On foot. Well, they'd have to be if they don't have tracked personnel carriers – there isn't a single half-decent road between here and the bridge. There was, during the previous Liboonese occupation last century, but it's gone back to jungle.' She read on. 'Damn! They got a half-track across, pulling what looks like an ex-Royal Artillery twenty-five pounder, before the bridge was hit. The rest of the artillery units are probably down in the bottom of the Barawat River and unsalvageable or else they're stuck on the other side. As of half an hour ago, the Liboonese force on this side of the bridge seemed to be preparing to move but they were still encamped there. We've got at least thirty-six hours before they could march here, if that's what they intend, and probably twice that. There wouldn't be much point in arriving exhausted.

'Give me some time to digest this, Tony, and you can take it to the brigadier with my compliments. No need to tell him that I sent for it unless he asks. Let him think that it came to me as a matter of routine.'

# Twelve

Hal had a mug of tea and a biscuit in the Signals office as a substitute for dinner and took to her camp bed in the late afternoon. Neither the lingering heat, the hardness of the bed nor the noises of the busy garrison could have kept her awake.

Hours later, she was jerked awake by the sounds of shots, shouting, whistles and the clatter of running feet. She came to quickly and used the torch to look at her watch, to find that it was after midnight. No matter what the emergency, the ranks were not going to see her in a short nightdress. She pulled on her uniform over the top, loaded her pistol and dashed outside, armed and barefoot, into the chill of an African night. There was hubbub from the direction of the seaward gate but the sounds of conflict had receded. She hurried painfully over the cobbles. One last shot sounded from down at the harbour.

Confusion reigned. What passed for street lighting was on and lamps were being brought out into the street. By their light, Hal saw that soldiers were pouring into the street, most of them hastily dressed, with or without their arms, milling around or waiting for orders. A cluster had gathered around something just inside the gate.

Sergeant-Major Hindley appeared from nowhere, miraculously immaculate. Either he slept in his uniform and standing up, Hal thought, or he had brought speed-dressing to a fine art. He barked an order and the men began to fall in in three ranks along the whole length of the street. Lacking a barrack square, this seemed to have become the new drill.

Tony appeared out of the officers' mess, wearing uniform trousers and a pyjama jacket and carrying a revolver. 'What's going on?' Hal asked him.

'Commando-type raid. They came in from seaward and took the guard by surprise. Sergeant-Major McDowell took a party and went after them but he must have been too late.' Tony paused and screwed up his face. 'You'd better come in here.'

Hindley had imposed a degree of order. Men were sent to man the battlements, to guard the gates, to fetch powerful lights and to recall the men from the slit trenches. A parachute flare drifted overhead. The defensive measures, Hal thought, were in the nature of locking the stable door, but they had to be taken.

She followed Tony into the mess. The largest room, which seemed to have been used as the lounge-bar, was uninhabited but there were bottles on the bar top and glasses on the low tables, ranging from full to empty. Smoke hung in the air and a cigar was still smouldering in an ashtray. The body of an African in a white jacket lay on the black and white tiles, looking colour co-ordinated except for the puddle of red seeping from under him.

'M'mono,' Tony said. 'One of the mess stewards. Poor devil.'

Hal had a terrible suspicion about what had happened but she had to ask. 'What were they after? Where's the brigadier?'

'They got him. That's what they came after, him and the senior officers.'

'Killed?'

'Snatched, it looks like. Nobody's found any bodies yet.'

Other men came in, officers in various stages of uniform, most of them brandishing handguns. They seemed very young. Hal became aware that her feet were bare but so were those of several others. Each new arrival checked at the sight of the body and then looked away. Somebody brought a cloth, apparently from a billiard table, and covered the corpse.

One of the officers had brought with him a fully uniformed private with a badly swollen face and blood dripping from a scalp wound. 'Hinks was one of the guards at the gate,' he said. 'They knocked him down but at least they left him alive. He saw them leave. Who did they have with them, Hinks?'

Private Hinks might be dazed but his memory was working. Holding a field dressing to his head, he rattled off a list of names.

'The party in here hadn't even begun to break up,' Tony

said. 'That sounds as if they got the lot.' There was a murmur of agreement. 'Hinks, you can go. Get the MO to attend to your head.'

'They got the MO, sir,' Hinks said.

'Damn! So they did! Find Lieutenant Halstead.'

'So who's in charge?' Hal asked.

The men looked at each other, waiting for a lead.

'The most senior officer remaining,' said Tony. 'Unless one of the others went to bed early and wasn't woken by all the rumpus, that's you, Major.'

Silence fell.

'Me?' Hal said stupidly. 'Tony, don't be daft.'

'Unless somebody else of your rank or above turns up, you're it.'

'Regulations are absolutely clear,' said a young man with a fluffy moustache. 'The next most senior officer will take over. Not can. Not may. *Will*.'

'There must be somebody with more experience,' Hal said desperately.

'None of us has seen action,' Tony said. 'The regs don't say anything about experience. And the way the brigadier ran this outfit, none of us has much idea what's going on anyway. At least you're fully briefed.'

Two more men had entered, along with Susan in a green T-shirt and combat trousers with her hair flying. They waited for Hal to give them a lead. Hal's mind was swimming. She had been jerked out of sleep and was now being pitchforked into a responsibility which was both unprecedented and preposterous.

Another woman, with Royal Army Medical Corps slides and the maroon stars of a captain, appeared at the door. 'They took the MO,' she said. 'I'm dealing with the wounded.' She vanished again.

'I've only just woken up,' Hal said at last. 'Will somebody, for God's sake, put some coffee on?'

'I'll rout out the mess steward,' said the officer with the fluffy moustache. It was as if nobody knew how to make coffee.

Hal's mind suddenly snapped into gear. 'One moment,' she

said. 'The raiders seemed remarkably well informed. They went to the right place at the right time.'

'And they seem to have had the right password,' said a voice.

'So who would be spying for them here?'

'Edmund Haiko, the other mess steward,' Tony said. 'He has family in Liboon. He'd be easy to intimidate and suborn. There's nobody else.' Again there was a murmur of agreement.

'Somebody find—'

'I'll do it,' said the man with the fluffy moustache. He hurried out, calling for a sergeant.

'I can make coffee,' Susan said.

Hal breathed a sigh of relief. 'At last somebody's trying to be helpful. But wait. I don't suppose our visitors will be back, but we'll play safe. As soon as we're secure, I want to see all the officers and warrant officers, in here, immediately. Understood?'

The heads all nodded.

'And I want poor M'mono removed.' Hal's mind was in overdrive. Ahead, she began to see an orderly pattern of events. If all these men – and a woman or two – wanted to be told what to do, so be it. 'And a check of officers' quarters, in the hope that somebody senior had left the party early and slept through all the fuss and flap.' She paused. 'Well, don't just stand there,' she said. 'Go and spread the word. All except you, Lieutenant Thyme and Captain Laverick,' she added to Susan and Tony. 'Susan.'

'Ma'am.'

'Do you have anyone who could sweep this place for listening devices?'

'No problem, ma'am.'

'I want this room done before I come back and the rest of the building immediately after. I don't expect you to find anything, but our security's been at fault once and I'm not taking any more chances. Set it up and join me; I want you with me while I change. Tony, can you find me a map and somewhere to pin it up?'

Susan followed, grumbling. 'I don't get a chance to change?' she asked as they left the building. Two minutes later she joined Hal in her room.

Hal had already doused her face in cold water. As one of the very few who had had a full sleep, she was becoming ever more alert. She started looking in her baggage for a clean shirt. 'You don't have to face all those men in a few minutes,' she said. 'I bet they'll all be in Number One uniforms by now with everything polished. You can go and change when this signal's gone off. Ready?'

Susan produced a signal pad, apparently from thin air. 'Ready, ma'am,' she said.

*'The following British personnel were taken in a commando-type raid at zero-zero-twenty-three today.* Give a list in order of seniority. *The following were killed.* Same again. *The following were wounded in action.* Same. We'll get the details when the meeting resumes. Paragraph. *A further report will follow as details become available.* Paragraph. *As the most senior remaining officer, I am assuming command pending further orders or a senior replacement.* Sign it H. Brown, Major, stick my army number on the end and send it. Digitally encrypted. Got it?'

'Got it.'

'Trouble is,' Hal said, 'there's a time difference of – what? – three hours, isn't it? The beggars will just be going to bed. How do I look?'

'They'll all lust after you,' Susan said. 'Ma'am,' she added quickly. She borrowed Hal's hairbrush and set about tidying her pale locks.

Hal winked. 'That's roughly the effect I was aiming for. Come on. Let's go and beard the lions in their den.'

'Don't think of them as lions, think of them as lambs,' Susan said. 'They're all lambs, really.'

The big room was filling rapidly when they returned to it. Military orderliness had asserted itself and the warrant officers had arranged themselves neatly against the walls while the officers were seated on the low couches. *Dishabille* was no longer evident. There were shadows of stubble but otherwise, despite the hour, smartness prevailed and even medal ribbons were on show. Silence fell and there was a move to rise as they entered. Hal was momentarily flustered and her

94

mouth was very dry but she managed to articulate the words 'at ease' and there was an immediate relaxation.

She took time to glance around the packed room. The black warrant officer would be the sergeant-major of the African company. It took her some seconds to distinguish the soldiers from the support, but, discounting engineers, RLC, an AGC captain and quartermaster staff, she counted ten captains, all grouped together. These would have been the second in command of companies, which, allowing for one absentee, equated with eleven company sergeant-majors and an RSM. There should have been thirty platoon commanders but there seemed to be slightly fewer infantry lieutenants. For a supposed brigade, she thought, this was desperately below strength. All the same, sheer weight of numbers made this an even more daunting audience than the Joint Planning Staff.

Justin Carlsborough, the only officer on his feet and standing with the warrant officers, fixed her with an unblinking stare. She noticed that he wore the three pips of a captain. For a moment she felt uncertain of her authority but she had to put aside her stage fright and go on.

A uniformed corporal with Royal Signals insignia was removing an instrument that resembled a portable radio. Hal returned his salute. 'All clear?' she asked.

'Yes, ma'am.'

'Check the rest of the building, then dismiss.'

Tony had taped up a large mosaic of maps at the focal point of the room, above an ornate fireplace where Hal thought she remembered a mirror. The maps were slightly dated but they would do. Hal stood in front of them.

'Are we secure?' she asked.

Sergeant-Major Hindley snapped to attention. 'Quite secure, ma'am. From all accounts, the same number of intruders left as came. Any dark-skinned stranger will be dealt with.'

There was a stir of amusement.

'I shall have to watch out, then,' Hal said. The stir became relieved laughter.

'Not you, ma'am,' Hindley said seriously. 'They know about you. There's a company of men spread round the walls, fully armed. They have seven sets of night-vision binoculars but they won't need them – the moon's up.'

'Whose company did you take?' a voice enquired.

'I took the first hundred men available, sir. They'll be relieved at zero-four-hundred. And there's a section inside each gate with orders to keep the big gates shut, ma'am. If somebody arrives at the wicket and can't account for himself, they're to take whatever action seems appropriate.'

Hal decided not to probe the exact meaning of the last few words. 'Well done, Sarn't-Major,' she said. 'Next, do we know exactly what happened?'

'McDowell?' said Hindley.

Another warrant officer snapped to attention. 'I've been collecting reports, ma'am,' he said. 'Seems that a commando-type unit of about platoon strength came ashore in six canoes from a vessel what was lying off. According to Hinks, they had the password, so the guard opened one leaf of the gate. There was four men on guard under the command of a corporal. They was overpowered. The intruders come in here and carried off the brigadier, Colonel Bone, the majors, the MO and the chaplain. I took a party to follow them up but we was too late, on top of which they could shoot all they wanted while we was scared of hitting one of our own officers. So they got away.'

'What of our own men?' Hal asked.

'Two dead, ma'am, including Corporal Nash. Three wounded – one not expected to make it – and Michael M'mono knifed to death in here.'

'Give Lieutenant Thyme the names of the casualties,' Hal said. She looked around the faces. They looked back with alert curiosity. 'If any of you did not know that much,' she said, 'you know now. I am sending a signal, reporting the incident, stating that as the senior officer remaining I am assuming command for the moment and asking for orders.'

She paused, cleared her throat and rearranged her thoughts. 'I have some more to say before I let you go to get some much-needed sleep. Until we receive fresh orders and replacement officers, I shall be looking for support, help and advice. I understand that Brigadier Wincaster was inclined to treat information about the situation as confidential and disclose it on a need-to-know basis. I shall require intelligent co-operation from each one of you, and so I think it vital that you know as much of what's going on as I do.

'The army of Liboon began an invasion of Maveria two days ago but an air strike took out the bridge over the Barawat River. Without the bridge, the Barawat River is almost impassable. Liboon's small air force has also been incapacitated. But that seems to be all the help that we can expect from outside until the present crisis in the Middle East is resolved. We are on our own.

'We are outnumbered substantially. We have a strong defensible position, but they managed to bring across a half-track and a twenty-five-pounder before the bridge went. Apart from that gun it would seem to be infantry against infantry. An old-fashioned war, in fact. It seems to me that a policy of waiting will not do more than give the enemy time to find other ways to bring reinforcements and armament across the Barawat. We would be ill-advised to go out to meet a stronger force on open ground but we can at least prepare to give it a very warm reception. I hope to have a plan for discussion by morning.'

Hal paused. The officers were looking sympathetic, the warrant officers expectant.

Justin Carlsborough spoke into the silence. His voice was flat and apparently disinterested. 'With all respect, ma'am, I would like to point out that, though it's true that regulations require the most senior remaining officer to take command, this is an infantry regiment and women are not allowed to serve in the infantry. I suggest that regulations do not qualify you in this case.'

'That's just a technicality,' somebody said.

'Out of interest,' Hal said, 'who would be the next most senior officer? Which of the captains has the longest service?' She held her breath. Perhaps she was going to be let off the hook.

There was silence. It seemed that the rest of the room was caught in the frozen moment. 'That would be me,' a captain in the Adjutant General's Corps said at last. 'But no way am I taking command of an infantry brigade, however much under strength, over the head of an Int-Corps major.'

'Ma'am, you can hardly be expected to lead us against others of your own colour,' Carlsborough said. 'Who comes next?'

There was a rising mutter of protest.

Hal's back went up. She saw the men watching each other surreptitiously and realized that rivalry was in the air. Somebody had to take charge immediately if relationships were not to break down. 'Would you feel disqualified from leading troops against other white men?' she demanded of Carlsborough. 'Well? Would you?'

Carlsborough looked up at the ceiling.

Into the sudden silence, Sergeant-Major Hindley spoke quickly. 'Permission to speak, ma'am and gentlemen?'

'Go ahead,' Hal said.

The sergeant-major's voice became a bark. A warrant officer might be outranked by commissioned officers, but he could expect his confidence, authority and experience to be recognized. 'With all respect, army regulations are not subject to debate and command is not a matter for democratic election. In my time I have seen command in the field taken over for short periods by a chaplain and again by a medical officer. If that isn't enough, I would like to point out that Major Brown was sent here precisely because she has knowledge of the situation and the geography, and she speaks both of the principal languages. She is at least as well qualified to command this unit as any man here and probably much better.'

There was such a moment of silence as precedes a thunderclap.

'Thank you for nothing, Sergeant-Major,' Hal said.

The atmosphere shattered into splinters of relief. Suddenly, laughter was let loose. Hal guessed that each officer was relieved that some rival had not leap-frogged him in the promotion stakes. As an obvious non-rival, Hal was acceptable. When the laughter died, Hal spoke again.

'It would seem that I'm saddled with the responsibility until a replacement arrives – or, of course, until we can manage to liberate the brigadier. Similarly, captains must take over as company commanders and so on down the line. Those temporary promotions should be almost automatic but please refer any problems to me. I would like to see company commanders and warrant officers back here at ten-hundred today, together with the senior quartermaster and sapper officers. By that time I hope to have an outline plan ready.' She glanced at Tony Laverick. 'I would like the most senior of the mining engineers to attend. Before that time, I want to meet the Prime Minister.'

'Yes, ma'am,' Tony said.

'We have certain advantages on our side,' Hal said. 'We have the strong defensive position. We have, I believe, technical superiority, especially in matters of intelligence. Which reminds me. Is there a local radio station?'

'There was,' Tony said. 'Very amateurish. There were almost no sets outside the town anyway. It's dismantled now.'

'Keep it that way—' Hal broke off as the captain with the fluffy moustache entered the room. 'Yes?'

'I've been interrogating Haiko, the mess steward. There's no doubt that he fed information to the Liboonese, ma'am, but he's not telling us anything. However frightened he may be of us, he's more frightened of General Agulfo.'

'*Who?*'

The captain with the fluffy moustache seem perturbed by the sudden snap in Hal's voice. 'General Agulfo, ma'am. The one thing that Haiko let slip was that General Agulfo threatened to take his soul and feed it to the dogs if he told us anything.'

'But he has told us something,' Hal said. 'He has told us something very valuable. I am acquainted with General Agulfo. So are Lieutenant Thyme and Captain Laverick. He was at Sandhurst with us. And we can make a good guess as to how his mind will react to any given situation.

'I'll let you go now, gentlemen. Sleep while you can; I shall want you alert in the morning. Captain Carlsborough, please remain for a moment.'

# Thirteen

Susan Thyme had already gathered up the lists of casualties and captives and left to send the signal.

Tony hung on his heel. 'Shall I stay?'

'Please,' Hal said. 'You can be my dogsbody, as you were for the brigadier.'

The room emptied. Hal found Justin Carlsborough standing stiffly in front of her, looking thunderous. 'May I ask, ma'am, whether this is because I dared to question your assumption of authority?' he demanded. 'Or are you harking back to Sandhurst?'

'Neither,' Hal said tiredly. 'I will if you want to, but I'm quite prepared to let bygones be bygones. The present situation's too fraught to let old bickerings get in the way. For God's sake, let's sit down.' She waited until they had lowered themselves on to separate couches. 'I was hoping to trust you with something special, but if you're so full of hostility and suspicion, you'll be useless.' She thought of adding that she would have to report being unable to trust in Captain Carlsborough's co-operation, but she decided to leave this to be used as a later sanction.

Carlsborough's face reflected his indecision. 'I . . .' he began, and stopped. 'Tell me,' he said, and added, 'Please.'

'Very well.' Hal looked at Tony. 'Susan Thyme's deserted us and we seem to have lost our mess waiters. Do you think you could make some coffee? I'll bring you up to speed later.'

Tony sketched a salute and went in search of the kitchen or whatever functioned as the mess cookhouse.

'Here's the problem,' Hal said. 'As I told you, the bridge is out. The Barawat River runs in a deep gorge all the way

100

to the sea. The river mouth is broad and infested with croc-odiles. The Liboonese are without air support for the moment. They will want reinforcements and the supplies which are backed up on the other side of the Barawat River, and which I am determined they shall not have.

'General Agulfo, when we knew him, was not a subtle man. He tended to favour the direct and simple solution to any problem. There are several gullies in the cliff on the Liboon side of the river mouth. In this instance, the direct and simple solution would be to bring in the bulldozers and reshape one of those gullies to take traffic, using the spoil to build a small pier. Men and supplies could be shipped across and landed further along the coast, where the cliffs give way to beach and sand-dunes.

'The latest report from satellite imagery indicates that some such work has begun. A vessel was earlier lying off the river mouth, waiting to begin loading. That may be the vessel which brought the raiding party. You follow me so far?'

Carlsborough had lost his customary look of superior boredom. 'Of course,' he said. 'And where do I come in? Ma'am,' he added.

Tony returned with a tray bearing a coffee-pot and cups. Hal waited until the coffee was dispensed and Tony had resumed his seat. 'I seem to remember hearing that your father has a yacht. Does that mean that you've learned something about boats and the sea?'

'To the extent of skippering a large yacht in offshore races, yes,' Carlsborough said. 'I suppose that counts.'

'It certainly does. But perhaps you could suggest somebody else with comparable experience and less of a chip on his shoulder?'

Carlsborough winced. He shook his head. 'Please go on, ma'am.'

'There's a fishing boat in the harbour. Would you be capable of taking it down to the mouth of the Barawat and sinking that vessel, shooting up any canoes in sight and generally raising a little hell? Take your pick of men and weapons.'

Carlsborough was frowning, but thoughtfully. 'I would be

capable,' he said. 'Whether the fishing boat would be capable, I'm less certain about. Its sails seem to be in tatters and I understand it was left here because the engine refused to start.'

'There's a sort of combination warehouse and fish market down at the harbour,' Tony said. 'I had a poke around in there after the fishing fleet left in a panic. There are several quite decent lateen sails bundled up in there. The dozy beggars around here usually do everything under power. And I had a look down the hatch of the boat. There's a Kelvin diesel down there, all rusted up.'

'If I can get that engine restored,' Hal said, 'could you do it? Or would you care to recommend somebody else with the necessary seagoing experience?' She nearly added 'and more guts' but something told her that she had said enough.

'Yes, I could, and of course I will, ma'am,' Carlsborough said simply. He sighed. 'I seem destined to apologize to you. But if I seemed to have a chip on my shoulder, I am sorry.'

He seemed ready to say more but Hal chipped in quickly. A backhanded remark now could ruin what looked set to become a new relationship and it was not the occasion for breast beating. She had a full night ahead of her. 'Very well. You don't have to explain. Just get rid of the chip. You are hereby appointed admiral of the Malverian navy. Hand over your company – you *are* now in command of a company? – to whichever platoon commander you have most faith in. Go and get some sleep and then start thinking about men and armament. Skip the morning conference and report direct to me.'

Carlsborough put down his cup and got to his feet. After a momentary hesitation he saluted uncertainly and marched out.

'I take it,' Hal said to Tony, 'that we can find one or two good diesel mechanics? Perhaps you'd better go and root out the transport officer.'

'No need,' Tony said. 'Ramsay came to me yesterday afternoon, complaining that his two best mechanics had been arrested. I was going to bring them up in front of you this morning.'

'What's the charge?'

'Fighting. With each other. On duty.'

Hal found that the habit of decision was becoming established. 'Let's dispose of it right away,' she said. 'I'll go up to the brigadier's office – my office now, I suppose, for the moment. Ask Captain Ramsay to attend. Then have the guard commander wheel them in.'

Hal carried her second cup of coffee up the broad stairs. The brigadier's office was as vast as she remembered it, almost the size of the room below, and the huge desk still seemed lost in the geometrical centre of the room. It was littered with papers and the brigadier's personal odds and ends.

Hal seated herself behind the desk. Part of her mind half expected the brigadier to appear out of nowhere, pulverize her with sarcastic comments on her youth, colour and femininity and relieve her of any further need to struggle with the problems he had bequeathed to her. But the brigadier was not so obliging.

There were noises as of a regiment on the march. The door opened and a sergeant-major appeared. 'Caps off, left-right-left-right, left wheel, Halt!'

Stiffly at attention on the other side of the desk were two overalled figures. They had been allowed roughly to de-grease themselves since their arrest and several sticking-plasters had been applied, but otherwise they seemed to be much as the fight had left them.

They were followed by a blue-chinned captain who Hal remembered seeing in the room below. She ignored them for the moment. Tony had returned and she spoke directly to him. 'I take it that the unit has a clerk or two? Please find me one to do some night-duty. I shall be up all night, but there's no need for you to suffer. When we've dealt with this little matter, go and get some sleep.'

Hal returned her attention to the figures before her. One was a small, ferret-faced man with a thin moustache. He had a swelling over one eye and he seemed to have lost two front teeth. The other was larger, definitely female. There was a graze along one side of her face and finger marks on her throat were developing into bruises.

'Has the MO seen these two?' she enquired.

'Last duty he did, before they come and took him, ma'am,' said the sergeant-major. 'Privates Settle and Gurney, ma'am, charged with fighting on duty,'

Hal took another look at the female figure and suddenly felt laughter welling up in her. She hid her amusement. 'Hilda?' she said. 'Hilda Settle?'

Hilda remained stiffly at attention. 'Yes, ma'am,' she said.

'You do seem to have a habit of getting into fights.'

'She started it,' Private Gurney said loudly.

'Well, he called you a coon and a nignog,' Hilda shouted. 'And other things. He said the best part of you—'

The sergeant-major's voice stopped them both. 'Silence! Speak when the major speaks to you.'

Hal had to struggle not to burst out laughing. 'I'll take those remarks as a plea of guilty. Captain Ramsay, any comment?'

'They're good mechanics, ma'am,' Ramsay said. 'They make a good team. They just don't get on. But I'd be hard put to do without them.'

'Thank you,' Hal said. Her mind was racing ahead. 'I'll give you my decision in a minute. First, I want to know whether you two, working together and given the bits and tools, could restore an old Kelvin diesel engine, PDQ.'

'No problem, miss . . . ma'am,' said Private Gurney. 'If it's not too far gone.'

Hilda was more forthcoming. 'My da had a lorry with a Kelvin engine,' she said. 'I was the only one as could keep it running.'

'Right,' said Hal. 'There's an old fishing boat in the harbour. I want its engine running, reliably, by midday. Draw what tools, stores and other support you need and if anybody gets in the way, refer him to Captain Ramsay or to me. Sergeant-Major, post a guard, just in case the enemy makes a return visit.'

'Yes, ma'am. And regarding the other matter?'

Hal thought for a moment. The two culprits could not be

expected to work well together, and certainly not in amity, with a threat of punishment hanging over them. 'You two,' she said. 'Kiss and make up.'

'Hoy!' said Hilda. She looked at her fellow-accused with revulsion. 'No! I'd rather kiss the sergeant-major.' Her tone made it clear that she did not fancy either option.

Private Gurney returned her look with interest. 'So would I,' he said.

The sergeant-major began to swell ominously.

'Enough!' Hal said hastily. 'That is your punishment. Get on with it or I'll think of something much, much worse.'

Hilda seemed about to say that there wasn't anything worse, but in the end she made a gesture of resignation. 'If we got to, we got to,' she said and, seizing the reluctant Gurney by one ear and the nape of his neck, she planted a smacking kiss on him before returning to attention. Gurney's look of horror was a joy to behold.

'Right,' Hal said. 'That's an end to the matter. We'll record a verdict of Admonished. Go and get that engine running.'

'About turn,' snapped the sergeant-major. 'Caps on. Quick march. Left-right-left-right. Right wheel.' The military noises faded down the stairs.

Hal lay back on the brigadier's chair and laughed until her ribs ached. It felt like years since she had laughed with such abandon.

Hal went downstairs a few minutes later, still smiling. Tony was already asleep on one of the couches, alone in the big room. He slept neatly, she noticed, with his mouth shut and not the least trace of a snore. She took down his mosaic of maps and carried them carefully up to her office.

A thin man in a loose robe and steel-rimmed spectacles was waiting beside the desk. His face was marked by the pocks of some earlier ailment. His origin seemed to be mixed African and Asian and, although there was a trace of Asian sibilance in his voice, his accent was almost perfectly English.

'Joseph Mobo, ma'am,' he said. 'Civilian clerk.'

'Good morning, Joseph. Help me put these maps up,' Hal

said. They began fitting the jigsaw of maps together at one end of the long, blank wall. Hal still had security on her mind. 'How do you come to be here in Maveria?' she asked.

'My father was an officer in the Liboonese army,' Joseph said. 'He married the daughter of an Indian merchant. I was educated at a good mission school and then took service at the British Embassy. When the last military coup took place – one of many, to my sorrow – my father remained loyal to the president. That was his mistake. They shot him. My mother and I fled, intending to come here to Pembaka, but there were guards on the bridge and mines near the river to prevent any crossing of the border. She trod on one of the mines and died in my arms.' Joseph blinked behind his glasses. 'I was twelve. I swam the river, among all the crocodiles. I would not have dared, except that I did not care whether I lived or died. And it seems that they had already eaten their fill. Or else they did not care for Afro-Asian blood. Those were good days for crocodiles.' He smiled suddenly. 'It is all in my personnel file. Believe me, Major, I was thoroughly vetted.'

'I'm sure you were, Joseph,' Hal said. 'And I'm sorry about your parents. But information has leaked out of here and I have to be sure. I want some files looked out. Please bring your personnel file with the others.'

'Major, I understand and approve. Nobody hates the present dictatorship in Liboon more than I, but I am only glad that you are being more careful.'

For the next four hours Hal worked, assisted by Joseph. Joseph, as he said, had received a thorough vetting and his file was too full to have suffered tampering. Once she had established that he was to be trusted, she turned her attention to a study of the structure of the garrison and list after list of stores and armament and personnel. By the time her mind began to rebel, she had a good mental picture of her new command. She switched her attention to the mosaic of maps.

The garrison never slept. All night there were commands up on the rampart and once the tramp of boots as the guard was relieved. Then she was suddenly aware of voices in the street, footsteps in the building and a jingling sound. Daylight had crept up on her, fading the electric lights. An African in a waiter's white jacket came in with a breakfast tray. Coffee, cereal, toast and marmalade and some local fruit – either a lucky guess or somebody knew her preferences. Suddenly, she was ravenous. Thinking back, she had not had a proper meal since yesterday lunchtime. She wanted to ask for bacon and eggs, but they were probably unobtainable.

'More toast,' she told the waiter. When he had gone, she started on the cereal. The milk was goat's milk, rich and creamy.

When the second batch of toast arrived it was brought by Tony. He was smart and freshly shaved. 'I thought you'd still be sleeping,' she said.

He shook his head. 'I'll get by,' he said. 'I'm good at catnapping. I had to be. The brigadier thought nothing of summoning me at any hour of the day or night, for any reason or none. I've sent a runner to invite the Prime Minister and one of the mining engineers to come. You're looking tired,' he added.

'I slept yesterday evening. I'll catch up again later. Is there any word from Signals?'

'Your satellite images are coming through now. Susan promised to come over with them as soon as they're all printed. There's a hell of a lot of them. They'll have to parachute in some more printing paper if it goes on like this.'

'I brought what ought to be a ten-year supply,' Hal said. 'I dare say it'll last a week or two. See if you can get what's available so far brought over now. And get this desk moved back near the wall and see if you can find some chairs. I'm going to go back and freshen up.'

'Your quarters are over here now,' Tony said. 'The brigadier had a bathroom next door and sleeping quarters beyond. His batman turned scarlet at the thought of ministering to you, so Mamie – Sergeant Ashna – offered to take you on. I've had your gear brought round. I'll go and see how the printouts are getting on.'

Hal washed in a marble-tiled bathroom, promising herself

a long bath soon. In a large, cool bedroom she found that the uniform she had discarded the previous day was clean and on a hanger on the door of a huge, teak wardrobe. The brigadier's clothes and paraphernalia, down to his toothbrush, had been neatly stacked inside the wardrobe.

Back in the office, things had moved on. She must have taken longer than she thought to change and freshen herself, because chairs of a dozen different patterns had been brought from somewhere and arranged in rows facing the map wall. Tony and Joseph were matching up printouts and piecing together two more jigsaw mosaics on the long wall. The remains of her breakfast had been cleared away.

'I've had a message,' Tony told her. 'The Prime Minister is on his way.'

'Fine,' Hal said absently.

Susan Thyme arrived with the last of the printouts and sticky-taped them in place. Hal turned away from the wall, where she had been intently studying the mosaics as they came together. 'Dash back to your den,' she told Susan. 'Get off a signal, digitally encrypted. I want blow-ups of these last four sheets, more urgent than merely urgent, as big as they'll go.' She took a good look at the other woman. There was no doubting that Susan had also been up all night. 'When we've got that, go and get some sleep.'

The Prime Minister arrived, unescorted, a few minutes later. Mr N'koma was an old man, shrunken into a wrinkled suit of Western clothes, but his manner was alert and his eyes were bright. They took two of the chairs. Hal greeted him formally in Arabic.

Mr N'koma smiled, revealing a shining set of dentures. 'I shall be glad to use my English,' he said. 'So you now command the forces defending our country?' His English was very good although he had the vowel-sounds of the native African.

'I shall do my best,' Hal said.

'I am certain that it will be a good best. They are already saying that you will be a better general than the brigadier.'

Hal was struck, not for the first time, by the speed at which news and opinion can pass through a close community. 'Who knows?' she enquired. '"An excellent major, a mediocre colonel and an abysmal general" – somebody said that of General Buller during the Boer War.'

'They will not say it of you, I know it. And we pray for your victory. My grandfather was alive when last the Liboonese had power over this country. He has told me. It was not good and the history of hatred is a long one.' He heaved a sigh which almost filled his jacket to the point of fitting him. 'You will have much to do and so, if you wish to take the usual courtesies as being exchanged, we should talk.'

A waiter, new to Hal, brought coffee on a tray and poured for them. When he had left the room, Mr N'koma said, 'That is Saul Haroun. You may trust him.'

'That's good to know,' Hal said. 'Mr N'koma, I'm told that you hear all that goes on in Maveria.'

He smiled again. 'They give me too much honour. But the people tell me news and more so than usual in this troubling time.'

'On the wall there,' Hal said, 'are pictures taken from a satellite. I'm sure you know what I mean.'

'Very high in the sky.'

'Exactly. The pictures suggest that the Liboonese soldiers are still in camp near where the bridge was before it was bombed. But this,' Hal said carefully, watching his face to be sure that he understood her, 'I do not believe. I think that they have left a few men to keep cooking fires going and make things look as if they are still an army. I think that the real army is on the way here. Do you know if I am right?'

He nodded violently. 'They are marching,' he said. 'Not by the old road but keeping to the trees. They marched by moonlight, even, and only rested when the moon went down. That was near the mouth of Urma River.'

'I thought as much,' Hal said. 'Please gather as much news as you can and send it to me as fast as you can get it. But tell your people not to put themselves in danger.'

'Danger of death is better than handing one's country to an invader.'

'One man already betrayed us to the invader,' Hal said. 'We have him under arrest. But if there are any others who might spy for him, keep them away from the riverside. I do not want their commander to know what we are doing.'

The old man bowed his head. 'This I can and will do. My grandson will bring you news as I can gather it.'

'One more thing,' Hal said. 'How well do you know the geography?' He looked puzzled. 'The land,' she said in explanation.

'The land I know better than my own face. My face has changed with the years but the land changes very little. A few scars from the hand of man, that is all. When I was a young man I was a hunter and knew every yard of it. Since then, your people have made some roads and built a dam. Otherwise it is the same. Nothing changes the land in one lifetime.'

'Then please come and describe some of these places for me.'

# Fourteen

Hal returned to her office after an hour's absence. The room was filling. Again, the WOs had taken to the back of the room with the officers to the fore, facing the maps and mosaics. Captains all, she noticed, except one, looking barely out of his teens, wearing a lieutenant's two pips. Of course, she realized suddenly, this would be Justin Carlsborough's nominee to command his company. So Carlsborough was forging ahead, she thought aptly. Her mood lightened. After climbing to the ramparts to look out over the inland countryside, she had visited the wounded men in the makeshift sickbay. Real men wounded in real action had been a douche of cold water after all the theory and paper exercises and the remote overview of the Ministry. But if fighting men – and Justin Carlsborough at that – were doing her bidding, perhaps her first real command might not after all be the travesty that some part of her mind had been expecting.

She took a seat at the desk, at the end of the rows of chairs. The new faces were turned and looking at her with the now customary air of examining something from another planet. She looked along the shoulder-flashes. She counted heads again and returned to the same depressing answer. If this was a brigade, it was well under strength. The face of one captain and that of the one warrant officer were as black as her own. Her sense of relief was not because of the fellow-feeling but because their presence would make her own colour seem familiar and so more a part of the accepted scene. The ancient pattern of white-officers-black-other-ranks was already broken.

The last arrival was a civilian, a heavily built man, very

tanned, with a checked shirt and matching shorts. He carried a bush hat. She caught Tony's eye.

'Joe Tuckridge,' Tony said. 'Mining engineer.' Hal exchanged a nod with the newcomer.

The brigadier's personal odds and ends had been swept away, the papers tidied. Somebody had placed a carafe of water, chilled by rapidly melting ice, in readiness. Gratefully, she took a sip and then got to her feet to stand before the mosaics.

'Gentlemen,' she said bravely. 'I don't know all your names yet. I'll try to learn them soon. Meantime, please introduce yourselves each time you meet me and don't feel insulted if you have to do this more than once. I have a great deal to memorise.'

There were one or two sympathetic smiles and an air of relaxation. She had struck the right note. She decided that they were on her side.

'I've called you together because I want you to know the situation in detail and then I want to consult you about my plan of action. I look to all of you for support and to the warrant officers in particular for their experience. But that does not mean that our plans are going to be formulated by a committee. History holds too many examples of disasters beginning that way.

'On the wall are satellite images, taken shortly after dawn this morning. At first glance it looks as if the main body of the invading force is still not far from where the bridge used to be. The pictures show the heat and smoke of cooking fires and the flattened ground where a large body of men had camped. There are signs which might possibly be men. I don't believe those signs. I think that a party of men was left at the former campsite to create the impression of a much larger body stopped for regrouping. And I read that as an attempt to take us by surprise.'

Nobody threw questions, but there was a vaguely interrogative sound from the assembled men.

Hal sipped water at the desk, returned to the mosaics and went on again. 'I may as well tell you why I think so,' she said. 'We know that a single half-track towing an artillery piece made it over the bridge before it was blown. There is a double shape beside this supposed camp which could be the half-track and the gun. But it is not throwing a shadow.

'I requested images taken as soon as possible after dawn because shadows are often informative, but also because thermal contrast is greatest. On the thermal image mosaics, there is little sign of the heat generated by a large body of men. But if you scan over to here, near the Urma River, you see a pale speckling among the trees and one white spot which may be the half-track. I have asked for enlargements of those two areas.

'The Prime Minister, Mr N'koma, visited me this morning. What he has heard – don't ask me how – confirms my belief.

'So we may assume that the enemy is on the move. At one time there was an unmade road from the bridge to here. It's largely overgrown now but it would still be the easiest route for a body of marching men. We are meant to believe that they are waiting at the Barawat River for supplies and re-inforcements. But General Agulfo is not a patient man. He is impetuous. I think that they are marching beneath the canopy of the trees, trying to take us by surprise. That would be in keeping with General Agulfo's character as I remember it. Mr N'koma tells me that the area is forest but not jungle. There's little undergrowth under the acacia trees. If I'm wrong about all this,' she added, 'no harm will be done. We will have got ready unnecessarily early, that's all.

'On the basis of this information – or assumption – and assuming also a brisk rate of march, they would be in this vicinity late this afternoon. But they would be mad to attack immediately, exhausted from the march and in broad daylight.'

Hal was interrupted by the arrival of Susan Thyme with a roll of paper under her arm. Susan threw a smart salute. 'The enlarged printouts, ma'am,' she said.

'Smart service,' Hal commented. 'Put them up, please.'

Tony helped Susan to fasten the drawings to the plaster. The men were craning their necks to see. Hal took a quick look.

'Take a seat, Susan,' she said. She looked again and then faced the company. 'There's no doubt in my mind,' she said. 'They're on their way. Anyone with any doubts is welcome to look for himself. Incidentally, the thermal images show up the areas of swampy ground with greater detail and accuracy than the maps and I suggest that you get all your maps updated forthwith.'

Hal's voice was becoming husky. She took a longer drink of the water. It had been flavoured mildly with some citrus fruit. The ice was almost gone. 'Back to my plans,' she said. 'I have asked Lieutenant Thyme to remain because she and Captain Laverick were at Sandhurst, as I was, with General Agulfo who, we believe, is now commanding the Liboonese force.

'His obvious route to here was along the former road, but he is not taking it. My recollection of General Agulfo's thinking was that he was not a subtle man. He might avoid the too-obvious first option, in which case he would go for the second, but almost never the third. He was a competent officer but uninspired, and he had no talent for projecting himself into his opponent's mind.

'The River Urma lies between us. It is wide and its bottom is mostly muddy. It would not be easy to cross except at certain places. General Agulfo's first option would be to cross where the road to the mines crosses, upstream from here but below the dam. Mr Tuckridge, please explain the crossing. Mr N'koma tried to tell me about it but his technical knowledge and our common languages proved inadequate.'

'With pleasure, ma'am. It's what's sometimes known as an Irish bridge.' Mr Tuckridge's accent was unmistakably Australian. He was an exceptionally hairy man. His chin was shaven but blue and he seemed to be waging a battle of the scissors with hair in his ears and nostrils. His eyebrows were long and curly. 'It replaced a rickety affair remaining from earlier days. One material we had a lot of, left over from an abortive attempt to drill oil, was pipes. An Irish bridge is a lot of pipes stacked so's the water can run through them with a road, concrete in this instance, laid over the top. It gets covered when the river's very high, like now after the rains, but it can still be used. It would not be as easy to blow as a conventional bridge, if that's what you're thinking.'

'Thank you,' Hal said. 'That might be his obvious crossing point, but he knows we'd expect that. He might expect us to blow the bridge, so I'm glad of an excuse to leave it alone. We won't disappoint him. I want one unit with an LSW machine-gun emplaced overlooking the crossing. They'd better be well dug in and it would be good if they could look like they're a whole machine-gun company.

'A short way downstream, between here and the barracks where the river widens, there's an almost forgotten ford, unused since the first bridge was built. The river there is comparatively shallow and a long-ago rock fall made the escarpment climbable on this side, at least by mules. We can assume that Haiko, the mess steward who was passing him information, told him about the ford. That's the way I think they'd come. Would you agree?' She glanced at Susan and then at Tony.

'That would be in line with what we remember of him,' Tony said.

'I agree,' said Susan.

'One thing makes me wonder. I looked down from the wall just now and I saw crocodiles.'

'Only freshwater crocs, ma'am,' said Joe Tuckridge, 'and not too many of them. Back home in Australia, the freshwater crocs aren't nearly as aggressive as the saltwater ones. The difference isn't the same here, but there's still a difference. I wouldn't hesitate to wade there.' He paused. 'Well, maybe I'd hesitate, but I'd do it – with my eyes wide open.'

There was a general hiss of amusement.

Hal turned her attention to the quartermaster. 'Your name?'

'Masterson, ma'am.'

'Captain Masterson, what do we do for fresh meat?'

There was a murmur of surprise at the apparent change of subject but the quartermaster answered without demur. 'We have our own sheep and goats in a big pen outside the north wall. The native boys take them to pasture by day.'

'If we slaughtered all that we don't need for milk, could we prevent the meat going to waste?'

'We could freeze a lot of it, ma'am. We have some capacity so long as the electricity supply holds up. We could salt a lot more. The rest would have to be sun-dried.'

'How do we stand for an electricity supply?'

'We have our own generator within the town,' said Masterson. 'And we have an ample supply of diesel for it, if you're preparing for a siege.'

'I am not thinking of a siege,' Hal said. 'The reverse. I am thinking of going to meet the opposing force. But not going very far and doing it strictly on my terms. Mr Tuckridge, you seem to know about crocodiles. You're Australian?'

'Yes, ma'am. I've seen more crocs than I ever wanted, and closer.'

'Saltwater crocodiles are even larger and more aggressive than the freshwater variety?'

'Generally,' said Tuckridge. 'In Africa, freshwater crocs can grow pretty damn big too.'

'The mouth of the Urma River is infested with them, so I'm told by Mr N'koma. So tell me, if the blood from all those sheep and goats was to be poured into the river, what would happen?'

'My guess,' said Tuckridge, 'would be that the saltwater crocs would start swimming upstream, looking for the source of the blood.'

Hal looked at the Engineer captain. 'How long would blood take to reach the river mouth?'

'Westerly, ma'am. Very approximately two hours, at the present rate of flow.'

'Allow two to three hours for the crocs to swim upstream against the current,' said Tuckridge.

'And you wouldn't have to pour it into the river,' said Captain Westerly. 'Any of the town's storm-water drains would discharge it into the river. Not the foul drains, mind – they go through septic tanks.'

'Thank you,' Hal said. 'If we can time it right, that should be an option. But I wouldn't want the crocodiles to turn the opposition back. I want the Liboonese to start coming across in force. I want them to walk into our arms.'

'I can't speak for the crocs, ma'am,' Tuckridge said, 'but they probably wouldn't start attacking straight away, not until there was somebody or something thrashing or bleeding in the water to draw them to the place.'

'I hope you're right,' Hal said. 'Now tell me about the dam.'

She was looking at Joe Tuckridge but it was Captain Westerly of the Royal Engineers who replied. 'It's just an earth dam lined with clay, with sluices at the top to let off the surplus when the reservoir's full, like now.'

'What would happen if a hole was blown in the dam?' Hal asked.

There was a sudden stir of interest.

'In ten minutes,' Westerly said quietly, 'there'd be about fifteen feet of water above the ford, running fast.'

'But the town would be without water?'

'Not at that time. The pressure – the "head", to be technical – is much too great for the town's supply to come directly off the reservoir. There's a balancing reservoir underground, between here and the main reservoir. It was made in a natural depression but when the locals boys started using it as a crocodile-free swimming pool and the men used it as a fish-pond, we put a concrete roof over it. Going carefully, and with most of the native population still away, it should last for about three weeks.'

'We begin to see a picture in the tea-leaves,' Hal said. 'One more problem. The gun. They'll want to keep the element of surprise. Looking across the river from the wall just now, I could see a clearing, but that's too close to site a twenty-five-pounder without us being aware of it. Much further off, beyond the trees, would be a possibility, but I think that would be too far off for accuracy.'

'Definitely, ma'am,' said one of the warrant officers.

'Thank you. There's just one other large clearing to be seen.' Hal got up, walked to one of the mosaics and put her finger on the place. 'Here. That's where I'd put the gun. Any comments?'

117

There was a negative murmur.

'At that distance,' Hal said, frowning, 'its movement would be out of earshot from here by day. But they wouldn't move it by day. And in the quiet of night, we'd surely hear the half-track, even from there.'

An officer with prominent facial bones said, 'Captain Robertson, ma'am. They'll move it into place at last light. The noise would be covered by the howler monkeys.'

'I thought howler monkeys were South American and that they howled at dawn,' Hal said.

'Not these ber-beggars,' said Tuckridge. Again there was the hiss of suppressed laughter. 'There are two troops of them, always disputing territory, and they make more noise than the South American ones. I've worked in Brazil and in Colombia.'

'Then Captain Robertson is almost certainly right. Do we have any men with Special Forces experience?'

A hand went up among the warrant officers. 'Pennington, ma'am. I was a Royal Marine Commando until I was injured in training. I'm fit as you like now, but not fit enough for them. We have two men came from the SAS and three from the Paras, same reason. There's others.'

'Thank you,' Hal said. 'The opposition won't want to lose their element of surprise. I suggest that the gun wouldn't be fired until the infantry were in place and ready to attack. Then they would aim to breach the wall and go in fast. Sergeant-Major Pennington, would you volunteer to get together a party of the toughest men you can gather up, depart immediately, lie up near where we expect the gun to be positioned and move in on my signal?'

'With pleasure, ma'am.' Pennington was a well-built man with a close-cropped head and a precise moustache. He seemed to radiate confidence and physical well-being.

'Good. I'd have liked to capture the gun and the half-track but I don't see any way to bring them back here, or to make much use of them afterwards. Disable them where they are. How you get back to us afterwards, with fifteen feet of water over the Irish bridge, I don't know.'

'The reservoir has an upstream dam,' Westerly said, 'to

prevent the water flowing back up the river when the level drops. They can come back over that if the water level hasn't fallen quickly enough to suit them.'

'I'd like to volunteer to go with them,' Tuckridge said. 'I know the country and I know how to handle dynamite. I could fix that gun and half-track so's nobody could ever repair them.'

'Is that acceptable, Sarn't-Major Pennington? Then I suggest that the two of you go and get organized,' Hal said. 'Give Captain Laverick a list of your radio code-words. He'll give you the timetable when we've determined it.' She waited until Tuckridge and Pennington had left the room. 'There will have to be some reshuffling of Sergeant-Major Pennington's responsibilities, but I can leave it to you to organize between you.

'Now, gentlemen. In a minute, we'll talk details and times and who does what, when. First, help me to think. We are a raw unit with unfamiliar leadership, so let's try to anticipate every variation that fate may throw at us. Let's consider the geography. In General Agulfo's shoes, I'd want to assure myself that I hadn't been outguessed, so I'd put an advance party *here*.' Her hand made a sweep on the map between the town and the ford. Her training in tactics was flooding back to her. 'They won't know the lie of the land as you do, but as soon as they're up from the river they'll want to be sure that they can't come under fire from the two areas of higher ground which will be silhouetted against the sky, so their commander will send a party to each of those places. So, unless anyone can show me a reason to the contrary, we'll place our units in waiting *here* and *here* and *here*...'

'Ladies will no longer be excluded from the officers' mess,' Hal said. 'By order.'

'All ladies?' Tony enquired.

Hal thought back to some of the women she had seen in the streets and lanes. 'Women officers,' she amended hastily.

The change to the brigadier's edict was swiftly promulgated. Hal lunched with Tony and Susan in the mess. Lunch was served by a private with an apron over his uniform. Hal was still attracting glances from other officers. She thought that they seemed approving without being noticeably lecherous. The feeling in the air was hushed and expectant.

Hal kept her voice low. 'How did I do?' she asked the others anxiously.

'Good God!' Tony said. 'Don't you know when you're inspired? We're all most impressed.'

'Half the time,' Hal said, 'I thought I was gibbering. Tony, I don't want anybody walking around unnecessarily outside the walls and especially not going in the direction of the ford and giving away our intentions. We don't know who may be watching. Mr N'koma has promised to keep people away from the opposite bank, but an advance party of the Liboonese could reach there at any time. So a minimum number of heads on the battlements, please. Pass the word around,' she finished with a yawn.

'You should get some sleep,' Susan said. 'You were up all night.'

'I'd like to have a walk round on my own. Those WOs should know the lie of the land all right – after all, it's on their route between the town and the camp and it must have been used a great deal in training – but I'd like to see for myself, just to set my mind at rest. Not in uniform. One black girl wandering around aimlessly could be looking for a lost goat or something. After that I'll take a siesta.'

'I can lend you a cotton dress,' Susan said.

'Outside the town,' Tony said hopefully, 'the women go around in long cotton skirts, but topless.'

'Dream on,' Hal said.

# Fifteen

'I've forgotten something,' Hal said. 'I know I have.'

'I'm damn sure you haven't,' said Tony. 'Or if you have, somebody else has thought of it. They've been beavering away all afternoon, organizing each other and liaising away like mad. They were so happy to be consulted for once that they're putting their hearts and souls into not letting you down. We've got contingency plans to cover contingency plans.'

'Well, ain't that just dandy,' Hal said lightly, but something inside her was lifting with pleasure and she thought that it was probably her heart.

The two were on top of the high wall, above the landward gate. Darkness had come with a rush but the sky was still washed with streaks of flame. The sound of the howler monkeys drowned out all other noises. Tony stood looking over the land but Hal was seated on a cushion with her back to the parapet. Tony was unlikely to be recognized among all the men keeping watch from the wallhead, but Hal was determined to take no risk of Simon Agulfo becoming aware of her presence. Not, she added to herself, that he would realize that the working of his mind was so predictable. Probably. Always assuming that she was reading him right. And assuming that it was not some other General Agulfo in command.

The last of the sun's light went out of the sky and the rising moon took over. The howler monkeys fell silent and they could hear faint sounds on the seaward side of the ridge as the platoons, one by one, moved into their appointed positions. 'Anything?' she asked.

Tony took a look through the image-intensifying

binoculars. 'Nothing,' he said patiently. 'We've already agreed that he won't come for hours yet. If you or I were in his shoes, we'd come just before dawn. Make the crossing in the last of the moon, start shelling out of the darkness, then blow the gates and make the assault in the first of the daylight. You might just as well have stayed in bed.'

'I couldn't have slept any more,' Hal said. 'I wonder what it is that I've forgotten.'

'Whatever you've forgotten, forget it. You may as well stand up now. You're just a black blob.'

'I am never just a black blob,' Hal said sternly.

'We are all just black blobs,' Tony pointed out. 'But you more than most. I can't see anything but I think I can hear the half-track. Or maybe it's the sound of the jungle drums.'

Hal jumped up. In the sudden silence of the night, there was a faint mutter. Then the night-time offshore breeze swallowed it. It might have been the blood in her ears.

'Go and get some dinner,' Tony said, 'and thank your stars we're not sitting around some crummy campfire, like Henry the Fifth.'

'"He that outlives this day, and comes safe home."'

'Right. Then you can come back and relieve me. Don't hurry. I'll send for you if anything happens.'

Hal looked and listened. The river was black except where it reflected a moonlit cloud above the hills. The trees beyond were black as a coalmine. The hills in the distance seemed to have grown. Even through the image-intensifying binoculars she could see nothing of interest. The darkness was blank-faced, as though nothing would ever come out of it, but that very blankness could be hiding demons in the shape of the Liboonese. She slammed her mind shut on such imaginings. The temperature was falling rapidly as the warm onshore breeze was replaced by a colder wind. She was more interested in a thick coat than in food.

'Will the men be all right out there?'

'They're well clothed and equipped. They have field rations with them. This is what they enlisted and trained for. Stop worrying.'

Hal cast one last look into the darkness. 'All right,' she said. 'I shan't be long.'

The officers' mess was deserted but the native cook and the enlisted waiter hurried to tempt her with fish, accompanied by vegetables washed in water which they swore was the purest in Africa. Hal was past caring.

It was more than an hour before she returned to the parapet. 'Our guesses may be right,' she told Tony. 'Susan's had a signal reporting on the latest satellite images and giving map references. I've been plotting them and it looks as if the main body's assembling at the track down to the ford. We were right about the siting of the gun, too.'

'I never doubted it,' Tony said. 'You always did seem to have a touch of the second sight.'

They stood for a while in companionable silence. 'Who's doing the adjutant's job?' she asked suddenly.

'We're sort of sharing it around,' he said.

'In other words, you're doing it as well as bottle-washing for me. Am I overworking the willing horse?'

'This horse is more than willing.'

Hal could feel the tension among the men around her. But this was not surprising – they were comprised of normally non-combatant troops. Every man who could fire a rifle had been pressed into service to release an infantryman for the ambush. At the range from the walls, such shots would be more to damage the enemy's morale than to kill, but it would all go towards harassing him with a dense hail of firepower.

'What's that noise?' Hal asked suddenly.

They listened for a moment. 'The sheep and goats are being brought in for slaughtering,' Tony said. 'I'll go for something to eat now.'

Hal shivered. Death had raised his head before she was ready for him. She was left with nothing to do but give her plans another mental scrutiny. As well as her coat she had brought a blanket and she was glad of it. The night-time offshore wind was now bringing air that had been chilled in the high hills. She swept the opposite bank with the binoculars and listened for non-existent messages on the radio. When Tony came back, she settled down on to her cushion below the parapet, out of the wind.

Hal could have sworn that she was alert for every moment of the night. She had undergone training at Sandhurst in conditions of severe sleep deprivation, but the years at the Ministry had softened her. The firing began with a suddenness that brought Hal's heart into her mouth. She jumped up from the cushion where she had been squatting, caught in the hinterland between thought and sleep. The moon had completed its traverse of the sky and was touching the hilltops in the west.

The sudden clatter of gunfire and the light of a parachute flare came from far to her right, up towards the dam, where the Irish bridge made the crossing. Hal, still bemused, made a sound of protest.

'Relax,' Tony said. 'They're trying to draw us off in that direction. Everything's going as you predicted. Look.'

Hal rubbed her eyes and stooped to the night-vision binoculars on their tripod, aimed at the ford.

The river was now silver against the last trace of moonlight. Long files of dark bodies had materialized out of the black shadows on the far bank and had begun crossing the ford to the island. The first men were already into the water again and approaching the near bank.

'Give the signal to Sergeant-Major Pennington to move in on the gun,' Hal said.

Tony turned to the radio and pressed a key. The small hiss of the carrier signal stilled. 'Funky finger,' Tony said into the microphone.

'What the hell?'

'Not my idea,' said Tony. 'Tuckridge chose it. I decided that at least it was unlikely to be duplicated.'

They waited again. Pennington and his chosen few would be closing in on the gun and half-track. Silently, she hoped. Lights and gunshots from that direction would be a bad omen. The arrival of shells would be worse. Her stomach cramped at the thought. She wondered whether ulcers were an occupational hazard for generals. From upstream, the drumbeat of gunfire continued, flares were setting the sky aglow and she could hear shouting. Both sides were putting on a show.

Figures, hardly visible in the poor light, topped the escarpment and fanned out across the road and the cleared ground, taking shelter among bushes and undergrowth and occupying the two dominant positions Hal had identified. Small parties detached and circled the two small hills. Hal forced herself to wait still longer.

At last it was time. 'Give the signal,' she told Tony.

'Hoof hearted,' Tony said into the radio, carefully distinguishing the two words.

'Who thought that one up?' Hal asked. 'Tuckridge again?'

'I don't know. Not Tuckridge, one of the juniors. What he actually said was "Who farted?" and somebody else said that it would do for a code-word.'

Hal remembered her father's words. The army did not like a joker. Before she could utter a reproof, all hell broke loose.

There was a huge explosion from away upstream, dwarfing the gunfire as the sappers blew a hole in the dam.

From far across the river came a flare of light followed later by a double detonation. Hal waited, heart in mouth, for the arrival of a shell, but it never came. She could safely assume that the gun and the half-track were destroyed.

An 81mm mortar sounded a hollow note and after a long pause a parachute flare blazed high above the river, followed by another and another. The scene was bright as day. Mortars were firing steadily, dropping their rounds among the men massed on the far bank, turning them back and deterring the men already in the water from retracing their steps.

The two parties on the hillocks were taken out with sub-machine-gun fire and grenades.

The infantry hidden behind the crest and in every rocky crevice overlooking the open ground took most of a minute to come forward into firing positions, but the men on the town walls and others on a spur that jutted out above the river, half a kilometre downstream, were in action immediately, pinning the enemy down. Return fire was haphazard but the night sky seemed filled with tracer and the sound of ricochets was all around. Hal ducked behind the parapet. Rifle fire and light support weapons raked the river, throwing up spray. Some men fell and floated downstream but there was a general surge from the river back towards the far bank. The first parachute flares died and were renewed.

'Where the hell are those crocodiles?' Tony muttered. 'When I send for crocodiles, I expect to get crocodiles.'

He was answered immediately. A man below threw up his arms and vanished in a turmoil of water as a large crocodile went on the attack. The drama was repeated. Panic spread rapidly. Men threw away their arms and crowded on to the island. But their sanctuary was short-lived. Already the water was rising.

The troops on the spur shifted their fire from the river to the men still hesitating on the far bank. From the town wall, rifle and LSW fire was added to the storm of bullets. On the nearer bank, the vanguard of the Liboonese, cut off by crocodiles and rising water, tried to find cover among the low scrub, but the bushes and scrub were being raked through. Leaves whirled in the air. Cover from view, Hal remembered, is not cover from fire if the enemy saw you go there. The gunfire was almost continuous and drowned the cries of the fallen. Unmindful of any danger, Hal was on her feet. She found that she had drawn her pistol but hastily she re-holstered it. She wanted to cheer but remembered in time the dignity of command.

A recorded voice, very much amplified, boomed out over the sound of battle. It invited the Liboonese onshore to throw down their arms and surrender. Hal had supplied the words and a Swahili-speaking sergeant had read them on to tape.

There was a momentary lull. 'I know what I forgot,' Hal said suddenly.

'It can't have been important.'

'It's *bloody* important. What are we going to do with prisoners? We haven't even thought that far ahead. It would have seemed like tempting fate. But now we're going to have *hundreds* to deal with.'

126

After a few seconds, Tony said, 'There's the warehouse down by the dock. I'll send a runner to tell the sentries at the harbour to clear out anything that could be used as a weapon or an escape tool. He can come back and direct traffic down the hill.'

The island was covered now by fast-flowing water. Several kilometres downstream, a floating rope had been strung from tree to tree across the river, diagonally so that any man escaping from the river by hauling himself along it would come ashore at the feet of a British platoon. One platoon was judged to be enough. Any swimmer rash enough to hang on to his weaponry would undoubtedly have drowned. The first men ashore at that point were demoralized but uninjured. Then came those with minor bullet wounds and lumps of flesh amputated by crocodiles. Even the freshwater crocodiles, it seemed, had joined in the unexpected feast.

Dawn had begun, arriving so unexpectedly that the mortars were still sending up parachute flares. Men were coming out of the undergrowth, hands in the air, and gathering in a rapidly growing crowd along the roadway, milling around in search of some positive direction. Some were nursing their own wounds or helping comrades or even carrying the obviously dead. There was still sporadic firing as the infantry, mustered by the warrant officers, began a sweep through the bushes to root out any last resistance. The far bank was already emptied of the living and the mortars were searching for targets further off. The river had stopped rising. It was as empty and bland as if it held no secret killers and no dead.

'That's it, then,' Hal said flatly. It was the inevitable moment of let-down.

'Success.'

'Yes. And the objective? Death. So much death. And all of it at my door.'

'They were invaders,' Tony said. 'They knew what they were asking for.'

'Or were they conscripts? And what about our men?'

'I'll have a figure for our casualties very soon. I think that you'll find they're remarkably few. That's the benefit of a well planned ambush from cover.'

'One casualty would be too many.'

'That's the counsel of perfection. They were soldiers, all of them. They knew what they had signed on for. And so did you.'

'I signed on as an information gatherer,' Hal said. 'If I thought about it at all, I suppose I thought that the information I gathered might help to *avert* war. I didn't sign on to set men to killing each other. Tony, could I have managed with less bloodshed?'

Her voice was shaking. Tony stooped and looked at her in the poor light. He saw that she was weeping silently. 'Not a hope in hell. You've been under a lot of strain,' he said gently. 'The men mustn't see you like this. It might shake their faith in your infallibility, and faith is crucial. It would be like seeing the Pope with his trousers down.'

'The Pope doesn't wear trousers,' Hal said, laughing through her tears.

'Who knows what he wears under the robes. Come on, I'll see you to your quarters.'

Hal hung back, longing to escape but reluctant to go while others cleared up the mess. 'But, Tony, there are dozens of things to see to.'

'And dozens of men to see to them. The army has well-drilled routines for these occasions. You've done your bit. The enemy won't manage to regroup for at least a day, probably several days. Half of them are still running. Pursuit would be worse than useless. It's time to rest and gather our strength.'

'Wait.'

They stood and watched from the rampart. The wind was still coming cold from the mountains and Hal leaned back against his warmth. After the gunfire, the silence seemed absolute. Files of prisoners were mustered and marched away. Stretcher parties gathered the wounded. The men were redeployed into defensive positions. When they began to move the dead, Hal shifted uneasily.

'Let's go now.'

The town seemed empty as they trod the street. In the officers' mess there was a smell of coffee but nobody yet there to drink it. Hal was sagging with fatigue. Tony helped her up the stairs and into the big bedroom. 'Can you manage from here?' he asked.

After the surges of adrenaline she knew that she had little chance of sleeping and, if she slept, dreams would come to haunt her. She turned and leaned against him. 'Don't go, Tony,' she said. 'I couldn't bear to be alone. The dead would talk to me.'

He kept his hands at his sides. 'You know that I've always wanted you?'

'Yes. I think I knew.'

'You know what will happen if I don't go now?'

'I know, Tony. I . . . I'll welcome it. You've always been special to me. I'm surprised, now, looking back, that it didn't happen at Sandhurst.' She shook him gently. 'Tony, you're supposed to be the one saying this, not me. Please don't go.'

If Hal, guilt-ridden, clung at first to Tony in search of consolation, her mood was soon to change. Tony turned out to be a patient and considerate lover. She forgot for the moment her regret over the casualties and became lost in a timeless flood of passion such as she had never before known.

Hal awoke at noon to find herself alone. The horrors of the previous night had begun to fade into a regrettable duty properly executed, to be overlaid by the twin sensations of being both successful and desired. She was hungry again. The days of regular sleep and meals seemed to have receded into the distant past.

Sergeant Ashna – Mamie – had laid out clean clothes – before or after Tony's departure? Hal gave a mental shrug. She would have preferred her interlude with Tony to be discreetly cloaked, but on the other hand she could feel a temptation to shout it from the town walls, because, after all, no woman had ever been so loved. Time would take the decision out of her hands. She showered and dressed, quickly but with care.

Downstairs in the officers' mess she found many of her officers eating meals ranging from snack breakfasts to a full lunch. She was greeted with smiles and the company began to rise until she told them to be seated. Tony was alone at a corner table. She joined him. Well, it was only natural for a CO and her acting ops officer to eat together, wasn't it? They exchanged a covert glance, full of secret meaning. A different private was acting as waiter. Hal asked for as much of a full English breakfast as could be provided in a largely Muslim country.

'Everything's under control,' Tony said. 'Four hundred and thirty prisoners under guard.' He yawned. There were shadows under his eyes.

'What on earth are we going to do with them in the longer term?'

'I haven't the faintest idea. I thought of suggesting that we convert our old barracks into a prison camp but the perimeter would be difficult to guard and it would be very vulnerable to a counter-attack while Simon Agulfo's still on the rampage. They'd better stay where they are for the moment. The Medical Corps woman doctor you glimpsed yesterday, Lieutenant Halstead, is coping with the wounded, aided by three medical orderlies and one or two intelligent volunteers. She's set up a temporary surgery for prisoners in a small store next to the warehouse.' He finished with another yawn, hidden behind his hand.

'I heard a muttering sound from my window, somewhere north of here.'

'Tuckridge has got his bulldozers rebuilding the dam. The river will probably dry up in about a month from now, so it's important to start the reservoir filling again. We can argue later over who pays for the work.'

'Have you had any sleep?' Hal asked, partly for the benefit of their neighbours.

'Not very much,' Tony said. 'I'll go and get my head down when I'm sure you've got all you need.'

'What about our own casualties?' Hal asked anxiously.

'Amazingly light, considering. But, as I said last night, that's the benefit of an ambush from cover. Eight killed, seventeen wounded, one of them seriously. That's not counting scratches from thorn bushes, but including one snake bite that's responding well to antivenin. The names are on your desk. You'll want to visit the wounded later.'

'Of course,' Hal said. She closed her eyes for a moment. 'I'd better get a signal off straight away.'

'I've put a first draft on your desk.'

'Are our own men getting some rest?'

'They're being relieved in rotation.' Tony glanced around but general conversation had resumed and they were in no danger of being overheard. Even so, he lowered his voice. 'About last night . . .'

'There's no need to say anything,' Hal said. 'Not if you don't want to.'

'But I do want to. I want to tell you that it was the most wonderful experience of my life, physically and spiritually,' Tony said, and then spoiled the effect by an enormous yawn. 'I beg your pardon.'

'You're forgiven. Tony, it was the best for me too.'

He blinked at her. 'I don't see how you can know that. You kept falling asleep.'

Hal was shocked. 'Tony, I didn't! Did I?'

Tony's face broke into his broad grin. 'Got you! Now who's being credulous? You were wide awake and—'

They were interrupted, first by the arrival of Hal's breakfast – lamb sausages, a bacon substitute made from smoked goat and two fried eggs from a source which Hal was unable to identify – she could only hope that they were of avian rather than reptilian origin. She decided not to ask. Then a small group of officers, returning to duty, paused to offer congratulations. Hal took it that they were referring to the morning's victory, but there was a faint air of . . . What? Not quite amusement, nor complicity. Some of the congratulations seemed to be subtly aimed at Tony. Surely their secret could not be widespread already? But in the small, closed community of a garrison, few secrets were secret for very long.

As they moved away, another figure appeared. Justin

Carlsborough. For once, the captain was looking neither supercilious nor angry. He looked, in fact, tired but exuberant. He was smiling at her.

Hal disguised as a cough a small headshake, intended to clear away the thought that she might be dreaming. The day was continuing to slip away from reality. 'Join us,' she said. 'I'm relieved to see you. Let's have your report.'

Tony fetched another chair. Carlsborough dropped into it and accepted coffee. He looked tired and rumpled and he was in need of a shave. 'You'll excuse my coming into the mess in this state,' he said. 'I thought that I should report straight away.'

'Go ahead,' Hal said. 'I'll excuse you if you'll excuse me for eating while I listen.'

'I'm told that congratulations are called for. You seem to have scored a famous victory.'

'Thank you. And you?'

'We've played our part,' Carlsborough said. 'We spent the voyage southward in practising setting sails and mounting guns in daylight so that we could manage in the dark. We arrived off the mouth of the Barawat around zero-two-hundred. There was a large ferry boat anchored off the river mouth. They'd been loading it with supplies by canoe but at that time it was lying idle with just two of the crew sleeping aboard and nobody on watch. Presumably, they were going to load troops at the last moment and ferry them as far up the coast as the action was.

'Ashore, work was going ahead under floodlights, making a roadway and a dock. The idea would be to bring the ferry alongside to load some artillery, though I can't think how they were going to get it off again until they'd taken the harbour here, by which time it would have become superfluous.'

'Perhaps they were planning to fire it from the deck of the ferry boat,' Hal suggested.

'That could be. We came in silently from seaward, under sail, and opened up suddenly with rifles and LSWs. I'd brought along two Carl Gustav anti-tank weapons, just in case, and we knocked out the three bulldozers. Then we started our diesel, laid alongside the ferry and turfed the crewmen overboard.'

Hal was waiting, concealing with difficulty her impatience to learn whether or not General Agulfo could expect reinforcements, but at this her old compunction made a return. 'Did they make it to shore?' she asked.

'I expect so. Our first shot with the anti-tank mortars was high and it brought down a whole rock face, undoing most of what they'd done so far. With that and the bulldozers, we decided that we'd given them enough of a set-back.

'I left Private Falconer in charge of the dhow. He did a lot of dinghy sailing in his youth and seemed perfectly competent to handle something bigger.' Carlsborough smiled and his face became suddenly human. 'He had a crew of two NCOs under his command, which should have made for an interesting voyage back here. I took the rest of the crew on to the ferry, including that extraordinary woman mechanic I found working on the dhow's engine when I went aboard. She was a godsend, by the way; she got the boiler lit and did most of the stoking all the way here.'

'You brought the ferry here?'

'Yes. To judge by the charts on board, it had seen service between Dar es Salaam and Zanzibar. Whether the Liboonese chartered it, borrowed it, bought it or commandeered it I wouldn't know, but I didn't like to sink it. Bringing it here seemed the easiest way to deny the enemy the use of it. Do you mind?'

'I'm delighted,' Hal said. Problems seemed to be solving themselves. Perhaps it was going to be that sort of a day. 'How would you like to do another voyage? You can have Private Settle with you again as ship's engineer,' she added as an inducement. 'It should keep her out of trouble. Could you manage to carry just over four hundred prisoners under guard?'

Carlsborough's eyebrows shot up. For once his film star face showed shock. 'I was told that you'd scored a victory, but not the scale of it. Four hundred plus? I should think that we could carry that number at a squeeze,' Carlsborough said. 'Where to?'

133

'I don't know, yet. We'll have to get off another signal,' she told Tony. 'As for you,' she added to Captain Carlsborough, thank you. Well done. Now go and look after your crew, get some rest and then make ready to receive prisoners.'

Carlsborough got to his feet. 'I don't know whether to say "Yes, ma'am" or "Aye, aye". But I'll do as you bid. And . . . congratulations again. I'm delighted to have been proved wrong.' He gave a salute after the nautical manner and departed.

'A changed man!' Hal said. 'Extraordinary what responsibility and a chance to shoot up a few natives will do for the English gentleman.'

'Mr N'koma's grandson was here. The PM wants to see you,' Tony said. 'He should be here fairly shortly. And I thought you might want to get your – what shall we call them? – your tactical committee together again.'

'Not just yet,' Hal said. 'And don't call them a committee. As I said before, group thinking has been at the root of too many calamities. Call them my plan-checkers. Now, I know that we'll have to sally forth and smite the enemy once again – hip and thigh, whatever that means – while he's still wrong-footed and before he can expect us to get ourselves organized. But I'm not having our men chasing what is still a numerically superior number of enemy around in the jungle. Another famous cause of disasters has been underestimating the enemy – think of Singapore. And think about last night. As soon as they've started to regroup, we'll know where to find them. I'm going to Signals, then I'll visit our wounded. If Mr N'koma turns up before I'm back, ask him to wait.'

With Tony's draft signal in her hand, Hal climbed the stair to the Signals unit. She was greeted with smiles and a small round of applause quickly quelled by Susan Thyme.

'Apart from the routine signals,' Susan said, 'there are two urgent ones for you. The first acknowledges your taking command but goes on . . . Do you want to read it for yourself.'

The printout in Susan's hand ran to two pages. 'Give me the gist,' Hal said, 'and then send it over to my office.'

'Right. There's been an approach through the Foreign Office. The Liboonese say that they have Brigadier Wincaster prisoner and the brigadier has offered them a formal surrender. They therefore call on us to cease all hostilities and give up our weapons.' Susan waited. Her face was carefully serious but there was the hint of a smile in her eyes.

'They do, do they?' Hal said grimly. She settled at Susan's desk. Tony's report seemed crisp and factual. She added an opening paragraph to the effect that the Liboonese approach should be ignored. Tony's report, describing the action and its outcome, followed and she added a final paragraph. The 430 prisoners would be taken aboard an enemy vessel captured in action by Captain Carlsborough. Orders were awaited regarding where they were to be conveyed.

'Get this off right away,' she said. Susan passed the message to Sergeant Wilkes. 'What's the other message?' Hal enquired.

'From Int-Corps. Satellite pictures show only one small concentration of enemy troops and some scattered parties. Intercepted radio messages, clear but in Swahili, are ordering all troops to rendezvous at Urbala. That's the only other township of more than a dozen thatched huts, isn't it?'

'Yes. The native mineworkers live there and some of the cattle-herders.'

Mr N'koma was waiting patiently in her office. They exchanged formal greetings in Arabic. Mr N'koma was loud in his praise and exultation, but each was anxious to get down to business in English.

'I have news,' Mr N'Koma said. 'Too important to trust to my rascally grandson. Also you will have questions. So I come myself.'

'I'm happy to see you,' Hal said. 'Do go on.'

'Our enemy is at Urbala. They are sending my people out to sleep where they can be eaten by the lions and hyenas.'

'Are there lions and hyenas?' Hal asked.

'Very few. The herds have moved on and most predators

moved with them. Our local lions take a goat or a calf some-times, nothing more. But the men of Liboon did not know that,' Mr N'Koma pointed out indignantly.

'They are scattered,' Hal said, 'but we knew that their general was calling them to join him at Urbala. We do not know how many we killed this morning – many of them went down the river with the crocodiles – but we think that there remain many more of them than there are of us. Will Urbala hold them all?'

Mr N'Koma shook his bald, wrinkled head. 'It is little more than a village. The invaders have looked into the mine tunnels. I believe their chief thinks that many of his men could sleep there in safety. But I have more news. He keeps with him the Bwana Wincaster and the other men he stole from you.'

'Does he indeed?' Hal had assumed that the prisoners would have been transported directly by sea to Liboon. She spared a moment to hope that the brigadier had been given a lift in the half-track – and taken out of it before the assault by her commando unit. The old chap was hardly fit for a forced march in the tropics, but it would be regrettable if his own troops had blown him to shreds. 'Men will be watching us from across the river,' she said.

'This is true.'

'Do you have men who know the ground well?' she asked. 'Men who are not afraid? Men who could lead us by night? Men who can move in silence and strike out of darkness?'

'We have hunters who are just such men.'

'Describe to me the lie of the land,' Hal said.

# Sixteen

Back in London, confusion reigned in the MoD. Hostilities in the Middle East were slipping out of gear. An infantry division had been bluffed into advancing unsupported, had been cut off and was now conducting a stalemate defence among the mountains. A French unit had been shot up by a supposedly friendly fighter plane and the French were threatening to withdraw three full divisions in protest. And an American rocket, fired at a telephone exchange to demonstrate the accuracy of the system, had veered off course and hit a mosque. Things were not going well. The usually quiet corridors buzzed with talk and clattered with footsteps.

An assistant permanent secretary was gathering his papers. He had put out a hand to kill the computer on his desk when there came a rap on the door and a neat figure in black jacket and striped trousers entered, brandishing some flimsy papers.

'Good morning, Brigadier,' said the civil servant. 'But I can't talk now. There's a meeting of the Joint Planning Staff in about five minutes and I have to be there.'

Brigadier Welsh paid no attention but settled in the more comfortable of the visitors' chairs. 'What are we going to do about this Maveria business?' he demanded. 'That comes within your bailiwick, doesn't it?'

'Yes, but—'

'We get a signal,' said the brigadier, 'that the senior officers have been taken prisoner and this chap Brown's taken over. Then the Liboonese, through the Foreign Office, say they've got them – well, we knew that – and that Wincaster's offered to surrender. Not surprising really, if he was already a prisoner. And then, by golly, we get another signal saying to ignore the Liboonese and we've knocked them for six and taken a lot of prisoners and where do we want them delivered? And we know that the last version's the truth because of the satellite snaps and the radio traffic we've been intercepting.'

'I have to be going—'

'That last question's easy. They can go to Socoros Island, off the mouth of the Red Sea. We've already set up a prison camp there,' the brigadier explained, 'and nobody much to put in it. But as to the other business – I take it we don't go along with surrendering?'

'God, no!' said the civil servant. 'Dreadful PR! Do you have anyone you could send to take over?'

'We need everyone with two brain cells to get things back on the road in the Middle East. The Arab Alliance seems to be creating a deliberately confused situation, for some reason of its own, with separate little conflicts all over the shop. We'd better leave this Major Brown in place. Who is he? Harry Brown from Chiltern Abbey, the one who was at Harrow with my boy? I heard that he'd asked for a posting but I didn't know that he'd gone to the North Wessex. I had him under me for a year. I always said he'd go far.'

The civil servant had stopped trying to dodge round the brigadier. He would just have to be late and excuse himself by saying that he had been delayed while solving the entire Maverian question. 'We can soon find out,' he said. 'You should have his army number there on the signal.' He sat down at his desk and typed at the computer. 'That's funny,' he said. 'Somebody must be playing silly buggers.' He picked up the phone and pressed some buttons. 'I can't get the personnel program on the magic machine,' he said plaintively into the telephone. There was a pause while the receiver muttered at him. 'What? Well how long's it going to take?'

This time, he listened for a full minute before disconnecting. His face went from interested, through mildly concerned, via disbelieving and indignant, to horrified. Thoughtfully, he switched off the computer. 'We seem to have a real problem,' he said. 'Somebody's believed to have got in – *hacked in* is the expression, I believe – to the computers and planted a virus over the phone. That's to say, every military, naval and air force computer of every one of our allies and several others. The whole damn lot. It's a really bad one. It seems to start where the "I love you" virus left off. All you can get out of any of them is a few words of Arabic and a rude picture.'

'I thought they were supposed to be protected by anti-virus software,' said the brigadier. 'Bomb-proof was the expression they used.'

'I thought so too. But it seems that the less secret the program and the more often it's used, the less the level of protection. The personnel files are accessed all the damn time. And all the programs are linked together. The virus has been in the system for weeks and every time a back-up disk's been accessed it's been infected, but apparently each copy of the virus contained an instruction not to activate itself until today.'

It was the last day of the month.

The brigadier's prime reaction continued to be curiosity. 'How would they get the phone numbers in the first instance? The security chaps made a great fuss about keeping them secret.'

'The phone numbers wouldn't be difficult,' said the civil servant glumly. 'They'd only need one to get started. Probably got it from Directory Enquiries.'

'Surely not!'

'I was joking,' the civil servant explained patiently. 'More likely, they went in through one of the Ministry's websites. Once inside, I'm told that there are programs for testing every combination and finding a password within an hour or two.'

'When do they expect to get back online?' the brigadier asked.

'They don't know when they'll get back online.' He nearly added 'if at all'. 'They'll have to get the virus out of every program simultaneously or they'll only infect each other again. And they say that the virus is probably hiding a whole sequence of other viruses to take over as soon as the first one's eradicated. And then they'll probably find that some of the information's gone for ever. They may have to load all the data again from the original papers, which are scattered through basements from here to Inverness.' He put his head in his hands.

The brigadier had made it to his present rank because of his ability to communicate, and because a singleness of purpose can be a positive asset when in pursuit of a tactical objective. 'So what do we do about Maveria?'

The civil servant looked up. His mind was rushing ahead, but he forced it to think small. 'Your chap Brown seems to be doing all right. We were expecting the Liboonese to walk right in; a victory there would be a bonus. Leave him in charge.'

The brigadier was unhappy. There was a right way and a wrong way of doing things. 'Can't leave a major in charge of a brigade, even if it is very much under strength. Sets a bad precedent.'

The civil servant was getting desperate. By now, he could think of four – no, five – other places where he simply had to be, ten minutes ago. And promotions were cheap. If the Liboonese performed as expected, this chap Brown might never come back at all. 'Bump him up to colonel, then,' he said impatiently.

'Lieutenant-colonel?'

'Yes. There are native troops there, aren't there? We'll make him a local colonel – natives don't recognize anything less. Promotions come cheap in wartime and, God knows, whichever Brown he is, he seems to merit it. If you agree, the military secretary is in the building. I could fix it with him later.'

'Well done, James,' said the brigadier. 'I knew I could count on you. I'll send them a signal about Socoros Island, then, and leave the rest to you.'

'You do that,' said the civil servant. 'And I'll tell the FO to ignore the Liboonese. Would you give that signal about the success in Maveria to my secretary? No, better take it to the press office yourself. They'll have questions.'

'A press release?'

'Yes, of course. Some good news now may draw attention away from the other cock-ups.' He left the room at a pace that set his secretary blinking. She had never seen him move so quickly.

# Seventeen

Hal – now Local Colonel H. Brown, although she did not know it yet – presided over another meeting of what she called her plan-checkers that evening. Looking around, she realized that most of them had become individuals to her instead of just faces. She even remembered many of their names. It was a measure of her new-found influence that the men digested her every word in silence.

'First,' she said, 'I want my thanks conveyed to every member of this force – and to any civilians who gave us their help,' she added, looking Joe Tuckridge in the eye. 'This morning's action was a success because everybody played his part and followed the plan to the letter. I hope that we can repeat that success.

'We don't know how many of the Liboonese army were killed. The crocodiles may have been on our side, but they aren't giving us figures. We took more than four hundred prisoners, and those are already on their way to a POW camp on Socoros Island. The main force was largely scattered and is only now beginning to regroup. It still outnumbers us, however. If we hang about, they will not only recover, but reinforcements will find a way to get to them. Their first attempt to make a new crossing at the mouth of the Barawat River was frustrated yesterday. We must strike again quickly while the main force is still off-balance. They must never get a firm foothold in Maveria.'

There was a stir of agreement. The young officers looked nervous but determined. The more experienced warrant officers nodded.

'They're regrouping now at Urbala. They seem to have

141

driven out the locals. That hasn't endeared them to the local population. Perhaps as a result, a great deal of information is filtering back to us and we seem to have the co-operation of some skilled hunters.

'For the benefit of any other comparative newcomers, perhaps Mr Tuckridge would describe the layout at Urbala.'

Joe Tuckridge got to his feet. 'Surely, ma'am,' he said. He moved to stand in front of a plan which obviously emanated from the mining company. Tony had warned him that he would be called on.

'Starting from the Irish bridge,' he said, 'the road runs direct to the mines, mostly following the west bank of the Urma River. The road runs through swampy country, so, as part of our agreement, the spoil from the mines has been used to fill in some of the swamps. What we haven't got around to yet we've partly drained into the river and sprayed with insecticide. The risk of malaria or dengue fever has been brought down to a minimum. Beyond the bogs, you come to open savannah and, about where the grassland begins to take over – right where it meets the bottom of the foothills – there's an ore-bearing stratum and we've driven four more or less horizontal mine tunnels into the bottom of a rock slope. The tunnels are quite separate and don't interconnect.' As he spoke, his hands were darting over the plan, conveying his meaning as clearly as his words.

'The town of Urbala is less than a kilometre from the mouths of the tunnels. When we started mining there was nothing in Maveria, outside of Pembaka, but small villages. The township was begun in order to house the native workers at the mines. But a whole lot of cattle-herders wanted to be near the company shop and the doctor, so they moved in and built their own houses – they're only thatched beehive huts – and the whole place grew. Population now: about three hundred. It's surrounded by the traditional high circular thorn fence, to keep wild animals out and cattle inside.

'There are no company buildings there now. We were working from trailers and we brought them all back to a trailer park close to Pembaka when this crisis threatened. There's still a lot of machinery, too heavy to shift, outside the tunnels. I guess that's about all I can tell you.'

'Thank you,' Hal said. 'There will be some more questions, but we can save them until later.' Joe Tuckridge nodded and returned to his chair. 'In a moment, I'll tell you my plan and invite comments. Most of our men being inexperienced – though not quite as inexperienced as they were yesterday – we have to keep it simple. But first, I have some questions of my own. Captain Masterson, can we put our hands on any large glass vessels?'

'There are some carboys in the REME workshop,' the quartermaster said. 'If we need more than that, some of the men had a wine-making syndicate going. I think the winchester quarts were left in the old barracks.'

'How many Very pistols do we have?'

'Six.'

'And flares for them?'

'Any particular colour, ma'am?'

'No.'

'Ample, ma'am. More than a thousand.'

'Good. Next,' said Hal, 'does anybody know how to make napalm?'

There was a sound of indrawn breaths. Joe Tuckridge broke the silence that followed. 'Napalm's just diesel oil with an accelerant added. Leave it with me, ma'am. I'll work up something.'

Hal nodded. 'Three men were sent by General Agulfo to keep watch on Pembaka and the garrison from across the river. They have been dealt with by some of the hunters who were kicked out of Urbala,' she said sombrely. 'Their orders had been to report back if and when we moved, not before.' She hid a shiver. She very much wanted not to know how the hunters had come by that last piece of information. 'We'll be warned if any other spies are sent here. So, for the moment, we can take it that we can get away from here unobserved. That's important. Surprise is essential. We can't take on a superior and orderly force on open ground. If we find that our arrival has been anticipated before we've reached the point

143

of no return, we break off at once. The signal will be a red Very flare. Red flares are not to be used otherwise.

'On the subject of surprise, I don't think that General Agulfo appreciates how clearly the thermal images by satellite define the edges of the swamps and boggy ground, nor how accurately we could find our way, using the global positioning satellite units. Mr Tuckridge's activities have reduced the boggy areas considerably.' Hal moved to the thermal image mosaic. 'The contrast between wet and dry is obvious. I propose that our main force follows this route.' Her finger traced a complex path between the areas of bog. 'Mr N'koma promises me the services of a pair of hunters who know the ground well, to lead the way. They will already have pinpointed the Liboonese outposts. To General Agulfo, this area will seem to be one huge, impassable, fever-ridden swamp. He certainly won't expect us to come this way. The main force should plan to be in place by oh-five-hundred, the day after tomorrow. That would mean leaving here in daylight tomorrow afternoon, which I don't much like.'

A ginger-haired, bushy-browed man who she knew to be Captain Soames spoke up. 'We don't have enough trucks to carry the men, except in relays. We never needed them except for carrying stores between the town and the barracks.'

'I don't like the idea of relays,' Hal said. 'It would take too long. The noise could carry to Urbala.'

'Around dusk, the wind comes down from the hills,' said another man. 'It would be blowing from them to us. Cut the distance to be covered down a bit and the trucks could get in several runs while the howler monkeys are doing their thing.'

Hal looked around the faces while she thought. Tony was shaking his head. 'I don't like that any better,' she said. 'For all the distance the men could be carried before they'd have to get down and take to their feet. Sorry, chaps, it's not worth it. This is a pedestrian exercise.

'I want a second party to go round through the hills and come in from the rear. They will have to leave early. They also will be met by a group of hunters.

'The third party has the tricky job. Mr N'koma's grandson

brought me a message an hour ago. General Agulfo has been keeping Brigadier Wincaster and his staff with him, presumably to use as hostages. The prisoners have been put in the first mine tunnel as we approach from this direction. They're under guard, of course. There really is only one feasible approach to the first mine tunnel, so it will certainly be guarded. Sergeant-Major Pennington, would your commando group fancy another mission?'

'That's for sure, ma'am,' Pennington said. 'We was just getting started last time when it was all over. Only thing is, the lads wouldn't fancy walking into an ambush. Could we have a diversion of some kind? Draw the sentries out of cover, like?'

'A small party of the displaced people,' Captain Soames suggested, 'mooching along looking for some shelter to spend the night in.'

Hal thought it over. 'No, I don't like it,' she said at last. 'We'd be putting their lives on the line. At night, the guards would be likely to loose off first and ask questions afterwards.'

'I think that's true, ma'am,' Pennington said. 'In their shoes, I'd be real suspicious of a group coming along. And any shots would alert the whole camp.'

There was a protracted silence. They were all looking at Hal, waiting for her to produce the rabbit out of the hat. But the only available rabbit was not one that she favoured. She waited, hoping that somebody would be inspired. But the silence stretched out. There seemed to be no end to it.

'What about a lone girl?' Hal said at last. 'A black woman, walking alone and searching for her elderly parents, who were turned out of their home in Urbala?'

'She might get away with it,' said Soames. 'But she'd be facing another danger. She might get manhandled, badly.'

'The commando group would have to be close behind. All the same, I don't think I'd ask it of one of the local girls. And the few coloured girls in the unit only speak English. What about a black woman,' Hal said slowly, 'who speaks both languages and has had training in unarmed combat? It seems to me that I'm the only person who can do it.' She paused. The silence returned. She could feel the weight of it. 'Captain Laverick is my second in command,' she said. 'If I. . .become unavailable, he takes over.'

By three in the morning, some thirty hours later, Hal was acutely unhappy. They had been marching, with occasional rests, since dusk the previous day. The road, to which they were moving parallel, had emerged from the forest, skirted many miles of marsh – some of it partly reclaimed, some not – and was now entering the savannah. Hal was dressed in the traditional long skirt of the country women and over her naked torso she wore the shawl sometimes worn against the cool of the night. One advantage of the long skirt was that she could wear under it a pair of knee-high boots as a protection against snakes. Against that was the fact that she had had to borrow the boots from Susan and, as well as never having been designed for walking further than from a car to a nearby door, they had proved to be half a size too small. This had prevented Hal from wearing inside them anything but nylon sockettes which had ended up around her toes after the first half-hour. Her feet were killing her, but when she decided to remove the boots, brave the snakes and march barefoot through the grass, she was cautioned immediately by Sergeant-Major Pennington and others. Snakes might be a risk but chiggers would be a certainty. She might have risked the chiggers, but the sound of something slithering through the grass decided her. The boots might be just as painful as a puff adder, but they would not kill her.

She plodded on miserably, keeping to the soft ground. There was always the danger of being heard by scattered Liboonese troops heading to the rendezvous at Urbala. Even her elevation to full colonel, news of which had broken just before their departure, was no more than a slight comfort.

Later, Pennington halted his small unit. The men's faces were darkened so that even in the bright moonlight they seemed to melt into the shadows. 'You'd better go on alone, Colonel,' Pennington said. 'We won't be far behind.'

'Good,' Hal said. 'Please don't.' She handed him her wrist-watch.

'One other thing, ma'am, if you don't mind me making a suggestion.' Pennington coughed modestly. 'I'd ditch the shawl, if I was you. A woman coming along all wrapped up decent might make them think. She could be hiding a weapon. She could even be a man in disguise. But if she came along topless, I guess they'd have other things on their minds, besides turning their minds away from Europeans, if you see what I mean.'

Hal wanted to protest but she could see the sense in the argument. 'Keep it safe for me,' she said. 'I'll want it back the very moment I've done my bit.' She turned away and handed the shawl over her shoulder.

They had left the river behind. She limped on, step by painful step, following a rough path beside the road, keeping to the grass so that the sound of her soles would not betray her boots. A large animal crashed away through the bushes. The moon, as it dipped towards the horizon, seemed to be growing in size. The katabatic wind coming down off the heights played between her bare breasts, but as long as she was on the move she hardly felt the cold. There were too many other things on her mind. Would some chance encounter trigger a shot which would cause the whole operation to be aborted? Would the platoon coming over the hills arrive at the right place and meet the hunters? The company of Maverian soldiers had wanted a special task so that, when the invaders were repelled, they could hold their heads high. But would they really go through with it? Could she play her own part?

The foothills were very close now. Without her watch, she had little idea of the time, but they must soon be at the point of no return. At the first alarm, they would have to attack instead of retreating. If that should prove to be too soon, it might signal the death of the prisoners, but it was too late to think of that.

What on earth was she doing here, at the sharp end? As she asked herself the question she saw an answer that she had been hiding from herself. She was sending young men into danger. Some of them had died, some had been wounded, and there would be more casualties to come. Something inside told her that if she faced a share of the danger, even taking a risk of being shot by her own men in the event of a major fracas, she would feel less guilty.

Her danger arrived before she was ready for it. There was a small hillock between the path and the road. A movement drew her eye. A faint wisp of smoke drifted across the moon. At the same moment, a man rose out of some bushes, almost at her feet. He was lightly built. He wore a uniform that could have been British except that coloured epaulettes and a variety of cloth badges had been added. His head was uncovered and closely shaved.

The man looked at her intently for a few seconds. Instinctively, she raised her arms to hide her breasts.

'Who are you and where are you going?' he demanded in Swahili, keeping his voice low. His rifle, an American M-16 she noticed inconsequentially, was pointed at her midriff.

A country girl in Maveria would probably not be fluent in Swahili. She answered in Arabic. 'I'm looking for my grandmother.' He gestured to her to speak softly. 'Have you seen an old lady with a young boy?' she asked quietly.

If he understood her he was uninterested. He threw a cautious glance at the hillock, touched his lips in the universal gesture demanding silence and then looked down at the ground, which was slippery with mud. Water from a spring seeped across the path, towards the river.

Evidently he did not fancy the muddy ground for what he had in mind. He licked his lips and looked round again. Making up his mind, he leaned his rifle against a bush, took her by an arm, turned her away from him and signalled with a pressure on her neck that she was to bend forward.

There were certain sacrifices which Hal was prepared to make in the interests of the mission, but being raped was not among them. She could see no sign of her back-up among the deepening shadows. She made her decision and acted on it in the same instant. Instead of bending forward and offering her secret parts for his enjoyment, Hal leaned backward, reaching back over her shoulder to grab for his neck. She intended a shoulder-throw. Once he was on the ground, if she could nerve herself, the knife in her boot could do the rest. Or she could hold him at knifepoint or grab for his rifle.

She began the move just as she had been taught. Her grab found his thin neck. She locked on to it and put her weight forward into the throw. The man was lighter than she had expected and came easily off the ground and across her back, but the effort was enough to start her feet sliding through the mud. Instinctively, her grip tightened on the only available object. This was the man's neck, now coming under her armpit as she completed the throw. Her feet were still sliding forward. To avoid the horror of falling on her back in the mud with an enemy soldier on top of her, Hal jerked back.

She heard the neck break and felt the vertebrae part against her forearm. She jumped aside and the body fell at her feet. The man twitched, groaned and was still. Apart from a soft thud as he hit the mud, they had made little sound. Hal stood still and tried to calm the thumping of her heart. Now she felt the cold rasping at her bare skin.

Sergeant-Major Pennington materialized out of the shadow of the nearby trees, followed by the first few of his men. Wordlessly, Hal pointed to the mound. Pennington nodded. 'Asleep, with luck,' he muttered. 'Dozy buggers. You stay here, ma'am. We'll do it quiet if we can, but if you hear any noise go down flat and stay there. You two, stay here as R-Group.'

'No,' Hal whispered. 'You'll need every man. I don't need a bodyguard.'

'If you're sure, ma'am.'

As the last of his men appeared out of the darkness, Hal saw that each had a grenade in one hand. 'All right,' she whispered. 'But give me my shawl.'

Hal found herself alone with the body. She backed away, wrapping the shawl around her upper body and almost tripping over an American-style helmet. There was a boulder beside the bushes and she sat down, facing away from the corpse, and then turned again to face it. She wanted it in view or the least sound from its direction would have pushed her over the edge. She prepared to roll down into the shelter of the boulder at the first sound of trouble. She was shaking and she felt the tears come. Her signaller had been separated from the rest, somewhere along the way, and was presumably wandering around, lost. She was glad to be alone for the moment. Not to disgrace herself before the men, she wiped her eyes with the hem of her skirt. The other units should be in place by now. Any shot or grenade-burst would trigger a start to the fighting.

She heard nothing, but in little over a minute the men reappeared. The grenades had been put away but two of the men were wiping knives on cloth. She raised her eyebrows. In answer, Pennington nodded and drew a finger across his throat. 'Sleeping, all eight of them, leaving one man on guard to wake them if we came along. Well done, ma'am,' he whispered. He had to lift her to her feet. He added, when he saw her limping, 'Not far now. Don't suppose there'll be any more, but let's not take chances.'

Hal nodded. She handed him the shawl and set off again, dragging one foot after the other but still taking care to move in silence. The pain in her feet had become part of the natural order of things and was therefore tolerable. Somehow she covered another half-mile. Then Pennington caught her up again. He led her to the foot of the slope and found her another flat stone for a seat. He lifted his hands and she saw a tiny light glow on his wrist. 'Twenty minutes yet, ma'am,' he said. 'You stay here. You done your bit.'

'I'll have my watch back now,' Hal whispered.

Beyond the little town, the main body would be filing out of the swamp and deploying left and right, ready for the encircling movement.

Through the hills, a small detachment under Tony Laverick was approaching. Some of the men carried two winchester quarts apiece. Others were in pairs, carrying a carboy between them. Each carboy was in a net slung on a pole but, even so, the carrying was not easy. The men had swapped burdens a dozen times along the way.

Four tall, thin figures were waiting for them, hunters in loincloths with long spears. Each had at least one rifle slung over his shoulder. They were accompanied by Mr N'koma's grandson.

'No guards,' the boy said casually. 'There were, but no more.' Tony could see the dark stains on the blades of the spears. The rifles would make a welcome reward for the hunters. There would be plenty of ammunition to be collected where it lay. 'Come,' said the boy.

They followed the figures and came to the brink of the hill. There was the body of a man in uniform. The boy pointed down. 'There, your top man and his chiefs.'

They moved along the hillside. Below them, the town was a distant shadow on the grassland beyond isolated islands of big machinery. The town was in silence but not asleep. Scattered lights and movements betrayed the restlessness of a military force remaining half alert.

They came to another corpse. The boy pointed down. 'Tunnel where bad soldiers rest.' Tony realized that the hunters had used the bodies of the sentries as markers. Eight of the party, with two carboys and four winchester quarts, remained there; the rest moved on. At the next corpse, another eight men fell out. Tony went on with the remaining eight and found the last body. He looked at his watch. Crunch time had passed. He removed the red flare from the Very pistol, stowed it carefully where it could not get mixed with the others and reloaded with a white flare. He waited, fondling the Very pistol.

# Eighteen

When all the carefully synchronized watches arrived at the H-hour it might have seemed, for a few seconds, that little was happening.

The glass containers rolled, accelerating, down the grass and leaped into space, to smash on the rocks below. The main body of men deployed rapidly, partially encircling the town. The Maverian company ran to cover the town from the other side. Pennington and his small commando party raced in on the first mine tunnel. After those few, quiet seconds, the world seemed to explode.

Very flares from above ignited Joe Tuckridge's napalm at the mouths of three mine tunnels. Flame roared up into the sky. The tunnels filled with smoke and fumes. The only men to brave the flames emerged on fire and screaming. That was enough. The others were bottled in, choking and disorientated.

The first gunshots came as the flanks of the main body found Liboonese outposts. The shots were echoed as the Pennington commandos took out the guards in the tunnel where the British officers were being held. The restless town stirred quickly and there was some exchange of fire. The sound grew gradually into uproar.

The Maverian company had doubled round the back of the town, where the thatched roofs were nearest to the thorn fence. Flame was passed from torch to torch and the torches were thrown on to the nearer roofs. For good measure, grenades followed. The wind, coming down from the mountains, blew sparks from hut to hut. Very flares hastened the spread to huts deeper in the small township. Soon most of the huts were ablaze. Flame roared up towards the sky and from the town

152

came a sustained popping as abandoned ammunition exploded.

Men were still tumbling out of the burning huts, those who had paused to grab their weapons firing them off at unseen targets and endangering their comrades more than their enemies. The Liboonese, peasants themselves and also not averse to fresh milk and meat, had allowed the local cattle to be penned inside the thorn fence as usual. The lean, native cattle within the enclosure were already panicked by the flames and now menaced by gunfire. They stampeded round and round, bowling men over and trampling them underfoot. A gaunt cow hooked a truss of burning thatch on one horn and helped to spread the flames.

Fleeing men made for the gateway in the fence, but that had been closed for the night by several large thorn bushes. The guards on the gate had already fallen under the steady fire or made a run for it. Eventually, frantic cattle broke through the thorn fence in several places and men and beasts fled together. A herd of goats followed and wandered across the grassland between the town and its attackers, obstructing the field of fire.

In the growing light of dawn, Tony found Hal at last. She was still seated on her rock. Her head was down on her knees and her hands were over her ears. She jumped convulsively when he touched her arm.

'Pennington was supposed to leave you a guard,' he said angrily.

'I told him not to. He needed every man. And my signaller seems to have got lost somewhere.'

'You shouldn't have sent your R-Group away. We can't afford to lose any more COs. I'll deal with your signaller later.'

'I suppose. Tony, how—'

'It's all right,' he said. 'Not so many casualties this time. Marksmanship goes off by moonlight and the men were all mixed up with cattle and goats. Most of the Liboonese from the town have taken to the hills.'

'It's over, then?'

'Not quite. The tail end of the plan is still working out. The Swahili-speakers are going from tunnel to tunnel as the flames die down and the smoke clears. Their job is to leave the occupants in no doubt that if they don't come out, one by one and unarmed, they'll be having live grenades for breakfast. We're going to have rather a lot of prisoners.'

'More than four hundred?'

'My guess would be yes, definitely a lot more.'

Hal straightened her back, clutching the front of her shawl together. 'More problems! Carlsborough can't be back for days yet and that ferry could barely carry the last batch of prisoners. And anyway, I want Carlsborough to go down to the mouth of the Barawat again and shoot up whatever they're doing to prepare for a crossing.'

Tony could tell from her voice that Hal was near the end of her resources. For lack of any other helpful idea, he looked around to be sure that the familiarity was not observed and then patted her shoulder. 'Don't worry about it. It's all in hand. We're going to put them in the old barracks with a guard around the perimeter. The Liboonese won't be coming back in a hurry this time.'

'That's all right then. Tony, see if you can get these bloody boots off me.'

Tony knelt down and with some difficulty managed to remove the offending boots. When he studied her feet, she heard him suck in his breath. 'Bloody boots is right,' he said. 'Your blood's swilling around inside them. I've never seen such a crop of burst blisters.' He straightened up. 'I'll get a couple of field dressings on to them.'

'Leave them,' Hal said. 'I'd rather let the air get to them than have dressings stuck to them. Just don't ask me to march any further. My feet are on fire. If I'm needed somewhere else, you'll have to give me a piggyback. Meanwhile, lend me your shirt.' Hal could never have guessed at the consequence of those words. Later, she realized that there must have been a Liboonese fugitive hiding within earshot, among the boulders.

Tony removed his shirt and looked away, standing in front

of her in case there were eyes in the dawn's early light. 'Just hold on for the moment,' he said. 'There's nothing for you to do and the transport will be here in another twenty minutes or so, bringing the acting MO and the medical orderlies and to act as ambulances for the wounded. You are definitely one of the wounded.'

'I couldn't walk back again, that's for sure. Tony, when the transport goes back I want the Swahili-speakers on it. I want them back in Pembaka as soon as possible.'

'All right. But why?'

'Because,' Hal said, 'we seem to have scattered what's left of Simon Agulfo's force.'

'And they must be getting desperately short of ammunition,' Tony said helpfully. 'Whereas we have enough and some to spare. We took several tons of it off the ferry boat, all in our calibre. But we've lost the Maverian company for the moment. They took off in pursuit of the Liboonese. We won't get them back until they've blown off steam and exacted a little retribution.'

'That's not what I'm talking about. We can gloat later. Soon, Simon Agulfo – if he's still alive and at liberty – or his next in command will be on the radio, trying to get what's left of his force to re-form at some chosen rendezvous. First, I want the map reference of that position. Maybe we can send a detachment there before they move off again. Secondly, I want our Swahili-speakers broadcasting the same message over and over again but giving our choices of meeting place.'

'You are a devious woman. Relax,' Tony said. 'I'll fix it.'

'Pick several different places among the swamps,' Hal said. She yawned enormously while holding her feet up to the cooling breeze. 'You can get the map references off the thermal image on the wall of my office. Switch to a different map reference every couple of hours. That may help to keep them split up and with luck we may be able to gather them up in penny numbers from those places. With even more luck, some of them may wander into the bogs and sink.' Her voice began to fade.

'You're exhausted,' Tony said, 'and there's nothing for

either of us to do but wait while the plan works itself out. Could you sleep if you leaned back against my legs?'

'I could try. I think I'm too het up.' She leaned back against Tony's legs and closed her eyes. The noises of warfare had died down to an occasional shot in the distance. The flames had also died down and the smoke was blowing away towards the sea.

'Relax,' Tony said softly. 'There's nothing for you to worry about. Everything is going to plan. It's all in hand. Relax. Think about something peaceful. There's nothing for you to do.'

Hal's restless mental review of the situation in search of overlooked hazards began to fade and she succumbed to Tony's hypnotic words and tone. She could feel her muscles unknotting. She was almost asleep when Sergeant-Major Pennington made an appearance. 'Can you come please, ma'am? There's something you'll have to deal with.'

Hal's eyes snapped open. The ex-commando, usually totally in command of himself, was looking confused. 'What is it?' Hal asked.

'Can't we deal with it between us?' Tony asked. 'The colonel's exhausted.'

Pennington was distracted. He stooped to look at Hal's feet. 'Oh my God, ma'am! You should have said. We wouldn't've let you march, not with those feet.'

'Then you'd have walked into an ambush and our whole plan would have been shot,' Hal pointed out. 'What is it you can't cope with?'

'It's the brigadier, ma'am. We've recovered him and the other officers, just like you said. And now the brigadier thinks he's going to take over again.'

Hal's mind zigzagged. In a way, she would be sorry if her brief period of power was over. But after only a few days she was tired – tired of the strain of thinking for everybody, doing all the worrying, taking all the decisions and the responsibility for death and maiming. Small wonder if a senior officer's mind should fail at last. Somebody else would be welcome to take over. But then it came back to her. She had been ordered to evaluate the brigadier's continued fitness for command and she had sent the code-word that should have caused him to be replaced and sent on leave. Perhaps that order had been issued. Or perhaps it hadn't.

'Perhaps that would be best after all,' Hal said.

Tony made a sound of protest. Pennington coughed. 'That's not for me to say, ma'am. I just hope that all ranks are disciplined enough to . . . to . . .'

'How does the brigadier seem?' Hal asked carefully.

There was a silence. Clearly, the sergeant-major was torn between loyalties. 'Frankly, ma'am,' he said at last, 'I think he's lost his marbles.'

No matter how uncertain his present condition and status might be, Hal felt that she owed it to the brigadier's rank to go to him rather than have him fetched to her. On the other hand, she was incapable of walking and had no intention of exposing her bare feet to chiggers or puff adders. When her tired mind tried to recall the relevant quotation, she was uncertain which of them was the mountain and which was Mohammed, but she was sure that it was apt. Pennington, back in the guise of infallibility proper for a warrant officer, solved the problem by linking his hands with Tony's to form a chair. So Hal was carried in relative comfort to the mouth of the first mine tunnel. Time had passed and the fires were dead. The heavy pall of smoke had blown away, although the stench of burning hung over where the little town had been. The sun was up. Tidy formations of men were sweeping the ground for wounded. Groups of prisoners, many of them coughing and choking, were being assembled. There were a few shots in the far distance.

At the tunnel mouth, two figures in Liboonese uniform lay still. Another, bleeding from a head wound, was having a field dressing roughly applied by a British corporal. More than thirty liberated British officers were ranged beside the rock wall nearby. Most were seated or leaning against the rocks, but the brigadier had disdained such weakness and stood, isolated, like an angry guard dog ready to bite. It was clear

that the prisoners had not been treated with any consideration. Exhaustion was apparent and their uniforms were in
tatters with all insignia of rank ripped away. Sundry scratches
and cuts had gone untreated and there were visible signs of
infection.

Hal had tried to comb her hair out with her fingers. She
knew that she was in no state to be inspected by a pernickety
and irritable brigadier, no matter if his state was almost as
bad as her own. In Tony's shirt and a long skirt of native
cloth, with her feet bare and bleeding, carried along between
an officer and a warrant officer, she was an extraordinary
spectacle and she was uncomfortably aware of the fact.

She did not look forward to being set down on her feet,
but her two bearers knew it. 'Sit where you are,' Tony said.
'We can hold you.' Pennington grunted agreement. The two
men stood as near to attention as they could manage.

'Good morning, Brigadier,' Hal said.

The brigadier focused on her a look of such loathing that
Hal thought she could feel her hair frizzle. 'You, is it?' he
snapped. 'I'm told that you – a black woman! – took command
of my garrison in my absence.'

'As the senior officer remaining,' Hal said stiffly, 'I was
required to do so.'

'Is that so? We'll have an inquiry into that. What kind of
a sight do you think you are? An officer, improperly dressed,
being carried around by two men and one of them half naked.
What have you been getting up to? Get down, woman, and
stand up straight.'

Her two bearers made no move to put her down. 'With
respect, Brigadier,' Tony said bravely, 'I would like to point
out that Colonel Brown's feet were injured in spearheading
the party that carried out your rescue. She was disguised in
native dress for the purpose.'

The information seemed to make the brigadier angrier than
ever. He was literally dribbling down his chin. 'Is that so? Is
that really so? I'll come to you later, young man.' He switched
his glare back to Hal. 'Colonel now, is it? We'll see about
that. I'm resuming command of this unit, as from now. And

I want all British personnel back within the walls of Pembaka immediately. Do you hear me? We are in no state to chase an enemy around in the jungle, an enemy who's better acquainted with that style of warfare than we are and, moreover, who outnumbers us.'

Hal felt Tony brace himself for another act of courage. 'I don't think that those statements are quite correct, sir,' he said, overcoming his respect for rank and his ingrained fear of the brigadier.

'And who the hell are you to tell me what's right and what's wrong?'

Tony swallowed. 'Sir, you appointed me your intelligence officer and I am trying to give you some vital intelligence.'

Tony's rational statement made the brigadier pause. 'Go on then.'

'I doubt if they do outnumber us any longer,' Tony said. 'We sent a shipload of prisoners off two days ago. We have taken many more this morning. How many have been killed, we don't know for certain, but the number can't be small. Numerically, I suspect that we are on fairly equal terms, but the enemy is now scattered and must be desperately low in ammunition by now, whereas we have an ample supply. It is imperative that we follow up before he can regroup and get reinforcements and supplies.'

'I hear you. And that's your opinion, is it? But I'll make the decisions.'

Hal would have been happy to relinquish responsibility if it had been wise and proper to do so, but in a period of exhaustion some dormant senses may be aroused. There was no sound or movement but somehow a current was passing and she could feel her two escorts reacting against the brigadier's words and willing her on. There was even disquiet radiating from the brigadier's own silent companions.

'I don't think that you will, Brigadier,' Hal said. 'After you were taken prisoner, a signal was received. It confirmed that I was to take command. I am not relinquishing that command to you.'

'Damn you, that order was only sent because I was . . . unavailable.'

'If I get a signal confirming that position,' Hal said, 'I shall gladly hand over command.'

The brigadier was restraining himself with difficulty. 'Get me back to Pembaka and I'll send a signal of my own.'

Lacking any other way to show respect, Tony nodded. 'Certainly, sir. I see that our transport has arrived.'

Four trucks and seven jeeps were lined up on the roadway in the middle distance. Wounded men, British and Liboonese, were being lifted aboard. 'Return to your quarters at once,' the brigadier snapped at Hal. 'Consider yourself under arrest.' He strutted unsteadily across the grass towards the first of the jeeps, commandeered it and within a few minutes was driven away.

Hal could feel her two bearers breathing more easily.

'Can you make it to the transport, gentlemen?' Tony asked. 'Or do any of you need stretchers?'

'We can walk,' one of the officers said. 'Some of us may need a little help.'

'Which of you is the MO?' Hal asked.

One of the older men raised his hand. The wrist was heavily bandaged. He was unshaven and the grooves in his face seemed filled with dirt. 'Smithson,' he said. 'Major.'

'Major Smithson,' Hal said, 'is it your opinion that Brigadier Wincaster is fit to resume his command?'

Smithson was obviously embarrassed. 'The ordeal's taken it out of all of us. Physically—'

'Mentally,' Hal said. 'Can you say without reservation that Brigadier Wincaster is mentally fit to resume command of this unit?'

'I don't think that I should discuss . . .'

'Major Smithson,' Tony said, 'with all respect, loyalty may be very commendable but there are limits. Patient confidentiality hardly applies in present circumstances. Are you prepared, sir, to put everybody's lives at risk?'

The MO stood silent.

'Let me put it this way,' Hal said. 'You have been in his

160

company for several days. You've observed what this experience has done to him. If I were to be court-martialled, would
you be prepared to face the court and tell them on oath that
the brigadier was, at this moment, mentally fit for command?'

There was a long pause. 'No, Colonel,' said the MO at last.
'I could not swear to that.'

Hal could feel the relief coming from her two escorts. 'Thank
you,' she said. 'That's all I wanted to know. Shall we head
for the transport?'

As Hal was carried towards the vehicles, she asked, 'Who has
a radio?'

'I have, ma'am,' said Sergeant-Major Pennington.

'Would it have the range to reach Pembaka?'

'Just about, ma'am.'

'Tony,' said Hal, 'see if you can reach Susan Thyme. Tell
her she can send the brigadier's signal, but it wouldn't hurt
if it was delayed until we're ready with one of our own.
Right?'

'Right.'

'And tell her to get my things moved back into my original quarters. We don't want to push the brigadier right over
the edge.'

Hal was tenderly loaded into the front passenger seat of a
truck. 'You'll get a better ride than in a jeep,' Tony said. 'The
road's rough as far as the Irish bridge. I'll climb the hill until
I get a radio signal through.'

'Carry on,' Hal said.

'You'll be all right now, Colonel?' Pennington asked.

'Just fine, Sergeant-Major. And thank you. Services above
and beyond the call of duty.'

'It was nothing, ma'am. You don't weigh more than a
baby.' Pennington threw a smart salute and withdrew.

Some baby, Hal thought. She leaned back against the canvas
behind the driver's compartment. Men, freshly bandaged by
the medical team, were being loaded into the back.

'What happened to you?' asked a voice.

A second voice replied, 'I was with the party getting the

brigadier out. The guards gave up nice and easy and then didn't some silly bugger at the next tunnel loose off and get me in the bum with a ricco!'

'You was with that group, was you? Hey, is it true that the colonel broke a man's neck wiv her bare hands?'

'It's true. I saw her do it. Neatest thing you ever saw.'

The memory came flooding back. Hal could feel again the soft snap against her arm. She could feel the shakes coming on. She was certainly going to be sick.

'Cor. Some lady!' There was a protracted silence before the first voice went on. 'Did you see her tits?'

'Yeah.'

'What was they like?'

There was a brief hesitation while the other voice sought the *mot juste*. 'Bloody gorgeous,' it said reverently.

Hal leaned back, grinning to herself. The world was not disintegrating after all. Some things were eternal. And whatever was to come, somebody appreciated her.

# Nineteen

In the Middle East, hostilities were becoming ever more confused. Both sides had weapons of mass destruction ready to hand, but each was reluctant to incur worldwide condemnation by being the first to use them. The fighting had deteriorated into a game of move and counter-move, bluff and counter-bluff, with ferocious but localized actions being fought on a dozen fronts. Everything available to the Western allies was deployed.

This massive, slow-motion dance was more demanding of strategic back-up than a more conventional war, which could largely have been left to the commanders in the field. The Ministry of Defence would have been stretched beyond breaking-point even if its computer systems had been fully online.

The computer specialists had been working overtime, eradicating the virus, reprogramming the computers and loading again from hard copies the huge mass of data comprising all the knowledge of a major armed force. This was no simple task. The electronic invaders had been thorough and well trained. The original virus had contained, in addition to the delay instruction, a whole series of worm viruses designed to transfer between computers, each to emerge as soon as its predecessor was traced and countered. Some progress was made at last. The fact that Colonel H. Brown was young and female was on the point of emerging. Unfortunately, nobody had thought to notify the Contracts section of Works about the disaster and, as a result, Works had continued to send payment certificates, carrying late variants of the virus, over the wire to Finance. Within seconds, the Payments program reinfected Pay and Allowances, which passed the virus in turn back to Personnel. Systems, partially reloaded by hand, crashed

163

again and again, taking with them the back-up disks. Nobody could think where the lingering source of infection was located.

The spate of signals following the action at Urbala went unattended for more than a working day. The assistant permanent secretary, who had dealt with the previous signals and Hal's promotion, was taking some long-overdue leave. The file, containing no more than those signals, fetched up on the desk of a deputy under-secretary who, when it reached the top of the pile, went to consult the responsible military man. The original brigadier, however, was already en route to Oman, to replace another who had made himself *persona non grata* with absolutely everybody. The former's duties had been taken over by yet another brigadier who was trying to cover several areas simultaneously, aided only by staff who were being driven frantic by information that appeared and vanished again like the beam of a lighthouse.

The two, who were barely acquainted, shook hands. 'Now,' said the civil servant when sufficient courtesies had been exhanged. 'What about Maveria?'

'Who?' said the brigadier. His mind was full of the Canal Zone. Operations were not going well.

'Maveria,' said the civil servant distinctly. 'The protectorate where we've been fighting a war for the last few days. In your territory,' he added.

'Got you,' said the brigadier.

'I have a signal here, originating from Colonel H. Brown but signed on his behalf by a Captain Laverick, reporting that the Liboonese were driven out of Urbala, with a further six hundred and fifty-three prisoners taken, by a force under Colonel Brown's command. Brigadier Wincaster and his staff were recovered – neglected but not seriously ill-treated. Brown wants transport for the prisoners or alternatively a drop of supplies and additional medical personnel.'

'Our casualties?' the brigadier asked keenly.

'Eleven wounded, one seriously.'

'Seems a bit too good to be true,' said the brigadier. 'On the other hand, the last lot of prisoners seem to have arrived at Socoros Island as promised. And if that's the Colonel Humphrey Brown I knew in Cyprus, he wasn't the sort to exaggerate.'

'It seems to be true enough. There's a report on radio traffic picked up by Intelligence, which seems confirmatory. And there's a long signal from Brigadier Wincaster himself.'

'In that case, surely it's got to be true. What are we arguing about? A press release?'

The civil servant shuddered elegantly. 'Definitely not a wholesale press release just yet. You'd better read Brigadier Wincaster's signal. But I'll give you the gist of it. He intends to resume command of the garrison but this Colonel Brown won't give it up. The brigadier, using rather intemperate language, describes it as mutinous conduct. He wants the colonel recalled to face a court martial.'

'Well, I don't know about that,' said the brigadier.

The civil servant stared at him in amazement. 'Surely you have to support the more senior officer?'

'Normally, yes. But I know both of them, you see,' the brigadier said earnestly. 'Humpey Brown's a very able officer, feet on the ground and all that sort of thing. And a damn clever tactician. Wincaster, on the other hand, even when I knew him, was brilliant but eccentric. Most of his men would have followed him through hell and back, but one of them caught him in the dark, I remember, and swatted him with a rifle butt. That was in the days when rifles had butts, you understand. They never did catch the culprit, so he must have had some sympathizers. Not to put too fine a point on it, I always thought Wincaster was several men short of a platoon. Now, word's been doing the rounds that he's becoming completely gaga. Loopy,' added the brigadier, to be sure that he was putting his meaning across. 'He was only given Maveria to babysit until he could be persuaded to take his pension on medical grounds and get out of everybody's hair.'

The civil servant's face revealed sudden comprehension. 'Ah! That explains the other note in the file. It's a briefing note to somebody-or-other. It hints that Intelligence sent somebody out to vet Brigadier Wincaster – more of a job for the MO, I'd have thought – and that a signal was subsequently sent, ordering the brigadier to come home on leave. Only he wouldn't have received it, being a prisoner of the Liboonese by then.'

'Being captured won't have done his mental balance a lot of good.'

'To judge from the terms of his signal, none at all. So you think we let nature take its course and fetch him home on that leave?'

'It seems best,' said the brigadier. 'Brown seems to be doing the business. But there's another thing.' Being abnormally free from jealousy, that curse of all hierarchical structures, the brigadier was always mindful of the prospects of other officers. 'A colonel shouldn't be left in command of a brigade.'

The brigadier might defend countries, but the civil servant had a budget to defend. 'It's a very much under-strength brigade,' he pointed out.

'That shouldn't matter. A brigade should be commanded by a brigadier.'

The civil servant tried not to look impatient, but with the world going mad around him and the Joint Chiefs of Staff demanding more and more facts, which the computers were flatly refusing to divulge, he could have done without what he regarded as petty distractions. 'We'll have to think about that. It may turn out to be a temporary responsibility. I'll put a note on the file. If there's a vacancy in establishment—'

'Bugger establishment!' said the brigadier briskly. 'We're at war, or hadn't you noticed? But we'll let it stick to the wall for the moment. What about that press release?'

The civil servant thought quickly. 'We could certainly do with some good publicity. I suggest that we make as much as we can of the military victory and recovery of the POWs, how the enemy's losses far outnumber our own and so on and so forth. Not a word about dissent between commanders, of course.'

'Of course not,' said the brigadier. 'And for God's sake let's not let any journalists go there until Wincaster's on his way home.'

'Good point,' said the civil servant. 'A very good point. It's not easy to keep the media at bay, but we might think about starting a rabies rumour and threatening them with some really painful jabs.'

'That might buy us a day or two,' the brigadier agreed. 'That's how long it will take them to check it out.'

166

# Twenty

Being ordered to confine herself to her quarters might, Hal decided, make a convenient excuse for a period of bed rest in the near future, but for the moment there were pressing calls for her attention.

A small cluster of houses had been called into service as a medical centre. On being decanted from the transport, Hal hobbled to each door to satisfy herself that everything possible was being done for the sick and wounded of both victors and captives. The senior officers recovered from captivity were, one and all, determined to resume duty and discover what had happened to their responsibilities in their absence, but Smithson, the medical officer, had slipped and suffered a broken wrist and, being the only one clearly incapable of resuming full duties, supported his deputy in confining the others to their beds.

Hal's feet seemed to be aflame but there were more serious cases than hers. On the promise of attention in strict order of urgency she left the medical team to slave over burns, smoke inhalation, dysentery, exhaustion and bullet wounds and accepted transport to her original small office, where her personal chattels had magically appeared.

She was desperate for sleep but quite sure that her feet would keep it at bay. For hours she was plagued by a series of visitors requiring orders about the clean-up after the recent victory, the feeding and disposal of prisoners, the allocation of guard duties and preparations for the pursuit of the scattered enemy. She was tempted to refer all the less weighty matters for the attention of the brigadier, but that would have been to court defeat and might have counted against her in the event of an inquiry. Brigadier Wincaster, she gathered, was back in his office and issuing a stream of instructions which were being accepted and then ignored or referred to Hal. Tony was desperately trying to take some of the burden from Hal while paying lip service to the brigadier.

At last, an exhausted medical orderly arrived, tut-tutted over Hal's blisters and left them soothed and bandaged. By now it was late afternoon. She retired to the hard and narrow cot next door and, against all her expectations, fell into a deep sleep.

During the night she floated close to the surface – once or more, she could not tell – and was aware of her door opening, whispers and the door closing softly again.

She started into complete wakefulness in an African dawn. The garrison was stirring. Boots marched the street outside and other feet on the stairs overhead were trying to move quietly. Her door was open again and Tony stood in the opening, peering anxiously at her. His uniform was dusty and he looked drawn. Hal had gone to bed in a skimpy T-shirt and once the cool of the night was over had pushed her single sheet and blanket down. She pulled the sheet hastily over her bottom. 'Did you get any sleep?' she asked him.

He yawned. 'Some. The brigadier had had nothing to do in his mine tunnel but sleep and think, so he's in hyperactive mode.'

'Come in, for heaven's sake.'

Tony looked over his shoulder. 'Better not.'

Hal drew the sheet up further. 'For heaven's sake,' she said in exasperation, 'I'll be less embarrassed with the door shut, instead of having every passing private peering in at me. Anyway,' she added as Tony complied, 'I don't think there's anybody in Maveria who doesn't already know about our sleeping arrangements the other night, except possibly some wandering Bedouin in the foothills. What's going on?'

Tony looked around for somewhere to sit. The only chair was occupied by Hal's clothing – replaced by fresh during the night, she noticed; Sergeant Mamie's allegiance must have followed her. She drew her feet up and Tony perched on the foot of the cot with a sigh of relief. 'Everything,' he said. 'Everything's going on. The Maverian company has returned, bearing trophies that you would not want to see. As ordered, B and C Companies have gone to round up stray groups of Liboonese – they have your firm instructions not to engage any re-formed bodies of the enemy. But I wouldn't want to be in any small party of Liboonese; the locals are forming militia groups and paying off scores. Your signal went off – I took the liberty of amplifying it slightly; hope you don't mind.'

'Amplifying it in what way?'

'I thought that you were being rather too modest. I've ordered you some breakfast, by the way. But we're going to run short of food if we have to feed all those prisoners for much longer, so I've gathered up a few fishermen who didn't abscond with the rest of the fishing fleet and sent them out with the dhow to see what they can catch; and Mr N'koma will put the word around among the farmers that we're in the market for fresh fruit and veg.'

'Well done,' Hal said. 'But when I asked you what's going on, I meant what's *really* going on.'

'We didn't catch Simon Agulfo. He's trying to rally what's left of his forces among the foothills. Susan's unit intercepted a fairly factual report from him to his political masters in Liboon, but some of his officers have been radioing reports which, if the translations from Swahili are accurate, credit you with magical powers but also claim that their force was outnumbered ten to one. Did you know that they're calling you . . .' He looked down at the notes in his hand. 'I got one of the Swahili-literate sergeants to write it down for me. *Afriti-mwanamki*?'

Hal nearly sat up but remembered her state of dress. 'Are they really? I take that as a compliment.'

'Yes, really. What does it mean?'

'*Devil-woman*. What else is going on?'

'The medics are running out of oxygen for the smoke-inhala-tion cases, but those seem to be pulling through all right. The MO, Major Smithson, is up and dragging himself around the wounded although they've all been dealt with at least once and he's in a worse way than most of them. He should be ordered off duty.'

'So should you,' Hal said. 'All right, my compliments to the MO and order him to go to bed. First tell me exactly what's the state of play. Then *you* go to bed.'

Tony was saved from having to make an immediate reply by the arrival of a native waiter with a tray holding a repeat of her previous big breakfast. He placed it on the crate which seemed intended to serve as her dressing table. Hal, who had once again missed a whole series of meals, began to salivate. But first things still came first. 'Now,' she said when the door had closed. 'Tell me.'

'If you're sure you want to know. The brigadier's up in what used to be *your* ivory tower, fulminating and issuing orders countermanding yours. I've been trying to get each of yours implemented before he hears about it, thus presenting him each time with a *fait accompli*. That,' Tony said, 'has not improved his mood much, and he's been demanding, since about three this morning, that you be brought to him, preferably in chains and not necessarily alive. I persuaded the quack to take a few minutes off from pulling grenade splinters out of the backside of a huge Liboonese sergeant, using what looked like eyebrow tweezers, and to write out a note stating that you were medically unfit. But I really think you're going to have to go and confront the brigadier soon. Don't go without me. We may as well swing together.'

'Soon is a relative word,' Hal said thoughtfully into her pillow. 'Tony, I don't want either of us to swing, but if I have to swing I'd rather swing alone. So don't put your head through any nooses on my account. If you will kindly get out of here I'm going to eat that breakfast, get dressed and then go up to Signals and find out as much as I can about the present state of the enemy. I also want to read everything that's come in or gone out. After that, if I feel suitably aggressive, I may go visiting. Can you borrow me a pair of slippers large enough to go on over these bandages?'

\*       \*       \*

Much refreshed and neat as a pin from the ankles up, Hal climbed the steep stairs to the Signals unit. Her bandages were enclosed in a pair of huge carpet slippers, kindly lent by a corporal-chef in the RLC, so that her arrival was sudden and unannounced. She found the loft full of ordered activity. Tony and Susan were stooped over a map.

As she entered, the personnel began to rise. 'At ease,' she said. 'Sit, sit. Tony, what's the latest?'

'We were just analysing the latest signal, plotting the map references given by the satellite images for probable troop concentrations and eliminating any that can't possibly be the Liboonese.' Tony gestured over the map. 'This one's almost certainly a herd of animals, or maybe a troop of monkeys. Two others would be our own B and C Companies, aiming to collect from the swamp any of the enemy dim enough to fall for our decoy signals. Two images described as "faint" are close to positions we've been broadcasting as decoy rendezvous, so your nasty, deceitful trick seems to be paying off. By process of elimination, the one remaining image must be the Liboonese, beginning to re-form, and they're just where their radio signals appointed for the gathering point. We could divert C Company to chase them around a bit.'

Hal was tempted. It might be a fitting end to her campaign. But she thought again. Commanders in the field had fallen because of overconfidence. Townsend in Mesopotamia. MacArthur in Korea. Napoleon. She shivered. 'C Company have enough to get on with,' she said, 'without going in among the hills and defiles after an enemy who got there first. I don't want to put any more men at risk than I have to. Simon Agulfo doesn't seem to have got any brighter. Let's see if he's as gullible as you used to be.'

She studied the map. The Liboonese were re-forming in a valley which sliced into the foothills, joined by several defiles. 'Have somebody prepare a message,' she told Susan. 'In clear – I want Simon Agulfo to pick it up. If Sandhurst taught him anything, it would be to listen in to our radio traffic. Tell P Company to approach down this defile here, Q Company to come in from the north, under a mortar barrage to begin –' she consulted her watch – 'an hour after the message goes out. That should give them just time to scatter into the grassland where D Company can be lying in wait for them. Don't bother pointing out that we don't have any P and Q Companies. I'm well aware of it. If they don't fall for it, nothing's lost.'

'You are still a dangerous and devious woman,' Tony said.

'Oh God! I hope so,' Hal said.

'No wonder they're calling you devil-woman.'

'It's to the good. Never underestimate the power of super-stition. They don't know who I am yet, do they?' Hal asked sharply.

'There's no indication that they do. Only that you're female.'

'I hope my name hasn't got back to him,' Hal said. 'The name Brown is common enough, but put it together with my gender and the penny might drop. I wouldn't want Simon Agulfo to know who's against him just yet. If I know how his mind works, he'll understand mine.'

'You think so?' Tony enquired, raising an eyebrow. 'I'm damned if I do.'

'That's reassuring. We'll have to prepare a reception for them. I think we can trap them against an edge of the swamp, but I want advice from somebody with a lot of experience in the field. Can we find, quickly, two or three of the warrant officers from what I call my plan-checkers?'

'Leave it with me.'

Tony vanished. Hal turned to Susan. 'Show me the file of outgoing signals.'

Susan produced a file of papers. 'There are some incoming ones you ought to look at,' she said.

'In a moment.' Hal skimmed through the outgoing messages. It was all there. Tony had done a good job. A clear report on the action. 653 prisoners. A request for a drop of medical supplies. A request for transport of the prisoners, who would alternatively be sent in relays to Socoros Island. A request for evacuation of wounded. A signal to 'Admiral' Justin Carlsborough, request-ing an ETA for his return. A request for a satellite picture of the mouth of the Barawat River, in case the Liboonese were attempt-ing some other form of crossing, such as a pontoon bridge . . .

She turned over a leaf, going backwards through time. A mildly rude word escaped between her teeth. 'I couldn't not send it,' Susan pleaded.

'Of course you couldn't,' Hal said. 'When a brigadier gives you an order, you jump to it. Unless, of course, you're an idiot like me.'

'I thought that he was going a long way over the top. I couldn't get him to tone it down.'

'And thank God for that!' Hal said. 'If he'd toned it down he might have been believed. As it is, he's so far over the top that even the Ministry of Defence will stop and think twice before acting on it. I hope.'

Despite her brave words, Hal quaked when, a few minutes later, her persual of the signals was interrupted by the arrival of the brigadier himself. He arrived, stamping up the stairs with Tony drawn along behind like a leaf in the wake of a liner.

Hal was left in no doubt that the brigadier was in a towering, all-consuming rage and only holding himself in check by an effort of a will which she had not thought he still possessed. The wreck of a man rescued from the mine tunnel a day previously had been shaved, showered, fed and dressed in a fresh uniform complete with medal ribbons. His self-assurance had been more than restored. The combination of rank and fury would have daunted a Hector.

'So there you are!' he said to Hal. 'I have been sending for you.' The words flamed in the air.

Hal denied herself the relief of flinching. 'I'm just getting abreast of the situation,' she said. 'I would have been with you in a minute. Sir,' she added.

Her reply only fanned the flames. The brigadier advanced his face to within a few inches of hers. She could smell an aftershave. 'You have no call to "get abreast of" any situations,' he snarled. 'I have resumed command of this garrison and you have no more part to play. Go to your quarters.'

Hal gathered up all her inner strength and struggled to keep her voice firm and steady. 'I'm sorry, Brigadier,' she said. 'Command of this garrison was transferred to me and until I

receive orders to the contrary from London, I am not relinquishing it.' There was provision, she knew, for relieving a
superior officer of command on the grounds that his mental
stability was impaired. She wished that she had taken time to
study the wording in detail.

'You are receiving orders now, from me.' On each sibilant
he spat slightly on to her face, but he was past caring.

'Brigadier, I am not accepting them.'

The brigadier was dumbfounded. No subordinate officer
had ever refused his orders. He looked round for support. The
Signals personnel had been attending raptly to the argument
but all heads went down. The brigadier's eyes passed over
them.

Before being called to heel by the brigadier, Tony had sent
word to the warrant officers' mess. Hal, he knew, would be
in need of help and, in the desperation of the moment, he
could not think of a better source of calm wisdom and moral
support. Sergeant-Majors Hindley and Pennington had arrived
at the door. The brigadier seemed to welcome them as heaven-
sent. 'Arrest that woman,' he cried.

Sergeant-Major Pennington had been present when the
brigadier was freed. He had given his own opinion and he
had overheard the opinion of the MO, Major Smithson. His
friend, Bill Hindley, had been an early recipient of the tidings.
The two men stood their ground, unmoving.

'Well?' snapped the brigadier.

Pennington swallowed. Warrant officers, perhaps more than
others, are trained and habituated to accept and implement
orders without question. He gathered his resolution to him
like a blanket. 'No, sir,' he said bravely.

'*What?*'

Hal was sure that a stroke was imminent. If she was saddened
to see the state into which the gallant old soldier had plunged,
she was devastated to watch him heading into a confrontation which she was sure must do him nothing but damage.
'Brigadier,' she said, 'for your own sake, please don't force
this issue.'

'Yes, you'd like that, wouldn't you?' He rounded on the

two warrant officers. 'You two are under arrest. Go to your quarters.' He glared at Tony. 'Fetch the military police.'

'Brigadier, sir,' said Pennington. 'With respect, you won't find a man in this unit who'll move against the colonel.'

The brigadier was taken aback. Hal thought that he might be about to cry, but he drew himself together. 'This is mutiny,' he whispered.

Hal was appalled. She had not intended that anyone else would be dragged into what she had considered to be her own private battle. That the whole unit should be drawn into the terrible routine and punishment that would follow a mass mutiny was not to be thought of. She opened her mouth to capitulate but hesitated. The alternative, which would grant Simon Agulfo time to re-form, re-arm and reinforce, was equally unacceptable.

The brigadier turned to Susan. 'Lieutenant Thyme, I want a signal sent to London immediately.'

Susan nodded. 'Of course, Brigadier, but first I think you should read this copy signal.'

The brigadier snatched the flimsy paper out of her hand. He had to blink before he could read it. He raised his eyes to her face. 'Why wasn't I shown this before?'

'You were already a prisoner in enemy hands when it arrived. The original must be among the papers on your desk.'

He returned his glare to Hal. 'According to this, I've been on leave since the day after your arrival. Well, that doesn't change anything. Leave or no leave, I'm still your superior officer, and you've refused an order, the lot of you and . . . and . . .'

Sergeant Wilkes appeared at Susan's elbow and handed her a signal form. 'This has just arrived, Brigadier,' she said.

'What does it say?'

'You're wanted back in London, Brigadier. They're sending a long-range Lynx helicopter for you from *HMS Caledonia*. Major Smithson goes with you. Colonel Brown is to remain in command.' Susan paused and moistened her lips. 'The signal has been in transit for the last thirty-six hours,' she added.

The brigadier drew himself up and blinked his eyes clear.

He was silent for a full half minute. 'You see?' he said at last. 'They want me? Very well. I know when to respond to a call. Come, Captain Laverick...Tony...My boy. I'll have to get ready. There must be a thousand things to do.'

'Coming, Brigadier,' Tony said. The two descended the stairs together. The two warrant officers waited until they had cleared the stairs before following. Everybody breathed out slowly.

There was a noise overhead from the helicopter, heading for the parade ground.

Hal groped for a chair before her knees had time to give way. 'Let me see that signal,' she said.

Susan backed away. 'You don't want to see it.'

Inside Hal, relief was fostering an urge to leap and dance, to sing songs, tell rude stories or turn handsprings. Her new seniority put most of those actions out of court, but she could not resist one little joke. 'This is mutiny,' she said in a passable imitation of the brigadier's voice. 'Lieutenant, show me that signal at once.'

Wordlessly, Susan handed her the signal. It had been in transit for less than an hour.

'That's all I wanted to know,' Hal said. 'File it. File it somewhere where nobody will ever find it.'

# Twenty-One

The Prime Minister, his Minister of Defence and the cabinet secretary were in deep discussion. At last there seemed hope of a not-too-dishonourable settlement to the conflict in the Middle East, which, it was now clear, nobody was going to win and of which all parties were by now thoroughly sick.

'What I want to know,' the PM said, not for the first time, 'is whether the Israelis will go along with it.'

'They might,' said the cabinet secretary, 'although it would look like a climbdown after all the promises of retribution.'

'They can say that we pressured them into accepting it,' the PM said hopefully.

'Assuming that the Israelis will accept it,' the Defence Minister said, 'will we?'

'Definitely, yes,' the PM told him. 'It would get us out of an expensive and unpopular war that isn't going to get any better. Cleverly handled, we could come out smelling of roses. If cabinet goes along, we could sound out the Israelis tonight.'

The cabinet secretary made a note. 'And about Maveria?'

The PM brightened. Maveria was a much happier topic. 'What's the latest?'

'The Liboonese in Maveria are nearly all POW,' said the Defence Minister. 'When Liboon's peace overture was relayed to us by the PO, we sent Colonel Brown a signal – more as a courtesy than anything else, because there was more than enough confirmation of the position. His reply was puzzling at the time. He said that we should accept Liboon's terms provided that free elections, supervised by the UN, were held within a year, failing which Devil Woman would continue the war, invade Liboon and raze their cities to the ground. Not that they have what you or I would call cities, but that's by the way.

'Our embassy in Liboon confirms that there is rumour going around, rapidly becoming folklore, about a "Devil Woman" who breaks men's necks with her bare hands and breathes fire on their houses. She seems to be a sort of person-ification of the British Army and they're scared stiff of her.'

'Why would we be represented by a female figure?' the PM asked. He was sensitive about his masculinity.

'God knows. Britannia, perhaps. Or maybe the legend of Queen Victoria still hangs on in some places. Either way, it's difficult to square with the legend that Devil Woman has feet of flame. Amazing how they can sometimes get the wrong end of the stick. Anyway, it's working to our advantage this time. It seemed worth a try, and damned if they aren't ready to go along with the free elections.'

The PM produced his first smile in weeks. He saw his chance to shine as the leader who brought democracy back to another benighted country, a triumph to overlay all the fail-ures. 'So what's holding it up?' he enquired. 'I want to get this settled before they find a way to reinforce their men in Maveria and start it all over again.'

'The Liboonese commander is one General Agulfo – trained by us, by the way. He has little more than a full company left, more or less completely armed but running short of supplies. However, he's managing to hold out, dodging our chaps in the maze of defiles in the mountains. He can't win, but it seems to be a matter of pride. He isn't going to surrender to a mere colonel. It's a general or nothing.'

'Bugger that!' said the Prime Minister. Neither of his listeners was surprised. The PM, who could debate ehtics with a bishop with every sign of sincerity, took a pride in his roots and in being 'one of the boys' when it suited him. 'A brigade knocked him for six, and an under-strength brigade at that, so he can make do with a brigadier. Shove this chap Brown up to brigadier and let Liboon know that their General Whatsit can surrender to him or sit it out. Or should I go out and accept the surrender in person?'

Both his listeners concealed their horror at the idea. The Right Honourable Geoffrey York was quite capable of fanning the flames back to life. 'You'll be needed here,' the Defence Minister said tactfully. 'Your first idea was the best one. But can I hold off for a day or two? There are proper procedures for this sort of thing. I'm told that the computers will be simultaneously de-bugged and back online tomorrow, or the next day at the latest. I've had somebody dig out a hard copy of his record, but it's rather garbled – nobody bothers too much about paper records once it's on the computer.'

Silently, the PM begged God to give him patience. Charles was being even more of an old woman than usual. A fanfare of good publicity over Maveria might obscure any shortcomings in the wider settlement. 'Listen,' he said. 'He's a colonel, isn't he?'

'Well, yes. And he's certainly eligible for promotion. But—'

'You know his army number?'

'Yes, of course. Two of his digits seem to have been transposed somewhere along the way, but that can happen—'

'And he's just won a small war?'

'A very small—'

'An under-strength brigade under his command overpowered a whole enemy division?'

'Most of it, but—'

One of the few things the PM enjoyed about his job was the power to play God now and again. 'I don't give a damn which Colonel Brown it is. Put him up to brigadier straight away, on my authority, and tell the Liboonese to like it or lump it. Otherwise we'll send Devil Woman to give them a kick up the arse from the feet of flame. And let's get the press office on to it. They might even hint that, given a free hand and no allies, we can manage a clear-cut victory, whereas . . . Well, you know the sort of thing, Noel.'

The cabinet secretary sighed. He knew exactly the sort of thing.

# Twenty-Two

In London, the return of the military, naval and air force computers to full online capacity did not immediately uncover the fact that Hal was not exactly the stereotype that had been envisaged in the Ministry. It was only when her file was reconstructed, using papers recovered from a basement archive near Charing Cross, and then called up for the addition of her successive promotions, that shock waves began to reverberate in the establishment. By then, the media had been fed the official version of events and urgent demands were being made for biographical details of the faceless Brigadier Hal Brown who was being forcibly escalated into a national hero. Media representatives were already on their way to Maveria.

Brigadier Wincaster's departure had left Hal in undisputed command. Immediately, she had tried to assume personal responsibility for all the grisly aftermath of battle. This willingness to share in the horrors had endeared her still further to the men, but it was pointed out to her, gently but firmly, that there were well-grooved routines for dealing with such matters as the disposal of bodies. Her participation need not go further than the writing of a tactful letter to the relatives of the remarkably few British casualties. This duty she undertook with great concern, researching each man's history. Her letters became treasures in the archives of several households.

Hal then turned her attention to more mundane matters. The harassing of the Liboonese remnants she could leave in the carefully briefed and increasingly experienced hands of her junior officers. Another large batch of prisoners had been dispatched in the direction of Socoros Island, but she had retained some of the more intelligent and willing Liboonese as labour volunteers. It was her intention to renovate and restore the barracks before returning her troops there. She also hoped to hand back to their rightful owners the buildings which had been occupied in the town, in at least as good condition as they had been when first occupied, and to rebuild Urbala.

On the second day after the departure of the brigadier, Hal, still unaware of her latest promotion, returned to the office that she had reclaimed above the officers' mess. She had attended the MO's surgery to have her blisters dressed again and had taken the opportunity to visit the wounded of both armies. The Liboonese men, to her surprise and chagrin, had exhibited stark terror when she was first introduced to them, but when she conversed with them in fluent Swahili, asking after their families and promising that their continued survival would be relayed, they lost their initial fear of her and even honoured her with a tribal chant that brought the guard in at the double, under the impression that hostilities had broken out again.

Hal's feet were still painful, but Tony brought her back by Land Rover to the door of the mess. Susan Thyme was waiting at the door and, instead of her usual between-friends salute, she produced one of which any RSM might have been proud.

Hal accepted Tony's help in quitting the Land Rover and sketched a return salute. 'What's all this?' she asked. 'If you're after a pay increase, I don't think it's within my powers.'

'I always give brigadiers a proper salute,' Susan said with dignity. She produced a small sheaf of papers. 'You'd better cast an eye over these signals.'

Hal had encountered some very young-looking colonels, but in her experience brigadiers were gentlemen of considerable stiffness and no little maturity, bearing no resemblance to her black young self. 'Somebody's having you on,' she said. 'I'll look at them upstairs.' As she leaned on Tony's arm and hobbled into the building, it seemed to her that the two sentries, like Susan, saluted with unusual smartness and that their faces were less solemn than was quite proper. Everybody, it seemed, knew something that she didn't know.

Arriving at last at the big desk, Hal sank gratefully into the brigadier's chair. 'Now,' she said, 'what's all this nonsense?'

Susan had followed upstairs, impatient as a cat within sight of its feeding bowl. 'It isn't nonsense,' she said. 'Look. And there's another signal of congratulations from Colonel Bowman and a personal message from the Prime Minister and. . .and. . .'

'Gimme,' Hal said. She held out her hand and received the signals. As she read through them her eyes grew round and her eyebrows rose ever higher. 'You'd better stay,' she told Susan. She looked at Tony. 'The world is going mad,' she said. 'It does seem that I've been bumped up to brigadier. Mostly, I gather, because Simon Agulfo wanted to surrender to a general and we didn't have any generals to spare.'

'You deserve it anyway,' Susan said stoutly.

'Rubbish! But thank you all the same. And it seems that there's a . . . What's the collective noun for journalists?'

'A scribble,' Tony suggested.

Hal's sense of humour was beginning to take over. The whole situation was becoming unreal and therefore laughable. 'Thanks,' she said. 'There's a scribble of journalists on the way to witness Simon surrendering to me. And if Simon wants to surrender to a general and he's only getting a brigadier, God knows how he'll react if he finds that it's only me, who he last saw as a newly commissioned second lieutenant, now masquerading in a major's uniform. Susan, send off a signal requesting immediate dispatch of a brigadier's insignia, surrenders for the receiving of.'

'I'll give you the wording,' Tony told Susan firmly. One of the duties of an ADC, he decided, was to prevent his superior's sense of humour running away with him. Or her.

'What's more,' Hal said, 'I can't meet him until my uniform's right, so get a signal to Simon Agulfo. Tell him that I propose a ceasefire from eighteen-hundred this evening and he can come and camp on his side of the Irish bridge until I'm ready for him. Should I insist that he comes in sackcloth and with a noose around his neck, like the buggers of Calais?'

'No way,' said Tony, 'or this war will go on for ever. And it was burghers. Never, ever forget that.'

Hal was laughing. 'I was pulling your leg. Nice to see that you're still as gullible as ever,' she said.

'I was pulling yours,' Tony said with dignity.

'Of course you were. There's another signal, requesting that hotel accommodation be reserved for the journalists. Well, this is the hotel and I'm not getting out of it before I have to – not for a scribble of journalists.'

'We can find them billets,' Tony said, 'provided that they come and depart again before the townspeople flood back. When are they due?'

Hal looked at the signal again. 'They should be here by now,' she said doubtfully. 'With a bit of luck, they've got lost or turned aside to cover something more interesting like the birth of a pop star's baby.'

'The amphibian came in this morning,' Tony said.

Hal's carefree mood vanished in an instant. 'I heard it. I thought it was only bringing medical supplies. Get out there, Tony. Round up a posse or something. If the journalists are here, gather them up and bring them here. Make it clear that it's their only choice if they want a drink and lunch. You could drop a hint that rabies is rife in the town. The last thing we want is a load of wild stories, but it's what we'll get if we let them talk to the men.'

'You'll have to let them talk to the men sooner or later,' Susan said. 'Otherwise they'll be sure that we're covering something up.'

'We can try,' Hal said. 'With a little luck a politician will get caught in a lie or a two-headed puppy will be born and they'll go tearing off after somebody else.'

With the help of her senior clerk, the always helpful Joseph Mobo, Hal made her dispositions. By the time the journalists had been rounded up, dosed with some deceptively powerful local spirit and brought upstairs, the office had been rearranged for the reception of guests and all superfluous personnel sent about their business.

The journalists all looked sweat-stained and travel-worn but roughly washed and refreshed by their visit to the mess below. They consisted of eleven male and three female representatives of the press (mostly British but three from other EU

183

countries) and two separate TV journalists with cameramen and formidable recording equipment. They filed in and took seats sedately but with an air of suppressed excitement unusual in their hard-boiled professions. The cameramen set up tripods. Safari suits, new-looking but crumpled, were much in evidence.

Hal was already seated with her bandaged and slippered feet hidden under the desk. She waited until the visitors had settled and then cleared her throat and gave a conventional greeting. It was her first meeting with the press and she was aware of a tightening of her stomach muscles. The lenses of the cameras stared at her in challenge. They were all waiting. For her, she realized suddenly.

'Let me introduce myself,' she said. 'I am Hal Brown, colonel, local brigadier, officer commanding the British garrison in Maveria. On my right is Captain Laverick who is acting as my second in command. Major Lampitter, on my left, was one of the officers captured by the Liboonese and recovered.'

'Chosen at random, I may add,' Lampitter said with a twisted smile. He was a tall man with features that looked larger than life, but his colour was poor and his face was lined.

'That is true,' said Hal. 'I can give you some comments on the rest of the actions but not about their time as prisoners. Major Lampitter was the first of that group to become available this morning.'

'Because the others are still hospitalized?' a reporter asked. 'Jenkins, *Gazette*,' he added.

Hal nodded to Lampitter, who said, 'Two of our number are still bed patients but each is expected to be up and about within a day or two. The rest of us are on our feet and gradually resuming duty.' He could have added that the others, suffering as they were from dysentery, were not yet ready to venture far from the nearest lavatory, but while the fact might have interested the media it would have lowered the dignity of the occasion.

'How did you come to be taken?' Jenkins asked.

'Brigadier Wincaster was holding a meeting with his senior officers and an unexpected commando-type raid nabbed the lot of us,' Lampitter said firmly. Hal had had a quick word with him before the journalists were admitted. The brigadier was to be spared any further odium.

'What can you tell us about your period as prisoners?' another reporter asked. 'Were you badly treated?'

Lampitter glanced at Hal, who nodded again. 'I'm sorry to disappoint you, but there are no wounds to reopen and there would be no point reopening them if there were,' he said. 'We could hardly expect feather-bed treatment from an opposing army on the march. We had to keep up and to sleep where they put us. The older or less fit of our number were sometimes allowed to ride in their one vehicle, which is more consideration than we might have expected. Within their lights, they were hard but not unreasonably so. They fed us what they could, which was not much considering that their supply route had been closed to them and they were themselves on very short rations. There was no gratuitous violence. No serious wounds were inflicted or bones broken. Our casualties were suffering from exhaustion, dysentery, minor accidents and lack of medical attention, which was only to be expected in the circumstances.' He paused and then added hurriedly, 'Our condition would have been much worse but for the very prompt rescue by the party led by Brigadier Brown. Colonel Brown, as I suppose she was at the time.'

Attention focused again on Hal. 'You seem very young for a brigadier,' said one of the two women reporters. 'Even a local one.'

'Yes,' Hal said, smiling. 'That's what I thought myself. My mind went back to Balaclava. "Theirs not to reason why." I can only assume that the army knows what it's doing.'

'A safe assumption,' said one of the men, 'seeing that you've knocked hell out of a much larger force. I'm Hardy, by the way. *Daily News*.'

'We had several advantages,' Hal said. 'Technology, for instance.'

'You seem to have made exceptional use of it,' Hardy said. 'We note that you are still wearing the crown and two stars of a colonel.'

'I only learned of my promotion this morning.'

'In that case,' Hardy said, 'we probably knew about it before you did. Just before our plane took off from Athens, I was contacted by a Colonel Bowman who asked me to deliver this to you as a matter of urgency.' He got up and laid on the desk a small padded envelope. 'My briefcase was searched by airport security and I was asked to open the envelope. I noticed – quite accidentally, you understand – that the envelope seems to contain another star.'

Hal hid her smile at the idea of a reporter gaining that sort of glimpse by accident. 'Thank you,' she said. 'The urgency would be so that I can be properly equipped to receive General Agulfo's surrender. I understand that he was refusing to surrender to anyone of less than general officer rank. He certainly wouldn't have appreciated being confronted by a brigadier in colonel's clothing.'

The woman reporter who had already spoken said, 'I'm Judy Phillipson. *Sunday Journal*. I have a question. Did you have any difficulty with or feel any reluctance at taking action against an enemy of your own colour?'

Journalists are not generally sensitive to matters of political correctness but one or two eyebrows went up. The youngest reporter, who was falling in love with Hal's smile, gave a contemptuous snort. Hal felt Tony stiffen. She spoke quickly. 'No,' she said, 'I did not. When one of my officers asked me that question I asked him, in reply, whether he would have more difficulty fighting a white enemy than a black one. You may care to note that I am British-born, of British parents, and I have never had any other home or loyalties.

'The colour of my skin is irrelevant – except that, very indirectly, it may have given me an additional advantage. I learned early on that General Agulfo was in command of the Liboonese force. It happens that we were at Sandhurst at the same time and, because of some hazy association of ideas on the part of the staff, we were usually in the same group for theoretical exercises in tactics. I therefore had a very good idea how his mind works. On the other hand, I don't believe that he knows of my presence here even yet. I had only arrived in Maveria a few hours before the raid, but I found myself to be the highest ranking officer remaining after the raid and therefore required by regulations to take command.'

The *Sunday Journal* reporter, Judy Phillipson, raised her hand, pausing at her ear to replace a curl straying from a still perfect hairdo. 'At Sandhurst, were you and General Agulfo lovers?' she asked.

The question could have disconcerted Hal, but suddenly she remembered Simon Agulfo's hopeful proposal and she let her rich laugh warm the air. 'Definitely not,' she said. 'Contrary to what one reads in some of your papers, it is possible for a man and a woman to meet without forming an amorous relationship. Perhaps Miss Phillipson's experience is different?'

There was a murmur of amusement, becoming open laughter. Judy Phillipson had a certain reputation. Her lips closed in a tight line.

Hardy caught Hal's eye again. He was an insignificant-looking man but his eyes compelled attention. 'We were given a briefing in London before we left,' he said. 'It was all right as far as it went, but I don't think that we have the whole story. Are we to understand that you enlisted the help of the local crocodiles?'

'Their services were available to either side,' Hal said. 'It seemed a pity not to make use of such willing volunteers.' Under pressure, she explained the availability of the saltwater crocodiles and how they had been tempted into position.

Hardy took up the questioning again. 'We've been gathering whispers since we arrived here. London gave us a clear picture of the tactical decisions and their outcomes. We thought that we could detect the customary exaggeration when it came to your role. But now it seems that there may be some parts of the story that even London doesn't know. Is it true that you personally led the party which rescued Brigadier Wincaster and his staff?'

'Not really,' Hal said.

'Major Lampitter let slip that you did,' said Jenkins.

'Major Lampitter spoke out of turn,' Hal said. She paused to choose her words. 'I did not lead the party in the sense of taking command of it. That was the responsibility of Sergeant-Major Pennington. I merely preceded the party so that it wouldn't blunder into an outpost. The assumption was that one black woman could pass where a party of white soldiers would have given the alarm before we could get within striking distance.'

'Your own assumption?' Jenkins asked.

'Yes. It proved to be correct.'

'But you put yourself at some risk,' said somebody else.

'There is always a degree of risk . . .' Hal began carefully. There had clearly been some conferring among the reporters and a spokesman had been elected. Several pairs of eyes looked towards Hardy, who spoke again. 'Would you care to deny that you encountered a Liboonese sentry who attempted to rape you?'

'No comment,' Hal said stiffly. She could guess what was coming.

'Would you deny that you then broke his neck? With your bare hands,' Hardy added – superfluously, Hal thought.

The question brought back vividly to Hal the moment when she had attempted the hip throw. She remembered the sound and the feeling as the man's vertebrae had come apart and she thought that her stomach might disgrace her. She wanted to deny the story, if only to herself. It was not a feat she wanted permanently attached to her reputation. But her study of history had taught her that nearly all major scandals had flared up, not because of the original deed but over attempts to deny the truth. 'No comment,' she said again.

'Then we will have to rely on our other sources,' Hardy said gently. 'Is it true that your feet were hurt during the same patrol?'

'They suffered some blisters,' Hal admitted.

'We understand that many of the opposing force were trapped in mine tunnels by the use of some sort of napalm outside the tunnel mouths. Did you get your blisters when your feet were burned in the flames?'

'No,' Hal said.

'May we see your feet, please?'

'No you may not,' Hal snapped. 'Not because they are secret but because they look rather ridiculous at the moment.'

Judy Phillipson got up and, before anyone could object, darted round the desk and looked beneath. 'She's right,' she said, resuming her seat. 'They do look ridiculous.' There was laughter.

There would have been no point expressing resentment.

The deed was done. The mood of the room was far from hostile.

'Are you aware,' Hardy resumed, 'that you are now being referred to by the Liboonese as Devil Woman?'

'I had heard,' Hal said.

'And did you know that that *nom de guerre* is being amplified? They're now calling you "Devil Woman with feet of flame".'

Hal remembered her incautious remark just before her confrontation with the brigadier at the tunnel mouth. Some Liboonese fugitive must have been hiding within earshot. 'No, I didn't know that,' she said. 'And I think that's enough about my flaming feet.'

'But, Brigadier,' said Hardy through the laughter, 'you'll have to come out from behind that desk some time. Why don't you let us have a dignified photo session now? After all, those are honourable wounds incurred during the rescue of your comrades.'

There was some wisdom in his words. Hal sighed. 'All right,' she said. 'Provided that you all promise not to refer to me as Bigfoot. But I didn't burn myself in the flames. I got blisters from the long march in badly fitting boots, that's all.' Nobody was listening. The press can be very deaf to anything contradicting its preconceptions.

So Hal came out from behind her desk and the cameras closed in on her and on her bandages and the large carpet-slippers. She adopted a comic pose which looked well on camera and subsequently endeared her further to the British public.

The reporters, pacified by promises of individual interviews, were lured away at last to lunch. When the door had closed behind the last one, Hal said, 'Put the word around. Anyone caught feeding colourful stories to the journalists will be on latrine duty for ever. And I don't care if he's a colonel.'

'You won't stop it,' Major Lampitter said. He smiled and Hal saw him suddenly as he must have been before the ordeal of captivity. He was a good-looking man and younger than she had thought. 'You fit in somewhere between a witch doctor and a regimental mascot. I'll be surprised if fresh legends about you aren't still surfacing in generations to come.'

Hal said a rude word but she said it silently. Aloud, she said, 'Has anybody in this unit, do you suppose, ever seen a surrender being accepted? What am I supposed to do?'

'Leave it to us, Brigadier,' Lampitter suggested. 'Montgomery had much the same problem. Queen's regulations now cover it.'

The Liboonese soldiers, other than the few small parties who, lacking radios, were still scattered among the gullies and defiles of the foothills and the swamps beyond the Urma River, were conducted in single file towards where Hal sat, below the wall outside the landward gate. The position was shaded but it was also sheltered from the cooling sea breeze. Hal made up her mind to get the occasion over with as quickly as was compatible with the formalities.

Hal was flanked by Tony, her ADC, and by Major Lampitter, who seemed to have installed himself as master of ceremonies. All three were as smart as they could make themselves, lending dignity to the occasion in well-pressed uniforms, and Hal felt acutely self-conscious in the unfamiliar trappings of a brigadier. The journalists and cameramen, along with a host of non-combatants and spectators, were given a safe but grandstand view from the top of the wall.

The Liboonese deposited their arms on a growing stockpile and were led between two lines of purely British infantry. On this occasion the Maverian troops were excused duty, relieved of all live ammunition and banished to the rampart. There was no certainty that triumph over their old, tribal enemies might not have led to sudden bloodshed. By agreement, each Liboonese was to salute Hal as he passed on his way towards the prison camp in the British barracks, but it was noticeable that most saluted with averted eyes although the more courageous and less superstitious among them glanced curiously at her, and more particularly at her feet. Hal had already noted that her own native mess staff had taken to seizing any excuse to brush against her or touch her garments. Contact with her hair was considered to be particularly propitious. Evidently superstition about the powers of Devil Woman was continuing to grow.

Officers and NCOs marched with the men, but the officers fell out to witness the formality of surrender. General Simon Agulfo brought up the rear. He had made every effort to smarten his appearance and he wore a display of medals that was remarkably splendid considering the comparative shortness of his military service and its lack of hostilities, but his uniform was torn and sweat-stained. He unbuckled his belt and holster and threw them disdainfully on top of the pile before marching down the centre of the avenue between his former enemies and wheeling towards the table where Hal sat. He was thinner than her recollection of him and she could detect a slight limp.

She stood.

When he stepped out of the dazzle of the sun he recognized Hal and stopped suddenly a few yards off. For a moment, the world stilled. 'So,' he said, 'it is you! You are Brigadier Brown!'

Hal said, 'Yes.'

'A brigadier? Already?'

'And you a general,' Hal retorted.

His eyes narrowed and his full lips pinched together. For a moment, she thought that Agulfo was going to throw himself across the table to attack her. She sensed Tony bracing himself. But Simon Agulfo suddenly gave a shout of laughter that echoed back from the big wall. 'I might have known it,' he said. 'At times, I felt that somebody was looking over my shoulder. But you could always read my mind. What a blessing that we were never any closer than we were!' He came forward with his hand outstretched.

'Do I shake it?' Hal whispered.

'Not until he's signed,' said Lampitter aloud, after a brief hesitation.

Simon Agulfo checked, withdrew his hand and instead made a salute which Hal returned. For lack of any precedent, a document of surrender had been concocted and printed in an impressive typeface on the clerks' word processor. General Agulfo read the wording without touching the document, which was then half-covered with blotting paper to protect it from sweat

191

stains, while, with due formality, it was signed by both leaders and witnessed by Lampitter and Tony. They all saluted again. There was much clicking of shutters and a small patter of applause from the battlements.

'Now that I have surrendered,' Agulfo said, 'am I allowed to shake hands with an old friend?'

'Of course,' Hal said. The handshake was duly recorded by the cameras.

There was a moment of awkward silence. Nobody had thought beyond the moment. 'You have kept the pearls?' Simon asked.

A signal from Hal to a friend in Int-Corps had resulted in a phone call to her father. There had been an ecstatic note of congratulation in the envelope delivered by Hardy, along with a packet. It was Hal's intention to hand back the pearls. 'When I return a gift,' she would say, 'it stays returned.' But she had had time to study his appearance and body language. There could be no doubt that his pride had suffered a devastating blow. He could hardly meet her eyes.

His return to Liboon would not be to the rewards of a conquering hero. He might well be out of favour with his uncle, who, in turn, might not retain the presidency beyond the promised elections. Perhaps Simon would be in desperate need of funds. She wondered whether to offer to return the pearls, but on second thoughts she guessed that his pride, rather than his future, was in the balance.

'I treasure them,' she said. 'I am wearing them under my uniform.'

She had chosen the right reply. His old beam returned. He drew himself up, saluted again, turned and marched with dignity to rejoin his men.

# Twenty-Three

With an end to hostilities in the Middle East, the endless bickering began. Who had held the moral high ground and who had been in the wrong? Who had won and who had lost? With the propaganda outlet of every combatant claiming moral and physical victory and accusing its opponents, on the slenderest of grounds or no grounds at all, of genocide, torture, brainwashing and the use of chemical and biological weapons, the public, media and politicians alike were very soon sick of raking the ashes of history. Public attention in the West was therefore eager to turn to a story in which the facts were less clouded than usual, nobody had told much in the way of lies, the moral issues were clear-cut and good triumphed over evil in the end. The unique circumstances of the command added spice to an already satisfying meal. Hal became an overnight icon. The media clamoured for her return to face the cameras.

The politicians were less certain of Hal's positive publicity value. The uppermost strata of the military were openly pleased but secretly appalled. The revelation that Hal Brown had progressed from captain to the new and exalted level in the course of a few days, and that the freshly promoted brigadier was not any one of the various namesakes but was young, female, black and blessed with the forename of Hallelujah, had delighted the younger and more radical element but horrified the establishment. So Hal was left in place in the hope that the fuss would die down and somebody – anybody – would have some inspiration as to what to do about her.

Reporters visiting Maveria were granted interviews, which provided some local colour and human interest but added nothing of any weight to the story. Other reporters, who considered themselves God's gift to investigative journalism, pried into Hal's background without penetrating its apparent respectability. The *Sunday Journal* published several articles by Judy Phillipson, who was still boiling with resentment at having been slapped down by Hal before her peers. The articles suggested that there had been an affair between Hal and Simon Agulfo during their time at Sandhurst, but the suggestion brought immediate denials from the Royal Military Academy and the Liboonese embassy. Any suggestion of such an affair was hotly denied in letters to *The Times* from a number of those in a position to comment, including, surprisingly, Justin Carlsborough. Since it was quite obvious that Hal had done the Liboonese general no favours, the idea was seen to be pointless. A further suggestion from Ms Phillipson, that Hal's war against the Liboonese had been the revenge of a woman scorned, so obviously stemmed from spite that her editor hurriedly told her to drop that line before she brought another libel action down on his head.

'So she was in the right place at the right time,' said the Prime Minister. 'That doesn't necessarily make her the right person in the right place now. What are we going to do about it? Can we leave things to shake out in the normal course?'

'I'm afraid not,' said the Defence Minister. 'No way! Even if the top brass would stand for her as a cog in the military machine, which they wouldn't, it would be impossible. The girl happened to be the right person to step into the breach and fight a couple of uncomplicated actions. She has the training but not the experience to manage all aspects of a full brigade in peace and war, and you don't get that sort of experience from the top. Trial and error may be all very well, but not when error can lose wars and cost lives.'

'And money,' said the cabinet secretary.

'Could we demote her?' asked the PM.

The Defence Minister threw up his hands. 'Impossible. The promotion was confirmed. And in view of her popularity, you'd have an uprising on your hands if you tried it. In fact, you're going to have to award her at least one medal.'

The PM shrugged. Medals came comparatively cheap. 'If we explained to her that it was all a mistake . . .'

'That may have to be our resort, but you'd be giving her a stick to beat us with. At the moment, the media know that we had a computer hiccup and they know that Colonel Brown was promoted to brigadier on your personal instructions. They haven't connected the two yet. If they ever found out that while the computers were down we let a promotion slip through which we would normally have rejected as totally inappropriate, but which then turned out to be inspired, they'd crucify us. We'd be a laughing stock. Just now, the general feeling is that we made an unconventional but far-sighted move.'

The PM sat up a little straighter. An election was looming and he had no intention of relinquishing power to an opposition which seemed to have no concern for the good of the country but only for electoral victory. This, he felt, made them *ipso facto* unsuitable to govern. Margaret Thatcher had ridden to victory on the crest of the Falklands War. Perhaps he could emulate that triumph. 'Could you find room for her in Defence? The Joint Planning Staff were impressed with her analyses and she couldn't do much harm . . .'

'Prime Minister!' Charles Hopkirk almost squawked with alarm. 'She could do infinite harm before she even reported for duty. She would outrank two-thirds of the personnel there, most of whom have substantially longer service and greater experience than she has.'

'And we couldn't have her retired on medical grounds?'

'I enquired about that. She's fitter than either of us. Much.' The Defence Minister paused and lowered his voice. 'It might be easier to arrange a little accident.'

'Charles, have you gone out of your mind?' the PM demanded. A convenient accident would be a very attractive solution but these things had a way of surfacing in the course of time. 'What about a lecturing post at Sandhurst? Or the Intelligence Training School?'

The Defence Minister sighed. 'Same objection. She's just too damn senior. The only answer, it seems to me, is to find

195

her some backwater where she can be top dog without putting anyone's nose out of joint.'

The PM nodded. Charles might be churning his metaphors into a froth but his thinking was straight. 'Such as where?' he asked.

The Minister's thinking had not progressed so far. 'Some depot somewhere,' he said vaguely. 'Or a firing range. Or the Falklands. Or . . . how about Maveria?'

The Prime Minister's smile was spontaneous, for the first time in several weeks. 'Brilliant!' he said. 'The very place. We'll leave her where she is until somebody comes up with a solution. We can say that the Maverians asked for her.'

'They did,' said the Defence Minister.

Thus Hal remained in Pembaka and busied herself with the repatriation of prisoners, the repair of barrack damages and restructuring of the garrison. She made detailed recommendations about promotions and decorations, all of which were accepted for fear of bringing back to general attention a situation that was beginning to fade away. She sat on the committee which patched up an uneasy but permanent peace between Liboon and Maveria.

She also underwent a visit of inspection by her general and his staff. General Fulbright was fresh from his own, much less successful operations in the Syrian Desert and he was secretly jealous. He would dearly have loved to find fault, but such faults as he could find were so trivial that he would have shown himself in a poor light by drawing attention to them.

He congratulated Hal. 'Your second in command seems very competent. I noticed that you didn't include him in your list of recommendations for promotion.'

'I wanted to, very much, sir,' Hal said. 'But he's a personal friend. I felt that it would be inappropriate and open to criticism. I was rather hoping that somebody else might recognize his qualities. As you did,' she added.

The general looked at her for a moment. Hal smiled. 'I take your point,' said the general happily. He had found something to carp at. 'But to spoil a friend's chance of promotion because of that friendship is unfair to that friend and to the army. I shall make a recommendation.'

He left, reporting favourably to London.

So matters continued for several weeks. The garrison returned, reluctantly, to the old barracks, renovated by prisoner labour but still a poor relation compared to the quarters it had occupied in Pembaka. Hal's office, although spacious, was stark and institutional, equipped with minimal metal furniture. Her sleeping quarters were slightly better but little used. The hotel had returned to its previous function but Hal, deciding that she owed herself a little pampering and well aware that nocturnal visits by Tony to her official sleeping quarters would almost immediately be in the public realm, had retained the luxurious bedroom with en suite facilities. In payment, she presented her credit card. The accounts never reached her credit card company but were settled jointly by the Council and the Mining Company.

The old Beaver amphibian clattered in one day and a visitor was duly ferried out by Land Rover to the old barracks and to Hal's office.

His arrival brought her brightest smile to Hal's face. 'Colonel Bowman!' she exclaimed. 'What a pleasure!'

The colonel wondered whether she would be quite so effusive when he left, but he congratulated her sincerely on her battle successes. 'You carried off the television interviews very well,' he said. She was now his superior officer but he had known her since she was a student and he jibbed at addressing her as ma'am. 'You were modest, discreet and factual. Not a word was said about Brigadier Wincaster's condition. This gives me hope that we can have another discussion in absolute confidence.'

'Of course,' she said.

'You can guess the subject?'

'It's about my promotion, isn't it? I knew that somebody must have gone off his rocker.'

'You could put it that way. You know that we had a computer problem?'

'So they kept telling me,' she said, 'whenever there was a

foul-up with supplies or postings. But they always say that. I took it with a pinch of salt.'

He chuckled, partly with relief. This was not going to be as difficult as he had feared. 'This time it was true,' he said. 'A virus was planted, which wiped all the computers and nearly all the back-up disks.'

'And nobody had kept a hard copy of anything?' Hal asked incredulously.

'Copies had been kept, but they had been microfilmed, badly indexed and allowed to deteriorate, and they seem to have been out of date to begin with. Add to which, a search of the system had not extended to women officers when it was derailed by a maddening coincidence. There happens to be a Colonel Hubert Bathurst-Brown with an army number very similar to your own. When the question arose as to which senior officer was to accept the Liboonese surrender, the PM's advisers thought that he must be the Colonel H. Brown who was performing with such success, and – may I say? – brilliance.'

'Which leaves them with a bit of a problem,' Hal said.

'It leaves us with a problem,' he agreed.

He did not say whether Hal was included in 'us'. Hal decided that whatever she said would probably be wrong.

Colonel Bowman saw that she was not going to help him out. 'So I've been delegated to come out and resolve the matter. We are still speaking in confidence?' Hal nodded. 'You were not, in fact, eligible for such promotion. But in view of all the favourable – and well deserved – publicity, we can hardly admit that the promotion, successful though it was to prove, had been a mistake in the first place.'

'It is the truth,' Hal pointed out.

'But not a truth which the PM and others are anxious to reveal. Similarly, we can hardly demote you. But to leave you in place would be impossible.'

'Whatever we do will leave me looking like an idiot.'

'Not . . . necessarily.'

'So you've come to ask me to resign?'

Colonel Bowman nodded sadly. 'It seems a waste of a

brilliant young officer, but there's no easy alternative.' He found Hal's look difficult to interpret. If she had been white, he might have been aided by changes of colour. He soldiered on. 'It need not be a disaster. With your record and reputation, you would be welcomed into the very highest levels of civilian employees of the armed forces and associated organizations. And industries, of course—'

'Let me save you the bother,' Hal said.

Hal gave the colonel a tour of the barracks, showed him the more salubrious parts of the town and gave him lunch in the hotel before escorting him back to the amphibian.

On her return, she called Tony into her office and invited him to be seated. 'I think,' she said sombrely, 'that my army career is drawing to a close.'

'You're not having me on again?' They were alone and formality could be dropped.

'Not this time.'

'The money not enough for you?'

'Come to think of it,' Hal said, 'I don't even know what I'm being paid. I expect it's plenty.'

'So what's the snag?'

'There are several snags. The most important one is that I seem to be a little bit pregnant.'

There was silence in the office. They could hear Sergeant Mamie's typewriter at work next door and the voice of Sergeant-Major McDowell as he drilled a perspiring squad on the roasting tarmac parade ground which ran to the very brink of the escarpment above the Urma River. Tony looked at Hal and decided that she was serious. 'I thought we were being very careful,' he said at last.

'Not that first time. I thought I should tell you. You have an interest in the matter.'

Tony blinked and then looked solemn. 'I have a lot more than an interest,' he said. 'Did you think I was going to walk off and leave you to bring up my child alone? I expect the chaplain can marry us. I'll have a look in the regs.'

'Tony,' Hal said in a small voice, 'you don't have to do

199

this. What happened – at least the first time, which must have been the one that counts – happened at my invitation. I needed comfort and you gave it to me. I knew the risk I was taking, or if I didn't, I should have done. And I expect the army makes good provision for pregnant brigadiers. It seems to provide for everything else.'

Tony got up and carried his chair round to Hal's side of the desk. He took her hands. 'Listen,' he said. 'You, ma'am, are losing the place. I was going to ask you to marry me ages ago, but then you suddenly shot up to dizzy heights. You made me very happy when you invited me into your bed, but I was holding off from any suggestion of marriage in the hope that there might come a day when there was rather less difference between our ranks. However much I wanted to marry you . . .'

'Did you really, Tony?'

'You have always been my most favourite person in the world. At Sandhurst, I was sorely tempted, but it would have meant starting something that couldn't be finished the way it should. The time seemed inappropriate. But I was sure that we'd meet again when our careers were more settled. Even when you were pulling my leg, I knew that you were the only person I'd ever take it from.'

Hal had been sitting stiffly to attention but now she began to melt. 'That's sweet, Tony. But have you thought about it. Your career? Children?'

'Yes, I've thought about it. The army doesn't allow discrimination on grounds of colour any more. And it's not as if you were a native, you're as British as I am. More, in fact, because I was born in Kenya.'

Hal was distracted for a moment. 'Really? Or are you getting your revenge for the leg-pulling? Because when we first met you seemed quite puzzled by my skin colour.'

'We came back to Britain when I was three months old,' Tony explained. 'I've no hang-ups about colour. I see you as a very beautiful woman, I value you as a friend and I want you for a wife. Is that enough?'

Hal felt a warm contentment spreading through her. She

would have liked to encourage Tony to elaborate on his theme, but there was one topic to explore first. 'What about children?' she asked.

'I think I know what you mean,' Tony said doubtfully, 'although if you mean that we shouldn't bring children of mixed race into this world, it's a bit late to be thinking along those lines. We're committed. In theory, I feel that the sooner we all interbreed and everybody averages out at a pale coffee colour, the sooner all the world's racial problems will be resolved. That's fine as a principle, but when it touches your own you can't help worrying.'

'Tony, suppose that we had a black son? Would you take him into your club and introduce him around?'

It was a serious question and Tony gave it some thought. 'If I had a son and he had a green Mohican and gold studs in his face, I wouldn't take him *anywhere*,' he said at last. 'But if I had a black son and he was appropriately dressed and mannered, I'd take him anywhere. How does it look, from your perspective?'

Hal, in her turn, hesitated. It was not a subject on which she'd ever fully opened her heart before, but this was Tony. 'Just how you'd expect. Not very sensible. Cruel. Unfair. Sometimes dangerous. It's uncomfortable, knowing that you may be slighted or even physically attacked at any moment, and seeing the shift in people's eyes when they meet you. It hurts, knowing that some doors stay closed and that you always have to be that much better just to be the same. But it taught me a lot about self-reliance. I might not have been able to cope with life if I hadn't had a grounding in standing up for myself.' For a moment she was sitting with her father again in the sitting room of the married quarters and listening to his halting words of wisdom. 'Sometimes I think that starting from a disadvantage is more of a spur than a hindrance.'

Tony nodded. 'People who make fortunes usually start from nothing. They have less to lose. So, have we decided that we won't worry too much about having slightly sunburned children?'

'Yes,' Hal said. 'I suppose we have. By the time they're

201

old enough to worry about it, perhaps the liberalizing process will have got a stage further. But, Tony, suppose I left the army and married you, would I be holding you back? How would I fit in with other officers' wives?'

Tony chuckled. 'I don't see any of the officers' wives daring to quarrel with *Afritimwanamke*, the flame-footed ogress of Maveria.'

Hal stroked his hand. 'Don't make fun of it, Tony. This is too important.'

'All right. Well, the army doesn't allow colour prejudice. There's no denying that it can still happen, covertly. And marrying the wrong wife can be the death to a career. But you come from an army background, you're well educated, you've served with great distinction and you know how to behave. You'll win them over.'

'There is an alternative. A radical one. The Prime Minister is asking me to run for President!'

'Wow!' Tony said, then fell silent, deep in thought. 'You'd probably have a landslide victory. But are you prepared to give up your British citizenship? There must be something in the constitution.'

'There isn't. In fact, there isn't a constitution. The former President took over too quickly after we moved out. Constitution is a dirty word to a military dictatorship.' Tony was about to speak but she held up a hand. 'Listen, Tony. I wouldn't take it on unless you came with me. This country shouldn't be a protectorate. I'd want to work towards real independence. And I'd need somebody to head up the army and organize training.'

'Brigadier Laverick? It sounds good.'

'General Laverick at the very least,' Hal said. 'It bears thinking about.'

'It does indeed.'

They kissed. Sergeant-Major McDowell, who had been observing them through the office window, nearly let his squad march over the brink and into the Urma River.